Perseaus

Perseaus

C.C. Wyatt

Me Myself Publishing

Me Myself Publishing, USA
P.O. Box 9201
Chandler Heights, AZ 85127
info@memyselfpublishing.com

First paperback edition by Me Myself Publishing, 2018

This book is a work of fiction. Any references to characters, events, or locales portrayed in this book are either coincidental or products of the author's imagination.

Perseaus: a novel/C.C. Wyatt–1st Hardcover Edition

Library of Congress Control Number: 2018906679

Moldavite stone image on cover,
printed with permission of Inner Vision Crystals

{1. Florida–Fiction. 2. Visions–Fiction. 3. Skatepark–Fiction. 4. Dreams-Fiction. Characters-Fiction.} I. Title.

Summary: Pia Wade continues to find answers about the night she went missing, about the mysterious person known as Ferret and finds herself in a situation that will change everything.

ISBN 978-0-9967785-7-2 (hardcover)

Printed in the United States of America

To my girls with love,
and a special thanks to God,
my guiding light

CONTENTS

Preface   1

1. A Fearless Heart   3
2. Celeb or Not   6
3. Some Shake-ups   15
4. Trust on Alert   30
5. Look-alike ✓   40
6. We Meet Again   46
7. Them…the Echoes   55
8. Let's Get Serious   72
9. Unusual Pursuit   86
10. Broken Commitment   103
11. The First Episode   115
12. Moping in Tears   128
13. Ring the Separation   134
14. The second Episode   141
      Monday   146
      Tuesday   148
15. Memory Lane   152
16. Ball of Confusion   163
17. Human Shackles   174
18. On the Run   183
19. When Hands Join   191
20. Island, the Island   197
21. Them, Him, and Me   206
22. The Ring in Truth   212
23. We Stick Together   222
24. White Nightgown   237
25. Confrontation   241
26. Oh no, not Again   254
27. Let the Games Begin   264

28. Lights go Out   276
29. Bypass Death   285
30. Weeping Memories   294

Epilogue: Storm   308

Perseaus

There's no parting ways with fantasy;
Its brush through time is far reaching,
Like an unforgettable mystery, everlasting.

Preface

I was as happy as one could be the moment I got the news. I mean ecstatic-to-the-top-of-my-lungs happy, jumping-up-and-down and kissing-the-paper-it-came-on happy. There was no faking how happy I was. In my hand was a dream-come-true.

And the word spread like ants fleeing for dear life, about the unusual girl whom most people adored. That's if she was staying on the road of the straight and narrow. Their road! Which meant that the world was a safer place because of it.

The news this time: she had a full scholarship to attend an Ivy League School of her choice. And Harvard was her choice. "Harvard" and "scholarship" in the same sentence, things were really looking up for me. I was doing so well staying on *that road* until something happened. Not with the scholarship or Harvard, but rather, with me.

One morning I woke up with a whim on how I wanted to begin the next chapter of my life. Of course it

1

was a biggie. You see, what I did you wouldn't do if you wanted to avoid pissing people off. (Even if it wasn't their business.) Especially if you were me, a renowned oddball everyone's keeping an eye on.

But yeah, this oddball did just that, and like what any sane person would do, I dug my head in the sand like an ostrich to endure the backlash that sounded like this:

"You want to do what...? We're going to save your soul if it's the last thing we do."

"What do you hope to accomplish? Just let it be...."

"Girl, please! Why would you want to go down that road again?"

"The Lord's telling me right now to knock some sense into your head...." (This person had hit me upside the head for real.)

However, for those who were plain leery of me, my change of plans hadn't surprised them one bit. You could say they knew things were bound to change. Because to them I was ruined no matter what and could never be the same. That if I didn't go looking for trouble, in a matter of time it would come looking for me.

But I found sacred ground among those who were sentimental and blamed my nonsense on love. You know, that crazy kind of love, once hooked, you can't help yourself.

As for the rest, I was just plain crazy. After what I had been through, they believed traces of that out-of-this-world kind of craziness had to be in my blood.

Could be they're right.

Chapter One

A Fearless Heart

The lock clicked as I turned the key. It was mine now. All mine. Nothing else mattered. Not what people thought and the things they'd done trying to stop me. And not what I'd done to let nothing stand in my way. Whether I was making the biggest mistake of my life didn't matter, because it was my life, and my mistake to make. Because I was right about this, I was sure of it. As sure as I had ever been about anything.

The door whined as it eased open. My fearlessness was still intact. At this point it would be self-defeating to let fear take charge. It would land me in a rather sticky situation considering what I had done to get here: *broke my parents' hearts.* Never would I have imagined I had it in me to do it the way I had.... A little while ago, I waved goodbye to those broken hearts.

I entered the kitchen, slid my purse off my shoulder and placed it on the glass-top table, along with the keys. The old house creaked, and in a wince my head tilted up at the ceiling. Standing perfectly still, I listened to the voices...the voices whispering in my head. They were right: No matter how hard I tried, I couldn't get him out of my mind. Not him-him, the one I loved and could count on and trust my heart in the palm of his hands—but the other one. The one I knew nothing about; yet feared I could risk my heart and soul for a chance to learn all I could about.

Ferret...yes, Ferret.

Who else but Ferret?

That day I'd seen him at the bookstore felt promising—that finally, I thought all my questions would be answered. But time passed. Days dragged into weeks, weeks, into months. Now, about a year later, that moment at the bookstore felt like a lifetime ago. A lifetime of wondering had it only been a figment of my imagination—that I really hadn't seen him at all. The snapshot of him fixed in my mind was all I had, and I had my share of it driving me out of my mind thinking I had seen him. Even had me talking to myself: *That's him over there...watching me.... There he is...should I say something?*

Had been so certain I saw him I could have sworn on a stack of bibles.

But could I really...swear on a bible?

I exhaled. The question was what good was it to have an image in your head if you couldn't trust your eyes to confirm that it's the same image standing before you.

Freedom is letting go. For whatever reason the notion brought chills to my arms. I melted away the chills running my hands up and down my arms, thinking how things had changed. I was free now. It had been all I ever wanted, all I could ever think of. Free of the creepy visions, the dreams, and all the craziness that came with it. Free so I could again live a normal life, and now that I was, it was as if "normal" wasn't normal to me anymore.

The house creaked again. The house, growing older by the minute, I said to myself. Then a woman, about a hundred years old, in a creaking rocking chair barely moving, came to mind. I couldn't let fear creep in and get the best of me. I couldn't, and I wouldn't.

I peered out the window as birds landed on a tree branch, asking myself why:

Why did I break hearts to be here?

Why did it feel impossible to stay away?

Was it because the only place I could feel normal was here, at the beach house?

Chapter Two

Celeb Or Not

"You're so good at keeping things to yourself. Too good. No one should be that good. I'm your best friend, Pia. How can you keep your best friend in the dark about something as important as this? What if I was in a dire situation and needed to take a page out of your book to...to save myself? *Don't you see?* That would make you a lifesaver. And how could you not want to save me, *Stephanie*, your forever loving friend?"

"Steph! You oughta quit!"—I touched the brake, shifted the gear to *Drive*—"Just give it a rest already," I said then pulled away from the house in my new Volkswagen Beetle.

"Aah, c'mon, just get it out of your system. Tell me, you know you want to. So come on, tell me how you pulled it off...." Stephanie still at it.

"Stop pressing her, Steph. She'll tell you when she's ready," Kim chimed in from the backseat then went back to touching up her makeup.

"Yes, thank you! Stop trying to beat it out of me,"

I said.

When Stephanie first learned I was staying here, alone manning the house, while my parents were hundreds of miles away, she could not believe it. Could not believe my parents had agreed to this kinky arrangement—unless, well this's what she was dying to know. Dying to know why in god's name they would let me flush an Ivy League school down the toilet.

Yeah, she wasn't buying that my parents thought the beach house was the perfect place for me to start out on my own. And that being at the beach house was no different from taking up house anywhere else. Oh no, they wouldn't dare—unless... Again, that's what Stephanie was dying to know.

And it wasn't that I didn't want to tell her because I did, *really*...and I would, soon enough, just not now.

To be honest I was ashamed and wasn't sure how to explain without sounding like the worst person ever. How could you tell anyone that you're a blackmailer—and worse than that, your parents were your victims? I was feeling the brunt of it now. Like when you commit a heinous crime and not realize it until later when it smacked you in the face. Then you want to undo things, make things right, but if you did, you would've done it all for nothing and... It really didn't matter; Mom and Dad couldn't understand why I would rather be here than there.... They had to know but...but were afraid to admit it.

Blackmail turned out to be tricky though. Yeah, my parents could go on living as nobodies as they called it. And yeah, I'd gotten what I wanted: to be here, not there, and my parents' support.

7

The Volkswagen Bug I sat behind the wheel of, they'd delivered with a white bow on top. You need something to get around in, they'd said, but because of the monster inside of me, I felt undeserving.

Out of the corner of my eye, Stephanie was aw-so-slightly shaking her grumbling mind at me. Still wanted the gory details on how I pulled it off. *"You chose to go to school here out of all places? You could be at Harvard for heaven sakes,"* was how she put it a few days ago when she first heard about it. And I teased when I'd said, *"There's nothing more I would rather do than to go to school with my best friend and the love of my life."* But she expected me right away to laugh and say, "Just kidding!" Because why would anyone in their right mind turn down a deal of a lifetime? That was unfathomable in Stephanie's book, unless, there was a good reason. And she desperately wanted me to open my book for a tell-all. To help her understand what seemed straight-out insane.

But it wasn't easy saying I blackmailed my parents and used my diaries to do it.

Gazing through the rearview mirror, I now wondered what was up with Kim back there ransacking her purse.

I lowered the volume. "What is it? Did you forget something back at the house?"

"I can't seem to find my gold chain. I thought I put it in my purse." She stalled, put on a contorted face. She was backtracking. "But...come to think about it, I haven't seen it the whole time I was here." Right then she lifted her torso, dug into her pocket and ta-da, pulled out a gold chain. Holding it up, she exhaled a huge sigh of relief then said, "Been in my jeans the whole time."

I smiled through the mirror, then turned the music back up as I drove on to the airport.

No way could we have gone back to fetch a chain anyway. Kim would have missed her flight for sure. Her flight to Houston was leaving at 12:15 and it was imperative that she be on time. Her parents would be furious otherwise. You could say they were all packed and ready to say "Goodbye, Houston" and "Hello, Seattle." Kim's dad finally had gotten the transfer he wanted. This was fantastic because Kim would soon start college at Seattle University. The family sticking together: Things were working out for them.

Anyway, we had our lucky charms to thank for the few days we'd spent together. Kim happened to have been on Dad's flight when she had a layover. So naturally, she thought about me and called. Our talk then led to her calling her Mom—and what do you know, she'd wound up saying *yes*.

The clear blue sky disappeared in the rearview mirror as I entered the dark terminal. Vehicles lined the curb as soon-to-be-passengers unloaded baggage and grabbed last-minute hugs. I coasted through until I came to the drop-off point for Kim. I paralleled the car with the curb, threw the gear in park. I then hopped out and went around to the other side as Kim grabbed the travel bag she had in the back seat with her.

"Ooh, I'm going to miss you. I can't say it enough, right?" I said giving her a big-departing hug, one of many over the past twenty-four hours.

"I'm going to miss you, too," she said cooingly.

Coming out of the hug, I smoothed a hand over her honey blonde hair. A hair color she was experimenting with that looked good on her.

"It was really nice meeting you." Stephanie approached with arms open for a quick hug. "You have to come back to visit; it's been fun."

"Yeah, it's been fun; I hate I must leave so soon," Kim replied. But we all knew it would be awhile before we saw one another again. Washington was clear across the country.

Stephanie pulled down the white tank top to cover her bare waist; she then waved and hopped back into the car. Kim waved back then put on pouty lips in a sourpuss face.

"What is it?" As if I didn't know.

"I just...and I know you're tired of hearing this, but I wish you would rethink what you're doing. Everybody can't be wrong. Shucks, you think I would be going to Seattle University had I got accepted to Harvard?" Kim said, then put on a smiley-frowny face.

"If only I could make it happen by using a lifeline, I would. It seems crazy, I know, with Harvard being my dream too." Security beckoned me to hurry up, I nodded okay and he moved along.

Kim bit down on her lip, shaking her head. "But you should seriously think about this some more, Kiddo..." ('Kiddo', she had a habit of calling people that.) "...while you still have time to change your mind. But Cameron, I get it. You two are great together. But I'm afraid for you, you know."

"I do, but as I said before. 'Don't look at it like

10

it's the end of the road for me.' I'm starting a new life here, not ending it—and *I'm not* afraid of anything. My mind plays tricks on me sometimes, because some things aren't easy to forget. But it doesn't mean that I'm stuck or living in the past."

Kim exhaled exhaustingly. "All right, all right. Just promise me you won't go off to some strange island playing detective. Keep your feet planted here in the real world." She said, pointing a stiff finger toward the ground. "Just take care of yourself, okay? It's not asking much at all." She hugged me quickly with one arm. "Okay, I better get going before that guard bites your head off."

"Text me when you land!" I waved, hurrying around the car. I opened the door and hopped in, but I wasn't going anywhere fast, in an instant I was jammed in. I looked around for Kim and she was nowhere in sight.

Moments passed, and I hadn't moved an inch and was getting impatient.

"Look, get a load of this dude," Stephanie uttered, and I ducked my head to get a full view of the person on her side.

"What the hell!" was my eye-popping diction of this odd-looking man and his out-of-season attire. "Hmm, he could be a rocker," I suggested now.

Dark shades covered his eyes, and a red ball cap pulled over them. A wallet tucked in the pocket of his leather pants attached to a chain. It reminded me of a rocker. *But leather pants? In the summer?*

He lowered an overstuffed duffel bag to the ground. The constriction in his jaws, *agitated,* I thought, and I wondered why. Did he miss his flight, couldn't get another one? Why else would he come out of the

Departure terminal? Or was he fed up for having to wait long for a ride? He looked in direction of incoming traffic, suggesting he was looking for something. Glancing at his watch suggested he was concerned with time. But when he tapped on his watch a couple of times, I wondered was it working properly. Trying to figure him out was confusing.

"I can't tell if he's going or coming. I wonder if he knows." Stephanie made a face, snickering. Then before we knew it, he was at the car tapping on the window.

"Excuse me...can I get you lovely ladies to give me a lift?" Our eyes bucked at each other. We couldn't believe he had the nerves....

"Do we look like we pick up strangers?" Stephanie took the initiative of blowing him off.

"No, but I could really use one; I can give you gas money, anything."

"I don't know where you're from, but this is the United States...of the *America.*"

"Stephanie...?" I tried to stop her before she embarrassed the poor guy but holding back a burst of laughter choked me up.

He showed a bit of humor though; he chuckled, straightened his trunk, then backed away from the car. It was then the ring on his finger caught my attention. The olive-colored stone, it looked like some kind of emerald, but rare because of the raw, spiny texture.

I stared at it. I just couldn't take my eyes off it. Strange, but it reminded me of something, though I wasn't sure what.

Yet I kept looking at the stone, embedded in a wide, gold band...it was just...just something about it.

Something...powerful, the thought crossed my mind. More power than I imagined this character dressed in leather pants would have. He began fingering around the ring as if his finger itching. "What kind of ring is that?" came close to rolling off my tongue, when I instead told myself it didn't matter.

I had to get hold of myself. After all, the ring was on a total stranger whom I may never see again. Besides, I had refused him a ride, so why strike up a conversation about the ring? No matter the effect it had on me, thinking I had seen it before, trying to remember where— no, I should just let it be.

"You can try to get out now," Stephanie asserted, snapping me back into the moment.

I pulled out as much of the front end I could. "Did you see that ring on his finger?" I asked. Stephanie turned quickly to look, so obviously, she hadn't noticed. But now she couldn't see with him holding the duffel bag.

My wondering continued, more about him now. By focusing mostly on the ring, maybe I missed the point. I didn't know, but I tried pulling from my memory, like going through boxes of photos, because something was there.

Maybe we just blew off a celebrity, I thought. Come to think about it, he had somewhat of a star quality to his voice. Maybe he was dressed so he wouldn't be recognized; celebrities do that. But I doubted that for some reason.

Nothing about him rang a bell. Nothing stood out except those leather pants, and, for some reason, that ring.

Pissed that I'd only moved a little bit for whatever reason, I checked the rearview mirror just to see if he was still there. And he was, looking back at me. In a couple of blinks, I checked again, sensing he wouldn't be this time.

And, he wasn't.

Chapter Three
Some Shake-ups

After leaving the airport, we were in the mood to hang out, anywhere, if anywhere wasn't the mall.

So here we were, driving around in circles hoping to steal a close parking spot in the heart of downtown. And we weren't the only ones, which made the task impossible. So I got out of the loop, made a few turns and wounded up in a parking lot next to a river and a jailhouse. A four-story glass building that would throw anyone off. *A jail? Really?* No, it didn't look like one. Then again, the police cars in the area could give it away. Besides, the building blended well with other glass buildings in the area. Overall, it offered a safe, pleasant feel.

"Do you still want to do downtown?" I asked for no particular reason as we got out the car. We were a few blocks away, just across the bridge.

"Well, yeah...if you still want to."

15

We loaded a few coins into a parking meter then started up the walkway, taking in green grass, lovely shade trees and the fancy boats sailing the river. Looking across the river you could see downtown sprawling a few blocks like it rose on a hill.

We came to a stairwell below a drawbridge (one of many throughout the city) and climbed our way to the top. With a concrete enclosure, it was like going through an upright tunnel, our footsteps echoing against the metal steps. And the moisture trapped within these walls clung to our bare skin. We made our way up to the bustling street traffic, drowning out a mellow tone of the city below.

"I'm hungry. Let's get something to eat first," I suggested moments after reaching the top.

"Okay. How 'bout the Cheesecake Factory?"

"But it's way over there."

"Oh, so now it's too far? Have you changed your mind about hanging out downtown?"

Gazing up the river, I supposed so. "What do you say we take a cruise on the water taxi?"

Stephanie followed my gaze up the river as one approached.

"Just so happen I have passes Mom gave me." I double-checked my purse to make sure I had them with me. "You want to? We can grab something to eat, take it with us on the boat if we have to."

"Yeah, let's do it," Stephanie agreed.

We then hurried across the bridge and down another flight of stairs to finish our journey to the other side. We stopped at the taxi booth first to confirm the passes and the next departure time. From there we hurried to an outdoor grille for something to eat. I ordered a fat, juicy burger, and Stephanie ordered slices of pizza. Then we sat at a nearby table under an umbrella, ate and chitchatted about this and that.

"Sooo," Stephanie elongated the word.

"So, what?" I asked. As if I didn't know.

Stephanie bit off a piece of pizza then gazed off into the river. A few moments later, said, "I'm wondering how bad it could be, that's all. But I promise not to bring it up again. Not today."

"Oh, I'm so relieved, thanks!" I drooped in my seat, pretending to be exhausted.

"You know," she said moments later, "you're the bravest person I know, to come back here. Humph, if it were me, I would have been too afraid to."

"I know...and I should be, but I'm not," I remarked, hoping I wouldn't live to regret it.

"You haven't forgotten about Elijah's birthday party Friday night, have you?" Stephanie changed the subject.

"No, I haven't." Cameron crowded my mind, so I took a moment to say more. It'd been hours since I heard from him last. He was in Orlando for a skateboarding event and meeting with a long-lost relative. "I suppose I'll go; it's not like I have plans or anything. Where did you say it will be?"

"The Palooza. A cool place. It has a huge dance floor with psychedelic lights. A live band will be there. And catered food from this place called Simone Delights—I hear the food's good too. And, um, you should bring a date. If you want to."

"You mean...bring Cameron? Really?" I said

17

between chews.

"Yeah, whoever." She then grimaced, "Yeah, sure, bring him."

I smiled, couldn't believe she invited Cameron to the party. She'd despised him for so long—and now... This was her first time ever showing any kind of approval of our relationship. To her, Cameron had been nothing but trouble. And she even demonized him for having arranged our trip to the island, claiming he'd put my life in danger, overlooking the part I had played. Stephanie was a piece a work, full of surprises, but this turnaround was a delightful surprise.

"I'll see what Cameron say about the party."

"Do that." After a brief pause, "Hey, you think your parents will be back around the time you start school?"

I shrugged. "I don't know; it's hard to say. Dad is on international trips right now. As for Mom, she hasn't mentioned it. She's been busy getting ready for a new school season, herself."

My cellphone rang and I got anxious hoping it was Cameron, but it was a number I didn't recognize, so I got unexcited ignoring it.

"What is it?" Stephanie pried with concern.

"Oh...nothing, nothing...just hoping to hear from Cameron that's all. He hasn't returned any of my calls or texts."

"You think he's avoiding you after the argument you two had yesterday?"

"Mnh-mnh. We're over that. I can't even remember what it was about." Of course, I was lying.

"Yeah, right," she scoffed. "Or something is

wrong with your hippocampus."

"Huh! The things that come out of that mouth of yours!" I chuckled, and she chuckled. Then for a moment, things got quiet. In that moment I reflected on us, Cameron and me, the heated discussion we had right before he left for Orlando yesterday. But Stephanie pried into my moment.

"What's bothering you? I hate it when you keep things bottled up. What is it?" She waited, then scoffed. "Okay, have it your way, don't trust me with anything."

"It's not like that. I'm just having one of those moments I can't really explain to myself, let alone to someone else." I stared down at the table. "It's...a strange feeling I'm having."

"Look...maybe he just lost his phone or something."

"I hope not. He just got a new iPhone." I shook it off, "Nah. He's probably having so much fun with his long-lost relative he has no time to think about anything else." Not that that made me feel any better.

Before long, we were relaxing on the water taxi, loving the scenery and the breeze on our faces.

The tour guide was on the speaker telling the story of how the river came to be. An interesting story: Over a hundred years ago, after a night of violent winds, booming noises and shaky grounds, the river suddenly appeared. No one knew what happened that night. But according to speculators, the roof of an underground river collapsed, causing it to rise—just like that. Because one night it wasn't there, the next, it was. And this area had been booming ever since.

Now the tour guide steered eyes on that beautiful house over there and on that incredible mansion over there, owned by the rich and famous. And the passengers were like *"Ooh, wow, that's Paris Hilton's mansion..."* and *"Gloria Vanderbilt lives there...."* So much whooing and aahing, I could tell who were on the tour for the first time, daydreaming of a grander life. Which was natural, who wouldn't?

"This is nice," Stephanie closed her eyes to the river-scented breeze, smiling. "I could sail into the sunset."

"You and me both," I replied.

Stephanie opened her eyes a bit, chuckled, and then surprised me. "You won't tell me but...I already know."

"Know what?"

She scratched her nose. "What you did to your parents—everything."

"Mmm. And what is it you think you know?"

"How you threatened to use your diaries if they didn't agree to you moving here."

"You mean to tell me..." I looked around to get a range on our privacy. The boat wasn't full, and with the engine going we were good. "...you knew but pretended that you didn't all this time? How did you find out?" I whispered.

"I have ears." She moved a lock of hair out of her face. "And maybe it wasn't so much of a secret as you thought. But listen, Pia. I know you think you have your parents right where you want them. But I also know how much this is bothering you, thinking your parents don't love you after what you did. But you're wrong; it's not like that at all."

I rolled my eyes. "And you know this beee-cause..."

"The point is that your parents love you, and they would have supported you no matter what. And because they knew you didn't want those diaries published no more than they did."

"I...I blackmailed them. A rotten, low-down thing to do—I can't believe that I did it. What a monster I turned out to be, telling them either let me go or I would make their lives miserable by sharing my diaries to the world. I'm so ashamed that's why I couldn't tell you."

"That's okay. But your parents, they knew you really didn't want to."

"No. And my diaries, they're a sacred part of me, and private. But I knew my parents didn't want to dredge up what was dead to them, coming back blowing our lives up with all that craziness all over again. I knew they would have done anything to prevent that from happening. Because, as far as they were concern, the monster sunk the island...no need to summon it, end of story." I crossed my arms. "Some ultimatum I slammed in their faces; how selfish of me." I looked at Stephanie, "But why, why did they let me get away with it?"

"'Cause you probably would have published the diaries even though you didn't want to. Or worse, driven you straight into CJ's arms—and they definitely didn't want that." Stephanie then chuckled. "Scary, considering you have way better options," she said, referring to Harvard.

"But I wonder why they didn't come out and tell me." Peculiar, I thought.

"Hmph. I don't know," she said. "But the fact is they're your parents, and they sacrificed for you. You don't know how blessed you are to have parents like Mr. and Mrs. Wade. And it seems they really like CJ."

"Ooh, I get it now: your change of heart for him."

"Yeah, well. But anyway, even though I don't like the tactics you used to get what you wanted, I like having my best friend near." She put on a smile. "But now, I'm wondering what's in those diaries. You think your parents know?"

"Mm," I shifted to my other side, crossed my legs. "I don't know; I hope not."

"Yeah. But I still don't get why you would rather go to school here..." she went on.

But I dropped out of the conversation, thinking that I could have gone off and study the science of space and time, but I didn't, because I wasn't ready. I'm Pia Wade. But who I was as a person, I wasn't sure.

"Why Pia? Why was it so important...?"

'Why Pia?' had been what Cameron asked before leaving for Orlando. He thought my parents blamed him for my demented behavior as much as they blamed me. And when he asked, his longing, impatient eyes had burnt through my soul, as he waited to hear me say what he believed in his heart of hearts to be true. But how could I admit to him what I barely could admit to myself? He gave me his back with the screen door flying shut behind him. I went after him, pleading. "I'm done with it!" he said, and I knew. I turned to head back in the house and had come face-to-face with Stephanie.

I looked at Stephanie now, with "Why?" written all over her face.

"I would think you know the answer to that already," I answered now, though I was a bit distracted.

My phone. With the roaring engine, I barely heard it ringing as I hurried to get to it before it stopped. I failed, but the phone lit up again. "It's Cameron!" I quickly answered.

"Hey, where are you right now?" his said with a sense of urgency.

"On the riverfront. Me and Stephanie. Why? What's going on?"

"It's Sebastian. He had an accident at the park."

"But he's going to be okay, isn't he?"

"I hope so; I hope so. It's crazy, the timing in all. It's not right, it's just not right...all the time he's put in getting ready...." He was working himself up.

"Hey, calm down! How bad is it?"

"I don't know, it's not good. H-he got a terrible headache when he hit his head, so they rushed him to the hospital. They ran scans and...and they found an aneurysm."

"Oh my god, Cam, that's serious! Where are you now?"

"On my way back, going straight to the hospital when I get there."

"Well I can meet you there. What hospital?"

"No—I mean, you don't have to. You're out with Stephanie and all. And besides, he's at Holy Cross right now but won't be for long. They're planning to move him to another hospital; I should hear something before I get back in town. Listen, I'll get back to you when I find out

23

more. Okay?"

"Yeah, sure, just keep me posted," I said, and then he was gone too soon.

"Hey, what's going on?" Stephanie asked at once.

"Sebastian, Cameron's friend...he's in the hospital with an aneurysm," I told her, though neither of us knew him personally.

I had met him for the first time a few days ago. The stories Cameron had shared with me prior, about this person bigger than life and a mentor loved by so many, made him sound too good to be true almost. And I never would've guessed him a woodworker, carving out custom-made furniture, with his father who owned a furniture store. The two had been friends for a long time, since before Cameron lost his parents. Sebastian had become the big brother Cameron never had; they were like family. So naturally when Sebastian and I had gotten around to meeting, it was as we'd already met.

"*Omigod.* You don't expect something like that to happen to someone so young," Stephanie remarked about the aneurysm.

I nodded, "Yeah...I know. It's hard to believe. He fell and hit his head at the skatepark."

"Is that what caused it?"

"I'm...not sure."

After talking to Cameron, I wasn't sure about anything. And being stuck here on the boat, I wished time would stop dragging and speed us back to shore already.

Stephanie went down to the lower deck to get something to drink and was back in a flash with orange sodas. She handed me one then settled down next to me. Popping open her can, "What are you going to do when we get back?" she wondered.

My head swayed absentmindedly. "I should know by time we get back," I said, all while knowing all I wanted was to be with Cameron. When he'd said "no", it felt like a total rejection. So my day was as good as shot (I was shot) thinking about it.

I tried reaching Cameron once back ashore, and my call went straight to voice mail. I left a message, so he would at least know I called. And until I heard from him, I couldn't orient my mind on what to do next.

"Look what we have here," Stephanie said, gazing at a lissome illusionist, attracting a crowd of people. He was wearing a black, flat-topped hat, baggy pants, and red suspenders over a white t-shirt. An unusual surprise, meaning he was new on the scene; never ever had I seen a magician performing here before. "Let's go check it out," Stephanie said already moving in that direction as I followed.

The illusionist was performing a trick with a deck of cards. One by one turning up all four aces after he'd shuffled the deck of cards up good. Since forever this kind of stuff fascinated me. Wondering how it was possible to do such tricks if no real magic was involved; dark magic, I mean.

Another trick with the cards, I thought as he gathered them up. *What will it be?* He had my undivided attention. The fanning the cards trick, this one amazed me also. The cards fanned out as he moved his hand sideways and upside down, like the cards were all stuck together—and to him. This trick generated applause, applause, especially from thrill-eyed kids as he tossed the cards up in the air and they rained down to the ground.

The kids scrambled to collect every one of them then handed them back to the magician. And in return, he pinned on them a button, what looked like a picture of him. In the interim, the audience clapped, some dropped tips in his hat as he arranged for his next performance.

The cup and marble trick, I had seen this many times, too. *Under what cup is that doggone marble?* You know, the magician puts a marble beneath one of three cups and moves them around, you keep your eyes on the cup with the marble—you know it—but when the cup's turned up, you're amazed to see it's not there. Then ta-da, it's under another cup—or not. In this case it wasn't so where was it? The trickster reached in his pocket, pulled it out, and again the kids went wild over the oldest and easiest trick on record. Even the little ones all grown up, like me, still fascinated by a little magic.

The illusionist clowned around a bit before his next performance. Where he popped open a black hat, turned it around revealing nothing was in it. Then placed it on the table, waved a magic hand over it and behold, reached in, and pulled out four clear balls, one by one, the size of tennis balls. The audience applauded, and he bowed. Then he juggled the balls. At a moderate pace at first then he got faster, faster, faster. I had never seen balls juggled so fast, I don't think. And when his juggling slowed down, all eyes were looking up, astounded. The balls were floating in the air like bubbles and descending like so. And he went on juggling the balls and they began multiplying, they all floating in the air like bubbles. The sound of amazement filled the air because this...was...incredible.

Incredibly strange...and familiar. I stared at the magician, then up at the floating balls and again at the magician. I was panicking, panicking, and I didn't know why. Something about this trick, the magician—I just didn't know what it was or why suddenly it had a weird effect on me.

"Let's go, Steph," and at once I walked away.

"Hey. What's wrong? Are you okay?" Stephanie on my heels wondered what came over me.

"Yeah, fine! I just have to get out of here."

"But what's wrong? Did you hear from CJ?"

"No, not yet. It's just that...I got a weird feeling all of a sudden."

And of course, Stephanie's reply was, "What kind of feeling?" But I couldn't make sense of it. Not now anyway.

In no time we climbed one stairwell and descended the other to get back to the other side of the river and back to the car. However, before we made it to the car, Cameron called and, "Hey," I answered promptly.

"I'm sorry for taking so long to get back to you," he said.

"It's okay. Just tell me what's going on with

27

Sebastian." I settled down on a nearby bench, hoping for nothing more than good news.

"They moved him to Broward Health. There, they have the best brain specialists. They're prepping him now for surgery."

"Brain surgery—I still can't believe it. Is he awake?"

"Yeah, but I haven't had the chance to see him. He's still having bad headaches though. 'Like contractions,' his mom described it. Imagine that."

"Hmph...sounds unbearable." Like bad menstrual cycles but worst, I thought. "I hope surgery will fix him up as good as new. What are the doctors saying?" *Maybe I was asking too much too soon*, I thought as an afterthought.

"They think he has a good chance of recovering. If only it could be a speedy recovery. I hate to see him like this, missing out...he's been training so hard for this. You don't know, Pia."

I could hear him getting distraught, so emotional that in any moment he would need a shoulder to cry on. My shoulder, I wanted it to be, not me imagining his emotions seeping on it.

Cam went on, "He had a good chance of winning—he'd gotten better than he's ever been. I wish," he took a breath, "I wish it were me instead of him. Because he's going to be okay, I know it. That's why I would take his place to give him that chance."

"*Don't, Cam.* I know how much he means to you, but you shouldn't say things like that. Just think what I would be going through if it were you."

"I know, I know, and I'm sorry but..."

"You think if he had been wearing a helmet it would be different?" Countless times I'd complained to him about wearing one.

"That's the kicker, Pia. He bought a helmet today—he was wearing it! But somehow it came off in the fall. And you know what: The reason he was wearing it was because he had a dream a couple of nights ago that he fell and hurt his head."

"A premonition, he had a premonition," I uttered, astounded.

"Yeah, apparently...though we know the fall didn't cause the aneurysm. But the bottom line is that he's in no condition to defend himself. And...and it's not fair for the competition to go on without him."

"Cam?" I wanted to say something, but he ruled to get his point across.

"Perhaps someone should to step up and do it for him. I mean win this thing for him..." It was like his mouth doing the thinking.

As he went on, something boggled me...though...I wasn't sure what...but it was like trying to remember something. Though again...I wasn't sure what. This, all while I was still trying to listen to Cameron, when suddenly it hit me, and I—

"No, Cam! No! That someone can't be you," I blared.

Chapter Four

Trust on Alert

"...And why not!" he demanded as my mind rushed across the river.

I remembered. *The illusionist, the floating balls.* I had seen them before. Long ago in a vision, in the exact same spot I saw it a moment ago, today, and with the *same* magician. *Yes, the same magician doing that exact same trick with the balls. Right here on the riverfront.* Only I didn't realize it until now. And Sebastian, oh my god, talk about premonitions....

...No, not Cameron.

"Pia! Pia! Are you there?" Cameron's voice came through like turning up the volume.

"Yeah, yeah, I'm here, Cameron."

"What's going on? Are you okay?"

"No—I mean, yeah, I'm fine." I was tripping, nonetheless spooked. "Sorry, um...I'm...just a little confused here."

"About what? What got you so ballistic all of a sudden?"

I took a deep breath looking up at Stephanie; she's wondering what the hell was going on. I mouthed that things were okay, not to worry. But her disbelieving eyes weren't buying it; they rolled as she turned; she then slowly walked away. I immediately got back to the matter at hand.

"Are you really thinking about taking Sebastian's place in the competition?" How could I explain being floored by the idea of a sudden, all because of a vision I once had? And that it was a sign of something bad about to happen: first Sebastian, and him, next.

Crazy, yeah—I would be the first to admit it. But even if I unleashed the thought, he would tell me quick to pack my bags for Harvard. From the beginning he'd been afraid of my past coming back to haunt me. And if I said anything about the vision (or the premonition), suggesting it might be linked to what happened to Sebastian, well, this would only prove his point.

"Just the other day you said, 'Why don't you go for it? Don't you think you're good enough?' And so now you're telling me not to? Because of what; all of a sudden I'm not good enough?"

"*No, no.* Of course that's not what I'm saying."

"Then what are you saying? Look, I have to go. We'll talk about this later, okay?"

"Yeah...sure," I dispiritedly replied at the sound of beeps; he already was gone. Gazing at the ground, I lowered the cellphone. I didn't know what to think, didn't know what to do or what not to do. But what I did know was that I didn't want to relive the past; and didn't want to relive visions, which were part of my past.

I looked for Stephanie. She had wandered up a ways along the river.

Once more I gazed across the river, just as the water taxi undocked with new passengers. Fancy boats still sailed up and down the river. It was such a beautiful day, and, an unusual one. Today my past shined a blinding light on my future, and the inkling was to proceed with caution.

I got up and started moving toward the car, collecting in my mind all that made this day strange:

That creep at the airport and that ring he was wearing...something about that stone.

My premonition and Sebastian's, and them happening on the same day, was it coincidental?

And why now I feared Cameron was in danger was natural, because I had suggested wearing a helmet a time or two. But now it felt more strange than natural.

I didn't know what to make of it. *But it's not too late for Harvard:* the voices in my psyche reminded me. *Yes, I most go, anywhere but here:* I responded to the voices. But some things are easier said than done. Isn't that right?

"Steph?" I beckoned to get her attention. Remembering that we were on the meter, I hurried over to the car. Time had expired but I was in luck with no ticket pinned to the windshield.

"Where to now? The hospital? Shopping?" Stephanie asked as the doors closed behind us.

"Might as well go shopping," I turned the ignition and the engine roared to life.

Feeling a pang of disappointment, I gave

Stephanie the update on Sebastian.

We were home, finally, having avoided it for most of the day. Home was also at Stephanie's house. With my parents all the way in Texas, her mom, Miss Burke, was like a mom to me.

My parents knew they could count on her to help as much as she could, and she did, offering home-cooked meals. Today was spaghetti and meatballs with garlic bread. As I finished, Miss Burke reminded me that I could stay over so I wouldn't be home alone. But I declined. And shortly later gave her a thank-you hug for everything then skipped home. I expected Cameron to drop by later.

I eased open the squeaky door, which was getting squeakier by the day, I minded. I closed the door behind me and scooted through the foyer to the kitchen. Hanging my purse on back of a chair, I thought about Sebastian, hoping for him to pull through with flying colors. I went to the bathroom to freshen up. Leaning over the face bowl, I drenched my face a few times with water. Then with a towel began clearing away tough layers of tension. Back in the kitchen, I powered up the computer.

As it powered up, I reached in my purse for my cellphone. And when it started ringing, I lit up seeing it was Mom calling.

"Hi. How is everything?" she asked casually.

"Mm, fine...everything's fine." I wouldn't dare admit otherwise. I wouldn't hear the last of it. "Will you be visiting this weekend?" I asked.

"I don't plan to. What is it? You're missing your folks already?"

"Yeah, like crazy," I said mirthfully. "But I'll survive. I'll get used to living alone at some point."

"If you say so. Did Kim get off all right?"

"Yeah, she made it back safe."

"That's good. Hey, you haven't ordered the psychology book yet, have you?"

"Oh, no. I was meaning to do that today. I forgot. Sorry."

"Don't be. I found one today online. A used one, at the bookstore on campus there. It's already paid for so all you have to do is go pick it up."

"Great! I'll go get it first thing tomorrow," I said thankfully.

"Okay, but other than that, you sure everything's okay? No bad dreams or anything like that?"

"No, Mom. No dreams. I know you can't help worrying, but try not to," I said. But knew she couldn't be more worried than I was in this moment, following today's events. Though, it all could be just a coincidence. Trying to give today's events the benefit of the doubt was tough though.

"I'll pray on it. And don't forget to put the alarm on," Mom said.

"I won't. I do every night. Mom?" I sniffled. "I'm...I'm sorry about everything," I admitted for the first time since forever it seemed, in tears. "And I love you."

She smacked her lips delivering a kiss through the phone. "Love you, too, dear. Talk to you tomorrow."

I hung up realizing I had forgotten to ask about

Dad. What country he might be in or would he be back by the weekend, I wanted to know. Still holding the phone, I took the liberty to call, and a chance that he might answer. But no such luck. So I left a message, and then logged onto Facebook, messed around there until I heard Cameron's truck pull up.

What am I going to say to him? I wondered.

I had been wondering that the whole time. Now with Cameron bombed out about Sebastian and him being in no condition to compete in tournament—I knew it wasn't just talk. He was serious about stepping in Sebastian's shoes *and become him* if possible. "I would do anything for my right-hand man," I could hear him saying, as he had before and meant it.

So how could I convince him not to...when I told him just the other day that he was good enough to compete himself in the skateboarding competition?

I opened the door to a dog-tired Cameron. What he needed most was a quick, sedated shower then lay quietly to sleep. "So, how is he?" I closed the door. He then sandwiched my head stiffly between unusually cool palms and said, "Just calm down now," but...

'Calm down'? I was calm! He was so tired he was delirious, I reckoned. He then fixed a hand at the small of my back and guided me over to the sofa.

"They did the procedure, and everything went well with no complications," he offered. "He's still in intensive care though, but the doctor's optimistic. He was asleep when I left. I know you've been worried too, but what's going on with you...really? And be straight with me. I know you, so tell me."

Turning it on me was unexpected. I still had

questions about Sebastian, and, I needed to slow things down a bit. "No—I mean, did you get to see Sebastian after surgery...talk to him?"

"No. I haven't had a chance to see him. Knowing the surgery went well I just left...gave the family some alone time. 'Course I needed to take a break, and, see you."

"Mm-hmm." Looking at him I agreed he needed a break. "Cutting his head open, I can't get the picture of that out of my mind," I added.

"No-no-no. They didn't actually cut him open. They did a coiling procedure. They went through an artery to get to the aneurysm. Then pack it with teeny balls of metal to stop blood from flowing to it. They say it's a common procedure, done all the time."

"Um, *yay* to technology," I uttered.

"Yeah. But they say recovery is different from one person to another. But doctors are optimistic about Sebastian," he imparted reason to feel optimistic.

"So now tell me what's gotten in to you. Why now you don't want me to compete? And don't tell me it's because of what happened to Sebastian."

"Why not? Why shouldn't I be afraid that something like that could happen to you?"

"Because it won't. Look, we fall all the time. The sport involves falling, getting bumps and bruises every now and then. Even the best skaters have accidents occasionally. And, I'm no expert in aneurysms, but the fall didn't cause Sebastian's aneurysm; he didn't hit his head that hard. And, what I've learned from my aunt having an aneurysm, is that it forms over time."

The more sense he made the harder it was for me

to plead my case without hearing him say, "I told you so." If I breathed a word, Cameron, along with my parents and everyone else would—I couldn't bear the thought. Because they were right, Florida was a breeding ground for weird happenings it seemed, when it came to me. And trying to convince Cameron that he was in danger based on—well at this point, it wouldn't work in my favor.

"There you go again," he said, and I looked him in the eyes. "Where did you go just then?"

I bit down on my lip. I always gave myself away by zoning out like that, I thought.

"Did you have a vision? Is that why you don't want me to step in for Sebastian? It's the only thing that seems to make sense."

I shrugged, not sure how to respond to that. "What if I did? Would you reconsider entering the competition?" I asked. His response would decide mine.

"You don't understand; I feel that it's something I have to do. For Sebastian. Look, I'm the only one who can fill in for him. Dax can't because he's competing for himself. There isn't anyone else." He took a pause.

"Did you know he won the last three competitions he entered?" I shook my head. "Well, he did. And I can't tell you enough how much he was looking forward to this one. I mean, he's well known in the area, but he wanted to move pass that on a national level. And he was ready. This competition would have gotten him there. But now," his thoughtful, serious eyes gazed into mine, "it must be me. Winning it for him."

"*But it won't matter.* Because you would've won it. Don't you see? If he doesn't win it for himself it won't be the same, and it certainly won't change anything for him."

"You would think that because you don't understand our bond."

"Maybe your right! Okay? So I'm done with it. Nothing I can say to change your mind. Because what I think doesn't matter!" I turned from him then, as I grew mute and aloof.

"You're wrong, Pia," his voice filled with solace. "You *do* matter. Just tell me. Have the visions started again, the dreams?"

"No!" I said like a demand.

He narrowed eyes, "And that's the truth?"

"Yeah, mm-hmm." Technically, I was telling the truth.

"Pia?" *You know I know you,* was exactly what he was thinking.

Holding back to no fault of my own, was what I had to do. Trust your instinct: I had trained myself well to do just that. But I couldn't much blame Cameron. Last year when he inquired about my having visions, I wasn't truthful with him, not at first. I couldn't open up to him about something so sensitive. I didn't know what to expect, and the damage he could have caused. I didn't know so I couldn't trust him. I'd been stubborn then—had to be. And afraid. But things were different now. I trusted him and yet, I couldn't trust him.

"Are the visions back?"

"*No, I told you,*" I hissed.

"Okay, if you say so." He then leaned into me, encouraging my lips to his. I gave in and he folded me in his arms as his back fell into the nook of the sofa.

"Mm," I fingered his lips now and asked, "What do you say going to Elijah's birthday party with me Friday night?"

"Really?"

"Yes, '*really*.' You and Elijah are cool. So why not go?" I said then my lips smacked his cheek.

"Well...I suppose I can arrange that. Friday night, hm?"

"Yep. At this place called the Palooza."

"Okay, look. I'll go under one condition." I gave him a questionable look and he went on. "That you go with me to the arena tomorrow. You being there could only bring me good luck."

You don't need luck, would have been the normal thing to say. But my thinking wasn't exactly normal. Instead, I said, "So, is this your way of torturing me? Or is this your way of getting me to conquer my fears?"

He chuckled, pinched my chin.

"All right, all right, I'll go!" I said after his handsome smile. "But first I need to go by the campus bookstore to pick up my psych book."

"No problem. We'll swing by there first, then to the arena for some therapeutic sessions," he grinned some more.

And I snuggled my head beneath that grin. I was hooked no matter what the consequence may be. No matter what, I was hooked.

Chapter Five

Look-alike ✔

We curved around a monumental bed of flowers near the entrance of City Community College. Arrowed signs pointed to different sites on campus. The deli Shoppe, library, fine arts center and so on, but we followed the arrow to the bookstore.

The campus was small but attractive with huge palm trees, shrubs, and other stuff like artifacts. And the windows of the main building made the building look like a 3-story when actually it was a 2-story. This building housed the administration offices and the classroom. But all the buildings had the same variegated colors of peach and deep orange.

"Just let me out here," I said to Cameron, seeing no close-up parking was available. I hopped out of the truck and he moved along with a few cars in tow.

Closed. Will reopen tomorrow.
Sorry for the inconvenience.

What! This wasn't here a moment ago. Lights were on, so I looked through the window. Someone was inside. "Hey," I rapped on the door to get his attention. The young man pointed at the sign on the door. "I know I just need my book. You're holding it for me. The name is Pia Wade."

"Come back tomorrow."

"No! You don't understand. It's already paid for if you would just give it to me. Please, so I won't have to make a special trip back."

"All right," he then opened the door.

I entered, "Thanks for saving me a senseless trip back here."

He chuckled. "No problem," he sounded hoarse now. *Congested,* I thought.

"Why is the store closed?" I asked matter-of-factly.

He turned completely around to face me. "I have to go and there's no one to replace me. Pia Wade, you say?"

"Uh, yeah...Pia Wade," I stuttered when our eyes locked. Trying so hard not to stare, my eyes shifted around in my head, tracing his body from head to toe. Here I was again wondering *could it be.* His slim body, doing nothing but standing still, but there was something about the spirit of it. Something about those deep brown orbs looking back at me as I stood here in another bookstore flabbergasted and trying not to show it. But I couldn't help it. I was in torture-me mode, creating a moment of déjà vu whenever I thought I saw him. But for once I had to do myself a favor, and of course, please the curious expression on his face by saying something already.

41

"I'm sorry but...but your resemblance is so uncanny. I mean, have we ever met, or crossed paths at some point?" This was a bold move, stretching out of my comfort zone. But it was a sane gesture to fall back on after staring at him for so long.

He put on a dulcet smile. "The thing about me is that I never forget a face. Especially one as sweet and delicate as yours," he spoke hoarsely still. He stepped forward, wagging a finger. "But you do look familiar. Eh, you're that girl. *Yeah,* Pia Wade, that's the name."

"So we have met, I thought so." I was feeling anxious now.

"Oh no!" he said tucking a hand under an elbow. Fingers then tugged at crumpled lips. "that's not what I'm saying. What I mean is that you're the one who was all over news not long ago. You landed a plane on that strange island. Yeah...see I told you I never forget a face. I'm right am I?"

I didn't want to admit it, but oh, what the hell. "Yeah...the one and only. So, other than that, we've never met?" I immediately shook my head, taking in account how he may interpret that.

"I wish you could remember; it would mean I left an impression on you. The person you think I am obviously did. I can be him, if you like," he said then winked.

Yeah, right. Smart ass. I delivered a grim look then took a moment to look around the bookstore. It was cute, large enough to carry some of everything: clothes, books other than textbooks, beauty products, which surprised me. And surrounding the huge counter here up front were all the goodies: gum, cookies, candies, chips and so on. And next to the door was a cooler filled with water, energy drinks—you name it. *Cool,* my spirit nodded.

"Well anyway, that had to of been one helluva adventure?" He added keeping the conversation alive.

"Yeah...it was definitely an adventure," I bobbed.

"It's a miracle you got out of there in time...."

"I'm sorry, but can I get that book I came for?" Enough of the small talk.

"Sure." He eased around the counter, dipped down and came up with the book. "*Pia Wade. Got it right here.*" He held up the thick blue book with one hand, came back around and handed it to me.

I was blind to it before, but I noticed then he was wearing a Vans t-shirt. Cameron came to mind and that feeling of fear again washed through me. "Are you in to skateboarding?" I said as I turned making my way to the door. After all, Cameron was waiting.

"Aw! You mean the shirt. How did you know? Just so happen, it's my favorite sport."

I glanced back, "Just a guess. A word of advice: be extremely careful. Well, thanks again for saving me a trip."

But as I was about to open the door, he said something that stopped me in my tracks. "No problem, Pia. It's the least I could do. I'll be seeing you around." I mean it wasn't so much of what he said but the drastic change of his voice that I had to turn around to see had someone else appeared out of the woodwork.

And when I turned, he was so close that I elbowed him. So close that he could very well hear my heart racing, feel my breathing grow rapid. And his alluring eyes showed no shame for his close encounter...for his intrusion. Until suddenly he backed off, "I-um...sorry. I was just going to lock up, so no one would come in behind you."

"Ah, sure...for a moment I thought you...were someone else. You got your voice back so suddenly it kind of spooked me. Sounded...supernatural in a way." I thought I'd throw in that last part, though I wasn't sure why. Supposed I wanted to see how he would respond. I studied his expression waiting, and as I did the more he looked like him. "I'm sorry. I know how that must sound," I recanted, then opened the door and got out of there as fast as I could.

I looked around for Cameron. Before moving on, I turned and looked through the window. All lights were out and he was nowhere in sight. As I advanced up the walkway his voice whispered, *see you around, Pia.*

Cameron decided we would drop by the hospital to see Sebastian before going to the arena for a practice run. Sebastian was out of intensive care. Now in a semi-private room, he lay peacefully in bed next to a window garbed with white drapes. At his side were a middle-aged couple, I assumed were his parents.

I trailed Cameron into the room, noticing the IV and monitors hooked to him. A good thing they didn't have to open up his skull (the thought of it was gruesome enough); he would heal faster for sure now. Sebastian looked like himself as he slept, getting healthier and stronger so in no time he would awaken and do whatever

44

his heart desired.

"Hi. How's he doing?" said Cameron.

"Hey," the man greeted Cameron with a pat on the back. "He's coming along remarkably well. Still having headaches, but not as bad. He just went back to sleep. We're about to leave. I got to go and check on things at the store."

"He asked about you. If only you'd been here fifteen minutes earlier," the woman said now. "He'll be out for a while with the pain medication."

"And who might this be?" The man asked smiling at me.

"Oh, I'm sorry. This is Pia. And Pia, this is Mr. and Mrs. Scott, Sebastian's parents."

"It's a pleasure to meet you," I said graciously to the couple.

"Cameron talks about you a lot. It's just nice to finally get to meet you," Mrs. Scott added. She then reached for her purse in the chair then draped it over her shoulder, "I'm ready, Sid."

"We're going too and just come back later," Cameron said.

So we all left the hospital together. Along the way we made small talk, about our big adventure last spring mostly, and how things had been with me since. Then once outside the lobby, we said our goodbyes and went our separate ways.

Chapter Six
We Meet Again

Wave Skatepark in Miami was Cameron's favorite spot for skateboarding, but today he decided to stay close to home, and so we ended up at a place called Flow Park. An indoor park like the one in Miami but this one had one of the best vert ramps, Cameron was telling me as we got out of the truck. But I couldn't care less about a ramp. I would rather be doing something else. Like going to the movies. As I thought about it, it was one thing we hadn't done together.

"Is Dax meeting you here?" I wondered.

"Yeah," he said reaching for the skateboard in the backseat. "He's already hitting the ramp. There he is right over there." I looked behind me and there it was, his white Rodeo. Cameron remotely locked the doors and we headed for the entrance.

Midways I stopped, "Hey, hold up. Are you skating in those shoes?"

"Nah. Watch this for me," he said placing the

skateboard on the ground and ran back to the car.

Today was mild, humid. We had been getting sporadic showers for the past few days, and from the feel in the air and scent it carried, I suspected today a shower or two. Cameron was back from switching out his slip-ons for black snickers to go with the rest of his attire—blue jeans, black pullover and a determined spirit. He swept up the board and we continued in stride.

"Pia, try not to worry. Okay? You're just worrying over nothing. Just give it time, you'll see," he was saying as the door opened to a noisy bunch leaving the building. I had become more nervous; it showed obviously. I nodded letting him know I heard him despite the blaring bunch.

After paying a small fee to enter the park, Cameron walked me to my seat. I plopped down quietly and said, "Ok," expecting him to leave and do what he came to do, but he just stood there. I looked up, on his face was an expression for me to not to worry. "Go! I'll be fine. Just be careful," I said then.

"I'm always careful. Just relax and watch me do my thing. And enjoy it like you always do." He landed a quick kiss on my forehead then took off.

I smiled to myself looking the place over. *If you've seen one skatepark, you've seen them all,* I thought. They all structured with ailments hazardous to your health. Like ramps...all kinds of ramps and railings to do all sorts of tricks. And stairs...mostly paralleled with the railings. And bowls of various shapes and sizes you would find at some parks, not here though. And what would a skatepark be without a pro shop to outfit skaters with protective gear? And for what I'd seen, hardly anyone used them. I supposed it was a macho thing. Like with women wearing heels to look good and feel sexy.

Here at Flow Park was a ramp called the half-pipe, sectioned off from the rest of the park. As I sat in the third row of a row of bench, I looked right through it to the other side where there were more rows of benches. The ramp itself shaped like a "C," laid on the curve of its back. *Help! I've fallen and I can't get up.* I imagined poor somebodies curled up like a "C," screaming for real because...it was that scary. This ramp had to be at least twelve-feet deep and I despised it so; the same ramp that nearly claimed Sebastian's life.

Now Cameron was on top of it, along the edge with his friend Dax. I couldn't help feeling queasy because the edge could easily take him over just for the hell of it. *No, he got this*, I recited. It'd been the case before, and I hoped it would continue to be so. Though what good that was doing, figuratively I was biting my nails and squirming in my seat.

They were planning something, Cameron and Dax, I could tell. Something big. It was all in their body language. I had seen them practice enough times to know. And *gosh* the anticipation pricked at my nerves. On skateboards lending over the edge, together they dove over it. And my heart went nuts as their skateboards carried them like a rocket, down one side of the wall and up the other. Smooth and effortless, they came within cutting inches of each other performing a crisscross. Frozen in awe, I couldn't believe it. I mean I knew Cameron was good, but I didn't know he was "that good." As if he woke up with superman's ambition, he was exceptional.

Over and over, he descended one side of the ramp and hurled up the other impressively that it seemed my nerves would have calmed down some—but no! I was on a constant roller coaster ride, reaching a height of being in a total wreck, to a low of what I didn't consider calm at all. Because I knew he would do it all over again.

I managed to put on a proud smile anyway, as the energy of people around me thrilled to death by what they were seeing sparked me. They were like "Wow, get a load of that... Those boys are good. If they're in the competition they're going to be tough to beat...." And whistling and shouting was in the mix. They were so in to it that some of the excitement rubbed off on me; the butterflies lodged in my pit began to fade away.

Cameron yelled to get my attention. He was pumping up the skateboard over his head, wearing a huge smile.

"Beautiful, Babe...looking good," I yelled through hands circling my mouth, as if they were a loudspeaker. A couple about my age sitting behind me, I suspected they recognized me. On a sly, they had been staring at me for a while now. It crossed my mind that it wouldn't be a bad idea to wear dark shades sometimes. I really didn't want to be bothered with people wanting to know more about my adventure on that island. But that wasn't the case with Cameron and Brian; they still loved telling the tale. I tried to avoid talking about it as much as possible. It was strange how I wanted to forget about it when it came to other people wanting to talk about it, which made me a hypocrite in a way, now that I thought about it.

"Whoa!" I responded to another pair who did an impressive flip. For what I'd seen so far, they all were as good as heck, lending credit to the rookies as well. Cameron and Dax had already done many tricks together like champions but were now performing solo.

And because they made it look so easy, and in spite of minor slip-ups here and there, I was starting to feel more at ease. So much so, I found room in my brain to think about the aeronautics of the sport. It seemed in order to move to great height, the weight of the body would have to be a significant factor. It seemed impossible for heavy persons to support enough speed to climb the other side of the ramp. They would fall hard. Really hard. Bottom line, too much weight on the board would steal some of one's mind control over the board. Whereas a lightweight person on the board could converge as one unit in motion flying like an eagle. It would be too painstaking for a heavy person to hold up. Like if a plane's carrying too much weight, it would go down.

"Yeah," I chuckled lightly to my brilliance. That's why all the skateboarders I've seen were thin to medium build.

Ouch! Ouch! It hurt my eyes to see one of the skaters, merely skin and bones, get a good beating as he tumbled off the slope to the bottom. "Is he okay?" I could hear muted and unmuted emotions say. Grabbing at one side of his arm then to rubbing his knees, it took him a moment to get up. One of the other skaters helped him up. He then retrieved his board, was moving on his own just fine.

No helmet, I thought to myself now. None of them ever wore helmets...hardly ever.

Scary how used to it they were. Just another day at

the park. In moments, that boy was back on top of the ramp, ready to give it another shot. By now, I was freaking out again visualizing every one of them mangled on top of one another at the bottom of the ramp. Just one huge mangled mess.

I got up and emotionally stormed out of the place. *A slip-up like that could have easily landed him paralyzed? Paralyzed due to broken bones at least.* But that didn't seem to affect anyone. That's the furthest thing from their minds it would seem. Never mind what happened to Sebastian. My emotional storm went on: *And what if the legs had bent a certain way on that boy? Or gone limp, making the fall that much severe? And his poor nose—My God what if the board had slammed him in the face leaving things a bloody mess? What if he'd landed in a coma?* Of course that was the furthest thing from their minds. The cellphone began jumping in my pocket as I went through the door. It couldn't have gone off at a better time; I needed a distraction to help me chill.

"Michelle Lambert?" I muttered, amazed to see it was her calling. What could she want? As if I didn't know. "Hello," I said moving to a more secluded spot to talk.

"Hi, Pia. This is Michelle Lambert."

"Yes, Miss Lambert; I recognize your voice."

"Is this a bad time? Sounds like you're at a bowling alley or something."

"I'm at a skatepark, actually."

"Oh. Well, I'll get to the point so I won't keep you. You are aware that our offer to publish your diaries is about to expire? Have you given it any more thought?"

"Well...it's like I said before. I can't see myself

sharing personal moments that I've written, to the world."

"I understand. Really, I do. That's why we are willing to work with you on that."

"Umm...what do you mean?"

"You don't want to publish the whole thing, we get that. So we'll leave it up to you to decide what goes to print and what doesn't. It's your call. Sounds like something you can agree on?"

"Ugh, yeah...I think I can. B-but...but what if you're not interested in what's left?"

"Good question. What you leave for us to work with will be the deciding factor. But listen. We want everything from the night you went missing to the day on the island, and anything relating to it afterwards. If you could offer more, then that would be a bonus. Okay?"

"I see. Well, I would need time to comb through it. How much time will I have to do that?"

"You think you can get back to me, say...two to three weeks?"

"Well, I'll try; it shouldn't be a problem."

"And if you need a little more time, don't hesitate to let me know. Call if you need anything or have any questions."

"Sure. Thanks Miss Lambert." Hmm...could be my diaries were going to be published after all. The idea of that happening uplifted me instantly. And as it turned out, was a good retreat for my mind going mad just moments ago. As I started to head back inside, I looked up and there he was. Immediately my uplifted state sunk like a bang sinking a cake in an oven.

"What do ya know, twice in one day, eh?" He came on to be as surprised as I was.

Tongue-tied, I had to force myself to speak. "I suppose I know now why the bookstore closed up so early?" I said eyeing the skateboard tucked under his arm, also noticing he had changed into gray active wear. I then pinned a stern look on him as he responded.

"And what is it you think you know exactly?"

"Well isn't it obvious? And just think; you were going to make me come back for the book."

"Besides the book, why does it matter to you? You still think I'm that person you've met? He must be very important."

"Don't flatter yourself. I just thought you had something important to do. Like a doctor's appointment...with your voice going in and out in all. But you seem cured now. Hmm."

"I don't have to explain myself. And you shouldn't worry over something that doesn't concern you—you think? Now back off now," he showed the palm of his hand when I stepped forward.

"What!" I shook my head, offended, but continued to move pass him. He looked off as the door to the men's restroom opened. The person surfaced wore a blue cap and active wear as well.

"Hey, I'll be in in a minute," Mr. Smooth-talker with a voice out of this world said to him. He then stopped me. "Pia...I know I remind you of someone. Whoever he is...well...if you need to talk—if I can help in anyway—"

I stopped him, "You know...what I don't like is you talking to me like you know me."

"Is that what I'm doing?" He shrugged, moved a few steps crabwise. "Yeah, well, I would like to. How 'bout that?"

His straightforwardness was a little too straightforward. I mean, who in the hell did he think he was? But, he did remind me of someone... Something about that was straightforward. If only I knew for sure. If only it was him, and he revealed as much.

"Think about it, Pia," he said walking away now. "I think it'd be worth your while."

"Oh, and why is that?"

With his back to me, he paused, "You know where to find me." He then opened the steel door, and the noise from within engulfed him then the door banged shut behind him.

Chapter Seven
Them...the Echoes

Steam blowing out of my ears, I scoffed at his remark and reentered the park myself moments later.

I moved through the aisle looking straight in the ramp specifically for him. But where was he? The person he spoke to earlier I saw him at the foot of the ramp. Yet he had to be in here somewhere. He couldn't have exited through a wall. No, he couldn't have done that; I was just overlooking him. *Exited through a wall:* on second thought that shouldn't be rule out. I, of all people, should know that anything was possible.

I sat in the same place, crossed my legs, and as I looked over my shoulder, there he was, coming down the aisle to my right. It looked as though he had just reentered the park from another door. As he went to join others on the ramp, I couldn't take my eyes off him, wondering where was has coming from just now. Legs crossed, I leaned forward and propped the side of my face with my hand. *'You know where to find me.'* Did he really think...? I mean, he seemed so assure of himself to suggest I would want to pursue him. When I didn't even know his—

Gosh! I could kick myself. Because not once but twice I didn't think to ask his name.

A group of people entering the park distracted me. Only for a moment, my mind then went to the top of the ramp, where he had joined, I assumed was, his skating partner. All the skaters had someone they liked practicing with.

My vision dropped to my knees as I began thinking about the magician on the riverfront yesterday. He really took me by surprise. Because it was like seeing a vision I had seen years ago all over again, only this time it hadn't been a vision, it was real.

I was starting to get that creepy feeling again. A feeling that something bad was going to happen. But maybe I was doing it to myself, generating my own fear. Because what you think is what you feel, and what you feel is what you think. And sometimes you give the mind more power than you intend it to have.

"Hey Nick!" someone said and my head snapped up. A couple of boys were hugging. They seemed surprised to see each other. As if it had been a long time since they had. My eyes then hurled to the top of the ramp, and like a jackrabbit, I jumped to my feet. Cameron and you-know-who were exchanging words as if they knew each other. As if, they were best buds. This had me more nervous than ever that I grabbed my arms and began kneading them. I couldn't yell and say—what exactly? So I eased back down, contemplating *what ifs*. What if he's really out to hurt Cameron? What if his plan was to do it here? And Sebastian, maybe his accident hadn't been an accident after all. His showing up here today couldn't be a coincidence. I had about convinced myself of this.

Cameron was off the ramp heading this way. But not really, with a hand gesture he said he was going to the restroom. "Okay," I nodded back and stayed put. As much as I wanted to head him off and warn him, I stayed put.

But in no time he was back in the routine. And I managed to relax a little, by feeding myself good thoughts. *Relax and enjoy yourself; everything's going to be all right.* Cameron, how could I tell him I thought otherwise?

"I've never seen them before." "Me neither. They must be new." A male and female sitting behind me said. "Damn! They're good," the male got a little excited.

And he was right. You-know-who and his friend *were* good. They were so coordinated they probably had been practicing together for years. No one could get that good overnight, I grumbled, though I had other thoughts going on in my mind. Apparently, they knew all the tricks; I could see Cameron and Dax taking notice. Everyone was. How could we not?

"Hey, I've never seen them around before. Do you know 'em?"

I could feel him leaning, talking to me, so this time I turned to put a face with the voice.

"Hey, Pia." This person I didn't know placed a hand on my shoulder, but I was surprised he called me by name. Then again, I shouldn't've been. But now was seriously thinking about wearing a disguise in the future. All that publicity still etched in some many memories—

and for how long? Maybe forever.

"Hey, hi," I just went along.

"Those boys are good. Do you know 'em? I saw you talking to one of 'em in the lobby." He was nice looking, neatly dressed, looked to be about twenty-something. His long, lean body he relaxed in a slouchy position now with arms straddled over a bench behind him. The girl with him had honey blonde hair, styled in a neat bob, and her smile was thin and pleasant.

"Not really," I said. "The one you saw me talking to I met earlier today at the bookstore. I was just surprised to run into him here." I smiled then turned back around, figuring that he knew me because he knew Cameron. But it didn't matter; I was back wondering about all of this being a coincidence.

"Whoa...that was a good copycat," a fella across the way yelled. But I frowned thinking the comment irrelevant. Because they all were copycats as far as I was concerned. How could they not be when the whole idea was to outdo one another? Besides, I missed what he was talking about—copycat or no copycat.

I put on a huge smile when I saw Cameron waving. I waved back with wiggly fingers; a flirty wave I called it. Then I noticed him looking at Cameron, and he then noticed me noticing him. The way he looked at me, if only I could read his mind. If only I knew for sure, what it was I thought I knew. And knowing that he and his friend were new to the area didn't help matters none. It only made me more suspicious.

The way Cameron was looking at me now, I knew exactly what he was thinking. So I played along. I folded my arms rough like, inflated and deflated my jaws with a whistle. Just to show that "yes" I was exhausted and ready to go. He then wagged his finger and shook his head. And I felt *oh so* like a little kid having to stay put—for god knows how long. Immediately I propped up my pouty face with both hands, acting like a kid. But I couldn't keep up the silliness for long. *A bargain is a bargain* I could hear Cameron say. And so he carried on, trying to show me there was nothing to worry about.

And it seemed so. So far, no one had left the place hurt or disabled. Seemed it was turning out to be just a typical day at the park. All peachy, no one worried that what happened to Sebastian would happen to them. Maybe, just maybe, I was worried all for nothing.

Cameron, Dax, and You-know-who and his friend were now kicking it around like best friends. Surprisingly I was doing better at not letting it get to me. They all were quite impressive today. And giving props where props were due was part of the game; I knew that.

I took out a pad and pencil just to put my mind somewhere else. "It's all about the motto," I mumbled, speaking of sports. I gazed off at them still kicking it around, and then started jotting down things:

Play well and be a good sport.
No matter what, keep the peace.
In solidarity, we are one.
It's what good sportsmanship is all about.

It didn't matter if they were newcomers, I then thought. Because new people had a way of drawing attention, sometimes in the most peculiar ways. *Yeah, they do, like now,* I thought. *Who were they? And where in the hell did they come from?* I couldn't help it...just couldn't help it.

I checked the time on my phone: one-fifteen. Another whole hour had passed, and Cameron still wasn't ready to call it quits. I went back to jotting down thoughts:

Don't make things more than what it is.
No matter what, always, always trust your instinct.
And never ever trust your opponent.
Never!

In a while Cameron signaled he was about ready. *Finally,* it was about time. I went over the notes, focusing more on the last part, before putting away the pad and pencil. *This was some session of conquering my fears,* I thought. Whether it helped or not, it remained to be seen.

"So what do you think now, huh? C'mon let's hear the verdict." Cameron approached all cheery-faced, roped an arm around my neck as he landed a kiss on top of my head.

"Please, hon, you all sweaty and smelly. Haven't I suffered enough?" I sniffed and covered my nose. "And I think you were incredibly good out there, really. I've never seen you skate like that." I expressed in a thrilling lovable tone.

"Now you're talking." He seized a quick kiss on my lips then. "It'd be okay; you'll see."

"Hey, Pia," Dax spoke coming toward us. He was as sweaty and exhausted yet wore a satisfying smile. Dax had a chiseled face with bulging cheekbones; a slim build, a little muscular, like Cameron's build.

"Unbelievable!" I said. "I could not believe my eyes. You two were awesome. When did you get that good? It's like you became masters overnight."

"Yeah, we were, weren't we?" Dax accepted the

kudos and virtually patted himself on the back.

I smiled up at Cameron. "Just keep being the best you can be—both of you." I glanced at Dax then back at Cameron. "But be better at being safe more than anything. You can't lose if you do that." My tone was mostly serious and I knew Cameron didn't need me to sound so serious. But he knew how I felt. That hadn't changed since we walked through the doors.

"Yeah...I feel you," Dax emphasized. "Hey, I got to get out of here."

"Gotta get to work?" Cameron asked.

"Mm-hmm." Dax glanced at a leathery watch on his wrist, "I got about an hour. Hey, I'll catch up with you later." He gave a fisted wave and headed for the exit.

"Yeah, later," Cameron said after him.

"Hey bro, you know you got it," a fella with dreads I'd noticed in the audience the whole time said to Cameron as he approached.

"Greg, hey man!" Cameron joined hands with him for a quick handshake.

"I heard about your man, Sebastian. How's he doing?"

"He's okay, and the prognosis is good. He's...hanging in there. I went by the hospital earlier to check on him, but he was asleep."

"That's good, good," he nodded. "I know how much he was looking forward to this gig coming up. But hey, you were looking good out there today. What's gotten into you? You looked determined, like a tiger. Is it true what I heard? You looking to steal that prize money?"

I looked at Cameron, chuckled, because Greg hit

it on the nail. It was if Cameron slipped into Sebastian's shoes and the fit was so perfect he became him.

"Yeah...I'm officially in," Cameron confirmed finally.

"Well then I'm putting my money on you, just so you know, so don't you let me down, now." He showed his pearly whites, grinning.

"If I let you down, I let Sebastian down," Cameron spoke from the heart, blushing.

"Yeah, I'm pulling for Sebastian too..." Greg took on a humble tone.

Cameron then took my hand, "We got to get out of here; I'll be seeing you, man."

"Don't let me hold you up," Greg graciously stepped aside.

As we inched toward the exit, I asked what I had been dying to ask. "Who were the new guys everyone was talking about? You and Dax were talking to them."

"You mean Winston and Ebay?"

"One had on gray, and the other one, burgundy...blue cap."

"Yeah, Winston and Ebay."

"Like the website Ebay?"

"Exactly," he said.

"Hmm," I frowned. "Which one is Ebay?"

"The one in gray. And the dude sounds like a broadcaster. We all were teasing him, telling him he should give up his skateboard. And he probably got tired of it, thinking we trying to get rid of him. He's competing too, you know? They both are."

"No kidding!"

"I wish. You saw how good they are."

"Mm-hmm, that I did," I said as Cameron shoved open the steal door. And as soon as we entered the lobby I could hear it, the pounding on the roof and the crushing thunder. "Ah-nah, it's raining hard...."

Mats by the doors were wet with people rushing in shielded with newspaper, clothes, plastic—anything they had gotten their hands on. Those standing by the doors ready to leave seemed undecided whether to dart through the rain or wait it out. But those needing to make a move for whatever reason darted out into nature's fury. I turned to Cameron when he placed a hand on my shoulder.

"I can run and get the truck and pull it up front," Cameron proposed.

"Nah, it's coming down too hard. Let's wait for a break then we'll make a run for it..." I was saying when I started hearing strange voices...echoic voices of men. I looked around wondering, trying to figure out where it was coming from.

"I know how hard it is to not get carried away in this mundane nature. For this being your first assignment, you handled yourself well," one of them said.

"You're a great mentor, Captain. I'm proud to be of service to you on this mission. I know how important it is to you," the other one responded. *"Captain, has the subject showed any signs of remembering?"*

"I'm afraid not. She doesn't know, but she's starting to feel it."

"I know you're hopeful."

"I'm keeping the faith. And letting it run its course."

"For however long it may be..."

"Cam, do you hear that?" I said as the voices

63

continued. Cameron must not have heard me. My lips moved, but even I didn't hear myself speak. The voices echoed in waves, and it appeared I was the only one hearing it.

The park doors opened, and the voices stopped, replaced at once with the noise spilling out of the park. Coming through the doors were Ebay and Winston—our eyes locked instantly. And it felt weird. Weird because, in a way, it felt like we were coconspirators of...something.... It was just that weird.

"It stopped raining just like that," Cameron chimed in. I could hear in his voice how amazed he was.

I turned, looked out, and I was too amazed to see it had stopped completely. And to see the sky was clear, except for one gray cloud hanging overhead, so low you could almost reach up and touch it. And it seemed odd it being the only thing blocking the sun, trying so hard to peep through it.

Through my peripheral, I watched as they arrived at the next set of doors; my head shifted a degree or two. *She's watching.* There it was again, the echo, at the same time he moved his lips. I held my breath, held it, because I knew that he, *Ebay,* was talking about me. I just knew. Also, I knew somehow that the voices...*were them.*

"Cameron?" I turned for his attention, but for the moment someone else had it.

They were outside now, and as they descended the stairs, I looked up in the sky. The sun now was in full view, and that gray cloud was nowhere in sight. *Where did it go that fast?* I wondered as my eyes again met his.

Moments later, "...Let's get out of here," Cameron startled me when he forced the door open.

With his hand on the small of my back, he guided me through the door. We descended the stairs then made our way through the parking lot.

A black Camaro. I made a mental note of the car Ebay drove as they left the premises. We were getting in the truck now.

"I'm hungry. How 'bout you?" Cameron said as his door slammed shut.

"You should be. That was some workout. You probably could eat a cow," I said buckling my seatbelt.

He smiled. "I feel like I could eat a cow. Where do you want to go?"

"It's up to you; I'm not really that hungry." Though not for food but for something else. "The new guys, was today your first time seeing them?" I asked him.

"Yeah." He glanced over at me, started the engine. "Why you ask?"

"I have a bad feeling about them."

"It's not them, Pia. You have a bad feeling about me getting hurt, and you're using them as a conspiracy theory because they're new to the area. And you must stop. You're running yourself crazy and you gotta STOP. Look...I don't mean to be hard on you, but what can I do to get you to see that?"

"Cam? What if I told you I met Ebay today at the bookstore when I picked up the book, and," I paused, thinking about this some more.

"So he works at the bookstore. What about it?" Obviously, he didn't have time for my pause.

*Well, I have reason to believe that he's behind everything, the island, and now he's come for me, and I don't know why, but I believe he's wants to hurt you—*I honestly believed this but... How could I tell him that?

"I saw him at the bookstore earlier. He works there, that's all."

"And? Come on with it! You know me better than that."

"And, he kinda came on to me." *Now how was I going to explain that?*

"What do you mean he came on to you? How?"

"I don't know how to explain it; it's just something about him I don't trust. And just now, in the park, I heard voices and I know it came from them."

"Voices, Pia? Really? It still doesn't explain things. Because it could be all in your head, you know that. I'm sorry but...what can I say that I haven't said already?"

"Nothing, just forget about it. I don't want to fight with you about this."

"Neither do I but you can't make accusations like that without proof. You say you heard voices."

"I know! I know," I sighed. "Let's not talk about it right now."

He shifted the gear to *Drive* and pulled off, not speaking another word. And it was for the best; I wasn't prepared to go another round with him about—everything! I would only make a mess of things. And it would end with him proving his point: why I shouldn't have come back to Florida in the first place. And I knew he hated being right about this. All he wanted was what's good for me. So the subject remained hush-hush for now.

We winded up at a Chinese buffet, close to the house.

The place was an ideal feast with a well-lit buffet situated in the center of the restaurant, people indulging around it. Blacktopped tables with red chairs surrounded it, also a few wooden booths off in corners. Dim lights and soft Asian music made for a cozy setting. And the candlelit tables added charm. We reserved a booth then went through the buffet. We returned with our plates loaded with egg rolls, fried rice, salmon, string beans.... Loaded with a little of everything frankly.

"Oh, I forgot to tell you. The publisher called today," I said spreading a big burgundy napkin over my lap.

"Oh, yeah? Still trying to get you to publish the diaries, eh?"

"What else? I haven't told my parents yet, but I have a feeling they might be okay with it."

He nodded, "Hmm, are you sure?"

"Well, she obviously figured I wasn't interested in the original offer. Now she will accept whatever I feel comfortable publishing. So I agreed to go through the diaries, take out what I don't want published, and they will take it from there." I grinned. "All they want now is the story starting from the day I went missing to the day we went to the island."

"That should have been enough from the start. They were trying to manipulate you, 'cause they never needed every little detail you wrote in the diaries anyway. New York Times bestseller list, here she comes!"

"Mmm," I nodded a huge smile, "I can see that."

"Cam, I didn't tell you because I was afraid to, and I probably shouldn't now, but I am. Because you may think it's a coincidence, and it could be."

"You had a vision?"

"No, not exactly. But it's about one I had a few years ago, of magician doing a trick with balls, floating in the air like bubbles. Well...I saw it, just as I had in the vision, on the riverfront, yesterday...I saw it yesterday."

"Pia," he looked me in the eyes. "You haven't been back long and already you're hearing voices, and now this. I don't know what to think; maybe it was a coincidence. Have you thought for one minute that you could be making yourself sick? I told you this could happen. The brain is complicated, weird sometimes, like an alien."

"So what you're saying, my brain conjured up the magician?"

"No, of course not! But...but it's intuitive."

"Like Sebastian's dream..." I muttered.

He bit off a piece of biscuit, stared at me as he chewed. "Can you at least help me understand what is it about Ebay that bothers you?"

I sighed softly, lowered my head. "No, I can't. It's just a feeling I'm trying to make sense of. You know how that is with me." I began drumming my nails on the tabletop, fed up with myself for not being more convincing. "But what if it's not over? What if it didn't matter whether I had come back here or not?" Holding his eyes to mine, I needed him to look deep and see the principle of my concern. And not ignore what we'd experienced together not so long ago. As far as I was concerned, we were in this together, forever. It was our destiny.

"Look, I would pack you up and drive you back to Texas myself if I have to. Or should I call your parents?

I don't know what I should do right now, Pia," he said, stunning me because obviously destiny wasn't communicating with him. Not as it had before.

"I don't want to think like this, but in order to protect you what choice do I have? You were safe back in Texas with nothing happening. When that island disappeared, so did the dreams and the visions. And now...I don't want to be responsible for anything happening to you. How can I live with myself if something happened to you because of me?"

"I want you to trust my instinct. What if it's you, not me, who's in danger?"

"So you're here to protect me? Don't you see how you're turning this thing around?"

"You...don't trust me," my tone reduced to sadness and disappointment.

"I *do* trust you, but this is not about trust. Pia...you have to find a way to let this go. It's all you, Babe, look—"

"Want me take 'is for you?" a petite female, Asian accent, interrupted offering to clear our table. We accepted and as soon as she was gone, I urged Cameron to go on.

"So you really think it's all in my head?"

"I just want you to be happy, blissfully happy. Lately, I've been thinking how happy you were the day of your prom. Remember? Like it was yesterday." He reached for his wallet on the table and took out a photo. It was photo of him, my dashing prince in a black tuxedo, and me, wearing a champagne gown. The bodice sparkled and chiffon fanned out from the hip. My Cinderella dress I called it, and it had been perfect for the occasion.

"Yeah, I do," I said reminiscing. That day he really surprised me to tears when he stepped out of the limo filled with partygoers. My parents and Cameron had arranged the surprise. I thought I was going to the prom without a date, and the whole time they had me believing that. I had just gotten off the phone with Cameron. His last words were "Have fun, and I'll see you at the end of the rainbow." And when he materialized moments later, it'd been like magic, seeing him and rainbows through tears of joy.

"Yeah. It was your Cinderella moment. How could I let you down? Don't you know I'd never let you down?"

I nodded. "I remembered saying that I wanted the moment to last for all eternity. And you said, 'In the power vested in us both, it will last for as long as you wish. I promise you.' And then I said, 'A promise is a promise.' And then we sealed it with a kiss."

"'A promise is a promise,' he repeated.

Gazing into his eyes, I said, "That was a special moment. One I will never forget. But Cam—"

"It doesn't have to be a 'but' don't you see. All you have to do is just let it go; I strongly believe that."

"How do you do it? How do put it all behind you so easily, like it never happened?"

"I haven't. Not how you think. But it helps knowing how lucky we were. Never would I ever want to be in that kind of situation again, Pia. And if I can prevent it I will, because next time we may not be so lucky."

"I know...it's just so unfair." Tears welled up and

I began blinking to keep them from cresting big-time.

"Pia?" Cameron got up immediately, moved to my side of the table, and drew me into his arms.

"I'm afraid. I just can't bear the thought of something happening to you...after what happened to Sebastian." I sobbed all over him, realizing only I and I alone would have to protect him, and I didn't know how to do that. He wasn't dropping out of the competition. So the best way to help was to let him focus on competing, not me. I couldn't live with myself if I were the reason he ended up like Sebastian or worse. I was on my own. *I was really on my own.*

"I know, I know," he said wiping away my tears. "I know."

Moments later he got up to go to the restroom, and my phone purred a melody. *Where are you?* A text message from Stephanie, I stared at it until it faded out with the light. I then settled my back against the vinyl. *What if I was right about someone, or something, out to hurt Cameron?* It's what my instinct was telling me, and it hadn't failed me yet.

I pressed the button to get back to Stephanie's message, and then tapped the section to reply. I typed *I need your help* then hit "send".

Cameron came back and we went to checkout. As we left the restaurant, a sweet melody awakened my cellphone again. Stephanie: *All ready for battle. I'm here for you.*

What! My eyes gleamed because...

She surprised me. She really surprised me.

71

Chapter Eight
Let's Get Serious

Cameron dropped me off at home before going back to the hospital to see Sebastian. But first he would go home and get cleaned up. I decided not to go to the hospital with him this time around.

As he pulled off, Miss Saunders my next-door neighbor was coming out of the house to get groceries from her car.

"Hi, Pia. How are you today?" she waved. She's a nice, big-boned woman that wore stylist frames to go with her pulled-back hairstyles. Like today, a ponytail. Looking out the window, I would see her coming or going. But when we encountered each other, like now, it was usually brief. And because Miss Saunders was naturally funny, I would always walk away giggling or with a big smile on my face. But lately, she was more concern about my well-being.

"I'm fine, Ms. Saunders. Can I help you with something?" I offered.

"This is the last of it, but thanks. Hey, how would you like to come over, visit for a while?"

"I would but I'm expecting Stephanie..." I looked up the street I saw her coming. "Well here she comes now."

"Okay, another time when you're not busy. And I'm over here if you need me for anything. And I mean *anything*," she said emphatically, slammed the trunk and headed inside the house.

"Thanks, Ms. Saunders," I waved.

When Stephanie arrived, she followed me in the house. I was eager to tell her about the plan I had worked up, hoping she was real about being there for me. Though I suspected I would have to do some convincing—no sinking islands or anything out of the ordinary. Just because it sounded as though she might be game for anything, didn't mean that she was. Just the same, her reaction to my text surprised me, given she had no clue what I was up to. But I had a hunch big sister was willing to take her protective mode to a new level.

I kicked off my brown saddles in the foyer, walked over and turned on the TV.

"Girl, what's going on?" Stephanie said coming through the door.

"Close the door. Do you want something to drink?"

"No, I'm good." She closed the door then stood aslant with her hands on her hips. "Do I need to get Ariana and Cristina over here?"

"No-no." I dashed into the kitchen, opened the fridge, grabbed a bottled water then hurried back. I entered the living room listening to the news report on the TV. About the earthquake that happened in Bermuda in 2009. *"...Seismologists are calling it a miracle that the tsunami moved out into the open sea...,"* the reporter was saying.

"You hear that? After all this time...that was about two years ago. *Unbelievable...*" I said, talking to myself mostly. It was so unbelievable it took so long that the reporting didn't seem real.

"Come. Sit," I said as I patted the sofa.

"Now I'm really curious," Stephanie said as she sat next to me.

"It's happening again." I picked up the TV remote and lowered the volume some.

"What? The visions?"

"Well, no...not exactly. Just listen, because I know what I'm about to say is going to sound crazy. And it is. It's always been nothing but crazy to me even though—but anyway, something is happening. And it's different this time, not like before."

"Okay." She looked at me with intentness and well sharpened sharp ears. "Did it just start today?"

I bit down on my bottom lip, shook my head. "Mnh-mnh. It started at the airport yesterday. I can't explain it, but remember that a weird guy that came to the car asking for a ride?" Stephanie nodded her head. "Well, I got a weird feeling about him."

"Well, so did I. I mean, wearing tight leather pants in the summer, and then he really had the nerves to ask us for a ride. I mean, what was he thinking?"

"Yeah. Strange. I think he was intentionally disguising himself for some reason. But that ring he was wearing. Remember, I wanted you to see it before we pulled off."

"Yeah, I remember. What about the ring?"

"I...I don't know exactly. Just that, I got a feeling that I'd seen it somewhere before, and it was so weird it bugged the hell out of me. Then the magician on waterfront; I didn't find it strange at first. But when he did that magic trick with the balls, I had a major flashback, and then I remembered seeing it before. That same magician, right there on the riverfront, and the floating balls trick—I saw in a vision I had years ago."

"Are you sure? Magicians do all sorts of amazing tricks like that all the time. I seem to remember seeing a trick something like that before. Magic seems unrealistic—I know what you mean."

"Magic is common, yeah, I hear you. But this particular one was exactly how I saw it in the vision... And then today at the skatepark I heard voices. Only me no one else heard them. You see?"

"Okay, so...are you thinking about hijacking a plane to go see if the island's back?"

"Stop it!" I hit the sofa with both hands. "You're not taking me seriously."

"I am taking you seriously. So going back to the island is out I get it. You said you needed help. With what?"

"So you're willing to help hijack a plane—impressive!"

"I'm glad to hear that's off the table. But I want to help in any way I can."

"It is because things are different now; it doesn't feel like before," I said.

"Before, it was all about the island. How would

you know how different it is without going out there to see?"

"I don't know, it's just a feeling. But I couldn't put your life, and my life, in that kind of danger again. But once I'm sure of what's going on I know who to contact."

"Then what, then?"

"You have to promise to not say anything to anyone." I looked her straight in the eyes for assurance, and she nodded okay. "I need time to figure this thing out..." I was saying when I heard car doors slam. We both hopped up and peeped out the window.

"Ugh. I forgot to tell you I called Cristina and Ariana," Stephanie now compelled to say after the fact.

"But what did you say to them!"

"That you were in trouble or something."

I sighed and went to open the door before they made it to the porch.

"Hey, there's a boat on fire on the water?" Cristina informed before I could say anything. "We saw a lot of smoke; it's not too far up the coast."

"Well let's go check it out!" Stephanie said.

"Hold up a minute, I gotta lock up," I said then rushed inside to retrieve the keys off the end table. I locked the backdoor then the front. We went through the backyard to reach the brick steps leading straight to the beach.

"How did you hear about the boat?" I asked indirectly.

"I got a text from Mike. He said it's up pass the boardwalk, but he wasn't sure what happened," Ariana offered.

"Omigod! Look how thick the smoke is, and

black," said Stephanie as soon as we came to better view. "I hope no one got hurt."

"I know. I wonder what happened," Cristina added as we all gazed off in the distance. It was far up the coast. And there were groups of people up and down the coast looking in that direction. As far as it was, I could see now flashing red lights at the boat.

"Come on," Cristina beckoned us. "Let's go see if anybody knows what happened."

"They probably don't know any more than we do," I felt.

"Yeah, but let's just walk and see anyway," she encouraged regardless.

"Sure, why not," I replied as we trudged down the beach to reach a group of people not too far away.

"So what's going on?" Ariana attempted to broach the subject of why Stephanie had called them in the first place.

"Ooh, it's nothing." At this point, I wasn't sure what I wanted to do or if I wanted to involve them.

Cristina frowned, "Are you sure? We're here to help in any way we can."

"Yeah, right. What did Stephanie say to y'all anyway?"

"Nothing!" Stephanie spoke up quickly.

"Look, I don't know. Maybe it's not a good idea, 'cause," I hunched my shoulders, "I'm not sure..." *I can't involve them,* right now I was thinking.

"Uh come on! What's not a good idea?" Cristina urged. And they all looked at me, their interest on fire like that boat up ahead, that I couldn't help smiling.

Shaking my head, "Nah it's—"

"*Uh, c'mon, tell us.* Let us be the judge." Ariana wasn't about to let me back out.

"And we promise to keep it between us. Anything you want," Stephanie now.

I gave Stephanie scolding eyes. *You had to of said something to them. You just wait...* She avoided eye contact, though, looking down at her gaiting feet. She had to of said something to get them eager "over nothing." And I say "over nothing" because at the time Stephanie had no idea what was going on. So I could only imagine what little bug she put in their ears.

The black smoke was starting to clear out, revealing more red flashing lights. Again, I hoped no one was hurt.

"Hi. Does anyone know what happened up there?" Cristina asked as we approached. We all paused to hear something. A couple about thirty-something, the male a good ten inches taller than the female, both wearing shorts and tank tops, spoke up.

"We heard an explosion from up there." From the resort, he was pointing; the same one Cameron and I snuck off into, I recalled. "And when we got down here we saw this. Not sure what caused the explosion."

"Was anyone on the boat that you know of?" Cristina asked now.

"No, I heard they got off in time," he said. "Thank goodness," the woman added.

Yeah, we agreed. We thanked them, hung around a bit then started back.

"I'm still waiting to hear what we can do to help," Ariana started up again. "And you know what I think?" I put on a quirky face and she continued, "I think you need a little convincing."

"Okay, go 'head and convince me. Tell me what it is I need help with and convince me on how you're going to do it."

"Well, we don't know the details. But I suspect you'll need a couple of fearless private investigators on your team. We're the best, Cristina and I. You couldn't go wrong with us on the case."

I busted out laughing, "You gotta be kidding me. Private investigators? The best in town?" I laughed some more.

"You're laughing but I'm not kidding. We have credentials," Cristina giggled. "Just let me explain."

"Please do." I delivered a smile to Stephanie who was looking ahead, smiling broadly.

"You probably don't know, but Ariana and I worked on the school paper in high school. And we would go and get stories from anywhere we thought was good for the school paper. Well, every year high schools in the county compete for the best paper in February. Norcross High had won two years straight by the way. We were coming up with ideas for a winning story this time too. Well anyway, Baines High was somehow stealing our story ideas. Every time we came up with an idea, it would turn up in their paper. And we were back at the drawing board looking for a good story. Well, it was obvious we had a mole in our department. Or, the office was bugged."

"Was it?" I found this story interesting

"Bugged? Yes and no. The school got someone to come in and search the office, but they didn't find anything. So this left us suspicious of everyone on the school paper. Ariana and I knew it wasn't us and we were determined to prove it. So we started our own investigation, kept it between us. We suspected Malcolm Olsen 'cause he would always leave before we began discussing new ideas. As it turned out, he was bugging the office. He set the bug then came back later to remove it."

"How did you figure that out?"

"Got it all on camera. We set the camera on the computer and caught him in the act."

"Ooh. He didn't hang around for the meetings trying to throw off suspicion. Sneaky *and* lowdown. But why did he do it?" I wondered.

"He claimed he was bullied into doing it; but Malcolm wasn't a pushover. Nerdy, but not a pushover. He got suspended but he should've gotten more."

"Wow. If he didn't do it because he was bullied, then I wonder why he did it. But excellent work cracking the case—I'm impressed."

"It was huge, all on the news and the local paper. *High School Girls Uncover Mole at School Paper* was the heading," Stephanie said proudly.

"Impressive, really. But, look, I know you're telling me this—"

"Wait! Is it because you don't trust us? Or you think we're just amateurs and can't handle it? That we might get hurt...something like that?" Cristina jumped in with a mouth full.

"If aliens are involved, we're not afraid of them either," Ariana said laughing.

And I looked at them all as if they were sneaky FBI aliens looking for me to give them their first assignment. And then I couldn't help it; I started laughing myself. Realizing it was all about my findings, my adventure. And if they could remotely experience what I did, it would look divine...*on their resume.*

"Oh c'mon, Pia. You're looking at future FBI agents," Ariana said with her chest out, wearing an overstated smile.

"We're majoring in private investigation."

"Mm-hmm," Stephanie said nodding.

"Really!" I had to admit I was surprised. "Okay, look. It's this person who goes by the name of Ebay." I was obviously giving in now.

"Like the website Ebay?" Cristina confirmed.

"Yep. But the thing is I don't think it's his real name. This is what I need to know. He's new in town, and he works at City College in the bookstore. So he must be going to school there. He was at the skatepark earlier. No one seemed to know him. And you have to be very discreet on this; I don't want him to link us together. Not now at least. I can't have him getting the wrong idea. I'll help as much as I can, but again, he can't see us together. And Cameron mustn't know about this. *Very important.*"

"It seems easy enough. Getting his name, is that all?"

"For now."

"So what is it about this guy? Why are you so suspicious of him?"

I gazed into the faces saturated with curiosity, and shook my head faintly. "I-I can't say for sure." What details I had or the lack thereof, I decided to keep secret and I hinted that Stephanie do the same. But the girls were smart, and I suspected they would put two and two together.

"And what about CJ? How does he fit in all this?" Cristina continued to dig.

"This is just between us. Okay?" Enough for now, they needed to understand this.

"Okay, okay. So what does he look like?" Ariana asked.

We climbed the sandy slope, back up to the house, as I gave more details about Ebay, and his partner Winston. Including how good they were on the skateboard. Then I got around to commenting on the incident at the school paper, "It must've really done a number on y'all. It's amazing that you really serious about becoming FBI agents."

Ariana chimed in, "It got our juices flowing and it's been flowing ever since. And I promise we won't disappoint you. And we'll be on the job first thing in the morning. Right Cristina?"

"Yep," Cristina said.

Yeah. Sleep on it, I thought. Maybe then it would sink in what they were really getting in to and change their minds.

After spending time with the girls at Stephanie's having a taco party, I was ready to tuck myself in for the night, when I got a surprising text from Cameron. Saying how exhausted he was and that he was in for the night himself. But what surprised me was this message: *So will you let me in?*

What? It took a moment for this to sink in. And when it did I got up and went to the window, looked out.

But there was no sign of him or his truck. So I texted back, *Where are you?* Then there's a knock at the back door and my reflexes jumped. I moved toward the door, "Cameron," I called out his name before looking out.

"It's me, Pia."

Well it sure sounded like him, so I flashed the porch light for a quick visual check. "Wait, I have to turn off the alarm," I whispered anxiously through the glass, surprised by this clandestine meeting. In a jiffy I turned off the alarm then slid open the glass door.

"Get in here," I ordered grabbing his arm. I couldn't wait to see what was going on. Knowing that it had to be something. I landed a quick peck on his cheek. "What are you doing here! Did something happen? Is Sebastian okay?" I went on autopilot not giving him a chance to get a word in edgewise. "Ah, wait! Did anyone see you?" But then, it's probably why he used the back door, being discreet because of the neighbors, I thought. But still I was curious why he popped up without warning. "What is it?"

"No, calm down, nothing happened. And no, I don't think anyone saw me. I parked up by the resort and came up the beach to here. I'm sure no one saw me."

"Oh, okay." I was relieved, though at the same time, I didn't want to further disappoint my parents; I had done enough already. And even though I was eighteen, officially a grown woman, and even though I did what I'd done...I needed still to be their little girl.

"So why I'm here?" He turned away, playing with his chin.

"Not that I'm not glad to see you, but yes," I grinned then stepped over to reset the alarm. "There's no getting out now without terrorizing the whole neighborhood. You should have thought this through before showing up like this. You're stuck here for tonight, you got that?" I said in an authoritative tone. His face bloomed with amazement to my reaction.

"*Yes, ma'am.* No disobeying here, I'm aimed to please."

"Aim to please, huh?" I scolded with both hands on my hips, trying not to smile.

"Well, yes, of course," he said sniggering. "Look, after what we discussed today, I just thought I should be near you tonight. I meant everything I said today, which boils down to me wanting you to be safe and happy. That's all, Pia. And, um, since I can't get out of here without setting off the alarm, I guess we're on the same page about this?"

"Safe and happy, it's what I want for you too. Yes, we're on the same page."

"Good." He then placed a soft kiss on my forehead.

"Let me see if I can find something for you to sleep in," I said, thinking Dad must have something around here he could wear. But then Cameron surprised me. He pulled off his pants, revealing long johns underneath. I was so tickled.

"You can either sleep on the couch or take the left side of my bed," I said going into the restroom. When I came out, he was on his side, covered up to his armpits.

"Is this your first time?" he asked.

"Mmm?" I quickly hopped under the covers. "After tonight it won't be. But still, there's a first time for everything," I reached up turning off the lamp.

I then curled up on my sleeping side. He moved closer, molding his body to my backside. "Just go the sleep; I got you covered."

With his arm over me, I felt an extra layer of protection. "Goodnight, Cam," I said smiling.

Chapter Nine
Unusual Pursuit

"Now remember. All I need for now is his real name. If you happened to get more then fine, but don't bring on suspicion, be as discreet as possible. I don't want the word getting back to him that someone specific was looking for him. Okay? Please don't mess this up for me."

I laid down the rules once more as Cristina turned into the college campus. I would have put this off had I not gotten a call from Stephanie. She'd called right after the passionate lip-to-lip sendoff I gave Cameron this morning. Stephanie wanted to join Cristina and Ariana on their investigative escapade and thought I would want to tag along as well. My first thought was *no, absolutely not*, because I didn't want us to be seen together. But my second thought was the reason I counted myself in: Maybe tagging along wasn't such a bad idea. That another pair of eyes on the scene would be good just to see that things went smoothly. So here I was in the back seat of

Cristina's cute little Chevy, in disguise, wearing a topless cap Cristina happened to have in the car, and shades.

Cristina pulled into a parking spot away from the store, shifted the gear in park. Then looked back at Stephanie and me. "I know how important this is to you. But if he's not in there, we'll work the person in there for information."

"But the fact that he works here on campus, it shouldn't be hard getting his name. Don't worry, we got this," said Ariana.

"Ariana has a point. And it should be easy especially if he looks as good as you described. Every girl on campus would know who he is," Stephanie giggled.

"Wait. That looks like his car there. The Camaro parked there on the corner. All right detectives. It's show time. Go do your thang." *And please don't screw this up.*

They got out and crossed the parking lot to get to the bookstore, situated between two parking areas. They stopped just before getting to the store; Cristina dug inside her purse for something...a notepad apparently. She began flipping through it. Ariana gave us a thumbs-up as they continued on.

"To take notes. Mm...to pretend like they have a list." Stephanie muttering to herself, I took it. Moments later she said, "I wonder how long it'll take them to get a name. It'd be simple if they wore nametags. You haven't told me, but for you to want his name, you must think you know this person?"

"Yesterday when I saw him, I got the feeling we'd met somewhere before. I don't know why I didn't think to ask his name then. And I probably wouldn't be going at it like this if...if he hadn't made it seemed like I was making a move on him."

"Why would he think that?"

"I ran into him again at the skatepark yesterday; we had a few words. And at the end he said I knew where to find him like I would be interested in seeing him again...or something."

"But why would he think that?"

"Exactly! I didn't do or say anything for him to get that impression."

"But it has to be more to this. I mean, why wouldn't you just ignore him?"

"Because. Because I have to be sure about him, and, I think you know why. Cam thinks I'm being psychotic. He thinks I'm letting what happened last year rule my life," I said sadly.

"Hopefully you're wrong and can forget about this. Because...he could be right, you know. You need to unwind. But I know you have to see this one through. But after this then what?"

"Then," I paused for a sec, "then if I'm wrong, I'll be okay with it. And I suppose I'd know for sure that I need to start working on myself...work on not being a psycho."

"Yep," Stephanie nodded. And few moments later she said, "You know, it's taking longer than I thought it would take. Maybe I should go in and see what's going on."

"Uh shit! That's him over there! Where did he come from?" He was on his way to the parking area cata-cornered of the bookstore. But where was he going? To keep him in sight I got out, stood by the car as I looked across a road that divided the parking area. "That's not his car. He's parked over there—and he's about to leave! Call and tell them to get out here now! We have to follow him!"

Stephanie had the phone in hand phoning them immediately. They marched out moments later, just as Ebay was leaving.

"Hurry, hurry up we have to go already!" Suddenly I got behind the wheel and started pulling the car out.

"That's okay drive." Doors slammed as Cristina hopped in on the passenger side and Arianna in the back. I hit the gas pedal much too hard and they all clamored, "Take an easy!" And I did, in a reckless-cautious kind of way. I couldn't let him get away. For that I sped through a yellow light to avoid those crucial second-by-second ticks that would have had me debating whether to run a red light instead. So I stormed through the yellow, hoping I didn't draw attention to any cops. And that I didn't draw attention to the one I was trying to keep up with.

"Hey, did you get his name?"

"No, we didn't get a chance; it was kind of busy."

"You know, if we're lucky, he'll lead us straight to his house," Stephanie hoped.

"Yeah." I kept my eyes on the road listening to Ariana and Cristina toss around ideas on how this pursuit could end. Capturing an alien, or better yet, winding up on a remote island like the one last year; oh, this would put them on the map for sure. But I wasn't hearing it. All they wanted was to be part of something extraordinary to help boost their careers. I chuckled: *these chicks were nuts.*

Between one- to two-car lengths, I stayed on

Ebay's tail. As we crossed into Pompano Beach, he put on the right bleaker. We were directly behind him now. "He's about to turn in a residential area. Could be where he lives," I announced though we all were peering through the windshield. "I just hope turning with him won't get him suspicious."

But then his blinker went off and he passed the street up.

"That was a dead-end street. I wonder if he knows where he's going," Stephanie wondered.

"I don't know, but this can't go on much longer. He might know he's being followed," I added.

"You've been doing good keeping a distance. If he suspected anything, he would've turned off just to see if we would turn, too. Or he could have slowed down and let us pass, but he didn't." What Arianna said made sense. That's what people would do. Some would even speed up.

We came upon a rising drawbridge that brought us to a standstill, but not for long. Only one boat was passing through. Shortly when we were back on moving, I couldn't help wondering if he was on to us. He made a left, drove a few blocks then made another left. He practically made a U-turn. And with our eyes glaring through the windshield at the Camaro two cars ahead, our wordless voices clamored—*what in the hell was he up to? Why was he heading back to Fort Lauderdale?*

"I can't believe this. Is he out joyriding or something?" Stephanie carped, not pleased with how this pursuit was going at all.

"I wish I knew," I replied reflectively.

"Either he doesn't know where he's going, or he's

on to us." Cristina's admission, I was afraid of that.

"Well that's not good. What now?" Stephanie said, and those words spoke volumes.

We probably should give this up, and now!

"There's always a plan B." There was a hint of cleverness in Cristina's voice.

"Mmm." I looked over at Cristina. *Plan B?* I wondered about but didn't pressure her for details. For now, no one did.

We came up on an area where traffic was moving bumper to bumper. It was Fort Lauderdale's most popular beach area. Moving at a snail's pace, this wasn't going as well as I had expected. And I was seriously thinking about calling this off before he really noticed us. But I had a feeling that he had already. And if I could make a quick move to get out of this mess, I would. I imagined him the type to be bold enough to stop in the middle of the traffic, get out of the car and come up to us—busted!

I didn't want to face that kind of embarrassment.

"Watch it!" Cristina yelled and I hit the brake.

"That asshole!" I was in an instant rage. "Did y'all see that?" talking to Ariana and Stephanie in the backseat.

"Yeah, the nerve of that man forcing his way in like that. That was too damn close," said Ariana.

"Look. Those glasses he got on are thick. The man is blind!" Stephanie said. And it seemed she wasn't joking.

"Little blind, sneaky mouse on a collision course, that's what he is," I tended to agree with Steph. He was puny behind the wheel after all and was obviously puny in patience.

It was just crazy around here today was what it boiled down to. Traffic wasn't moving fast enough. It was stop and go with longer stops than goes. And there were droves of jaywalkers taking advantage of the slow-moving traffic, moving to and from the beach. And it wasn't clear whether they were holding us up or something else. We couldn't see much pass them between gaps. Ebay hadn't gotten away from us. Just a couple of cars ahead, he was caught up in this mess, too. I balled by lips, slightly shaking my head, frustrated: This wasn't going well at all.

"Where you think all these people came from?" Cristina said.

"Mmm," I shrugged. "All over. This has to be a record-breaking year for tourist..." I reflected.

Finally, we were moving, slowly, but moving, thank goodness. Up ahead looked clear, meaning a car accident or anything like that seemed not to cause the delay. Those jaywalkers should get arrested, I thought. It had been them holding us up. Lanes going the opposite direction moved in a steady flow now; for this, I grew more frustrated, because we were just coasting.

"What the hell! Where did he come from?" I pressed the brake to a complete stop. The traffic guard appeared out of nowhere blowing a whistle and with his hand jotted out like a blaring stop sign. And I couldn't do anything with a car ahead of me, and as Ebay bent the corner getting away. "Did you get his tag number?" I asked now.

"Nah, I didn't. I can't believe this! He just popped out of nowhere and now he's getting away," Cristina was as baffled and pissed.

"What's going on now?" Arianna grabbed the

back of the seat looking for answers.

"It's the light," Stephanie said before anyone replied. "See? He's pointing up at the light. It's out."

"B-but...it was working fine a moment ago, and it was green when he stepped out in front of that car." This had me stupefied.

"Yeah, it was. I don't know...this seems awfully strange to me," Stephanie had to admit. "I don't get how he was there before the light went out. Almost like he knew it would..." she trailed off. I could feel her behind me trying to wrap her head around it. Like me.

"Could be he was there because it happened before," Ariana suggested. "We only drove two blocks. Maybe this was the problem why were backed up back there."

"Yeah. Maybe. But I don't get why he would stop traffic when the light seemed to be working fine." Stephanie clearly wasn't buying it.

"Yeah, well, we need to get moving to catch up with him," Cristina voiced urgency.

"With any luck, the other light caught him," I hoped.

"Go, go," Cristina hastened. The light was red, but the guard was giving us the go-head.

I pressed the accelerator (a little too hard) squealing the tires wanting to turn the corner as fast as I could. But as soon as I did, I wanted to undo it. Unfortunately, it was too late.

"Oh. My. God. I have never seen anything so dramatic, so extreme, with these gorgeous eyes of mine in my entire life." Cristina seethed, and then sighed heavily through her nostrils slumping back against the seat.

Stephanie and Ariana, seeing the horrible mess we now faced, were speechless. And there was no going backwards or much further forward.

"What the hell...I can't believe..." I muttered.

"That guard should've been preventing traffic from turning on this street. *I should get his name and sue him,*" Cristina spat exasperation.

"I feel ya. This, is, weird." I rolled to a complete stop, wondering why the traffic's backed up, because it didn't look to be moving anytime soon.

There was mayhem in all four lanes, but it was obvious why the other side wasn't going anywhere. A big RV had both lanes blocked. It appeared the engine died while changing lanes. People of the RV were standing around. And a couple of police cars pulled up to investigate. Up ahead people were in and out of their cars or just hanging out making new friends like at some club. A nearby restaurant and gas station served as a convenience for gas, snacks, and whatnots. This entire setting suggested we were stuck for a while. Which begged the question, how long had this been going on? Again, why didn't the patrolman block this street?

Suddenly people were looking up, pointing at something in the sky.

I began looking up through the windshield. "Oh Look!"

"I know, wow," Cristina gazed up as well.

"What?" The girls in the backseat were curious too now.

"An air balloon," I said as I opened the door and got out. They followed suit so we all were craning our necks up at the balloon, coming dangerously close to crashing into buildings. I couldn't believe it. This day couldn't get any weirder, I thought. So much had happened in the past thirty minutes, holding us up. And now a crashing air balloon—could it have anything to do with the gridlock?

As the balloon glided over the intersection, people abandoned their cars, took off running after the balloon would crash. The gridlocked mess we were in was the least of their concerns now. And the least of Stephanie's it appeared.

"Come on, let's go," she said. And why I was surprised, I shouldn't have been. This was turning out to be a weird and exciting day.

"No...you go ahead. Someone has to stay and keep an eye on the car," I gave them permission.

"Well, it's not going anywhere but suit yourself. We'll be back in time." Stephanie then took off with Ariana and Cristina in tow.

Recalling how we ended up in this mess to begin with, I began looking around for that black Camaro. And for a person in a white shirt, collar and sleeves trimmed in black, sitting behind the wheel...anywhere. He had to be lurking around here somewhere, with eyes like binoculars, senses like that of canine, gravitating to me.

Yep. He gave me the creeps all right

Where was he? I continued looking. He couldn't have gotten far, unless his car grew wings like a bat mobile and took to the sky. Nah, uh-uh, I needed to stop thinking like this. But how could I when I knew from experience that anything was possible? For this reason, my eyes soared across the sky looking for a bat mobile or any sign of him. And when I spotted nothing of the sort, I was relieved that my bizarre notion didn't reveal its ugly face. But that was until I looked up again and saw the plane...which...was...bizarre.

Bizarre because I had seen the plane before. Though it wasn't so much of the plane that bothered me, but the banner flapping on its tail. Here I was again seeing something I had seen once before, in a dream. A banner with huge black letters, sailing through the sky, broadcasting the same message as now; the message—

"I love you, Perseaus."

What? I couldn't believe my ears, a familiar velvety voice, touching me like a tap on the shoulder that at once I turned and, there he was. So close that when I tried turning further my shoulder brushed against him. "What—what did you say?" my tone damned rudely. Not where did you come from, or why were you all up on me like that? That didn't matter more than what came out of his mouth.

"I...love...you, Perseaus," he repeated but differently this time. This time it didn't sound sincere, as if he was saying it to someone personally. Someone, like me. "The banner..." he raised his head looking up at the plane. I stepped back now reminded that we were much too close. "It's what the banner says," he continued.

The words printed on the banner, exactly. I gave him a vile stare, bridling the fact that he showed up in this precise moment and uttered the words my tongue was processing—that he for real slipped the words off my tongue. Nothing about this was coincidental...

"Where did you come from—are you following me?" I flushed out, secretly begging him to endorse my suspicion since I was guilty of following him.

"Me, following you?" he said jeeringly. And that witting smile...was he on to me?

"Yeah. I don't believe all of this. I mean...us, ending up together like this, a coincidence, do you? So just tell me what it is you want from me." I took a quick glance; no one was paying us any attention. "And you can start by telling me who you are."

He looked away, his jaws moving like a heart near death as he crushed gum, one slow beat after another. Then he said, "I don't know what you mean. Are you still thinking I'm someone you've met?"

"Stop playing games and look at me!" I gave a scorching look.

He hiked an eyebrow in a swift turn facing me. "I know how hard this must be for you. And I'm willing to help in any way I can, but... Tell you what, let's meet somewhere later and we'll have that talk then."

I scoffed, "Meet you? I'm here now, and so are you. We're alone, sort of; this is a perfect time."

"Mm, you don't want to meet later?"

"Why should I?" I appended.

"Because you're suspicious of me," he interjected. "And...I want to ease your mind, shed some light on things—help you get to know me a little better."

"Will you start with you name?" I tried again.

"Oh...I thought you knew. I'm Ebay," he said. And believe me, it took all of me to restrain from calling him a liar.

"No. I mean, really, who are you?" I glared, waiting...

He bellied the jaws and vented a heavy sigh. "You. Don't. Believe. me." He shrugged, "Okay, that's fine.

What do you say to us getting together later? Let me at least try to ease your mind about who you think I am. That means you can ask me anything. But not here; it's too chaotic for getting to know each other," he said observing the area.

"Well..." I said, thinking I had nothing to lose. I needed answers, and all of this would drive me crazy if I did nothing. *Somewhere to meet...where? A public place, open, so my PIs....*

"Anywhere," he encouraged.

I looked off and saw balloon chasers streaming back to an unchanged condition, and wondering how it came to be, suspecting I knew the answer to that already. "The riverfront, downtown by the jail; do you know the area?" I asked, though I suspected he did. Who didn't?

"Yeah. Not far from here. That's a good place to meet," he said.

"Okay. But let's meet on the other side, where you catch the river taxi. Say...tomorrow, around eleven?"

"Eleven it is."

"Well...I'll see you then," I exhaled sharply.

A nod, then he saluted a goodbye with fingers as he turned and walked away.

I crossed my arms, massaging them lightly, watching as his unrushed steps carry him stealthily through cars to the other side of the street. He wended up the walkway, quietly and deftly, in a manner that anyone in his path might step aside and pay attention to. And see what I saw. Something dark and mysterious about him, but no one could see what I saw, or sense what I sensed. That could be because no one saw him, this untouchable being, unbeknownst to only me. But how could anyone notice anything other than this gridlock? I sighed, snapped back to reality it seemed. Still I had my eyes on him, on a passageway moving between buildings. I kept my eyes on him until the moment he disappeared. And it wasn't until then it dawned on me: *his car, where was it?*

He'd snuck up from behind—where did he come from?

Where was he going now?

But the most important question: Where was his car?

Thinking it had to be here that I'd missed it, I walked farther up the sidewalk to the end of the block: streets blocked in all directions. *He couldn't have gotten through this...no way, impossible....* That black Camaro...it seemed to have vanished.

The latest news about the air balloon started buzzing like bees. It had landed right smack in the canal; and thank goodness no one was hurt, and no property damaged. Only two people were in the air balloon, a husband and wife. When rescued from the wreckage, they were in hysteria trying to explain the air balloon had a mind of its own. The husband couldn't get control of it to save his life. "...And the balloon seemed determined to land smack in the canal," a man walking by just now told another man. He sounded as baffled as I was about everything that'd taken place.

The girls arrived giving me their scoop.

"Yeah...it's been one crazy day," I said and couldn't say it enough.

Shortly after we all were getting in the car. The traffic jam was fast becoming no more. As if suddenly, impediments at all channels lifted, giving the chaos permission to flow back into sanity. It reminded me of that day when everything stopped cold, me included, like a statue. And the only one thing moving was a ghost. A ghost...ventilating through a congested, lifeless street. When it disappeared, everything had turned back to normal. To this day, I still didn't know what that was, a vision...or not....

However, one could argue the air balloon stopped traffic here today, but it wouldn't be me making that argument.

"I saw him," I voiced from the backseat.

"You did?" Stephanie gawked in surprise. Cristina back in the driver's seat glared through the mirror at me; Ariana twisted her body to look over her seat.

"Yep. We're going to meet tomorrow."

"Where—what time?" Cristina anxious to know.

"The Riverwalk at eleven."

"You can't go at it alone, Pia. You have to reschedule because we can't be there," Ariana insisted.

"That's right. You have to be safe about this, so we must be there," Cristina backing up Ariana now.

"Well, I don't know if I can. It's not like I have his phone number."

"Then don't go," Ariana deplored. "Seriously...you need back up."

"Well, what about you Stephanie? You can go to back me up, can't you?"

"Yeah," Stephanie gave the girls a quick glance. "I don't have a problem with the time." She made a questionable face.

"Ah c'mon, you can't do this without us. You

need heavy back up. You don't know what this dude is capable of." Cristina went on making her case, as she drove in decent traffic, along the beach. "What if he sees Stephanie? I know you're not going in separate cars. And if he sees Stephanie, what kind of back up would that be? And he could have his own backup, you know."

Stephanie looked at me, and then we both busted out laughing. Our laughter rubbed off on them, because they started laughing too. I wasn't sure why I started laughing. In the moment, I supposed I wasn't taking their involvement in this seriously.

"I am serious y'all," Cristina said. "He could bring backup, and you're backup needs to show up in a separate car for this to work without issues."

"All jokes aside, I think she's right about us showing up separately," Stephanie aired her thoughts now.

I turned to Stephanie. "Yeah, I know. Look, I'll try to get in touch with him to set a different time. So what time can we all agree on?"

"What if you don't reach him then what?" was Cristina's next concern.

"He should be there," I said, avoiding the question; I wasn't sure about the 'what if'.

We crossed into Pompano Beach with our minds buzzing around other things.

"What is everybody wearing to the party tonight?" Ariana asked, reminding me that the theme of the party was "dress to impress." I had already picked out what I was going to wear and was completely satisfied with it. But as it boiled down, they weren't dead set on what to wear. Therefore, the idea to go to the mall crystalized. Except, going to the mall was the last thing I wanted to do.

But what do you do when you're no longer the person behind the wheel and you're *so* outnumbered?

You just give in, and on to the mall you go.

Chapter Ten
Broken Commitment

"Looks like they didn't have a problem getting the word out," I committed as we arrived at a recreation center, a new location for Elijah's birthday party. Elijah had to come up with something last-minute, due to a scheduling problem at the Palooza.

"Looks that way," Cameron replied.

I pulled down the sun visor to check my makeup and hair.

"You couldn't look more beautiful, Babe. Did I tell you how much I like that dress on you? And that I love it when you wear your hair down?" He gave a sexy grin.

"Um-hmm. A million times already, but who's counting," I said as I stretched my neck to collect a kiss, and then our eyes locked. "Do you really think so?" I emoted flirtatiously.

He then kissed my nose. "I will tell you a million more time if that's what it takes...."

"*Nan,* that won't be necessary." I fingered his nose. "It doesn't take much to convince me. I know what pleases you."

He jerked with wide eyes, "Do you now?"

I smiled, just being egotistic, I knew. However, it didn't neutralize the fact that I dressed for this occasion to impress him. Besides, he was always complimenting me, so I had a good idea what he liked.

Today I had on a white polka dot dress; the skirt of the dress was all white with a wide red belt around the waistline. Two-inch black sandals were on my feet. And around my neck, a sterling silver cross he'd given me for my birthday.

He, as handsome as ever, had on a buttonless, black vest, over a white, button-down shirt, and dark cargo pants.

We got out, making our way toward a set of doors with oval windows when midways Cameron stopped. "When we go in, let's put the rest of the world to bed and just have fun. And don't let anything come between our happily-ever-after from this step forward."

"You know I want that, Cam. So yes," I affirmed. Then our fingers interlocked joining hands, and we continued to the entrance.

An older woman about forty-something was at the door when we entered. Her jewelry, golden bangles, and looped earrings, I noticed at once because I liked them.

"Come right on in. Good you could make it," she said, her spirit bubbly. She then told us where to find things (like the restrooms) and gave an approximate time to gather to sing *Happy Birthday*. I really liked her too bubbly spirit; how it seemed to rub off on us. Putting us in the mood to really get in there and start enjoying ourselves.

We thanked her and moved further in, to the center of the building, which happened to be a huge living area.

I looked around admiring beautiful accessories that did wonders bringing out modest furnishings. For instance, the silk plants, the expensive-looking paintings on the walls, the metal vases situated on the floor here and there. Even the back wall had huge windows about eight feet high.

Beyond the windows was a luscious backdrop of shrubs, flowers, and trees. The room was alive with endless chatter and music coming through a surround-sound. Soft, inviting music, I supposed the woman at the door had put on.

"To get this party really going that music gotta go," I said to Cameron and he nodded, chuckled.

I took Cameron's hand as we mingled our way through, saying hi to people along the way. I was looking for Stephanie and the others. Then, through a nest of people to our left, I spotted Stephanie off in an open kitchen. She, Elijah, and a few others were over there having fun laughing and talking.

To the left was an island-style kitchen and it was huge. The countertops were granite and the cabinets, pure maple. And the island itself covered with silver trays and dishes, loaded with finger food—sandwiches, raw vegetables and dips, pretzels, potato chips, and so much more. A long counter, which marked the perimeter of the kitchen, had bar stools running its entire length. On top of it were punch bowls and more finger food, and on one end was the birthday cake. Deliciously decorated, suddenly I was craving a mouthful.

I got a tap on the shoulder, swung around, and there was Cristina, sipping something red that looked like red wine.

"See you made it," she said merrily.

"Yeah. *And look at you,*" I said admiring her hair, extended with luscious curls hanging down her back.

"Thanks." She took another sip from the cup and giggled.

"Is that straight?" I was suddenly curious what was in that cup.

She grimaced, "Yeah. I think so. It tastes straight to me—hi Cam! Glad you could make it," she spoke as though Cameron just popped up.

"Hey, ha-ha-ha," Cameron didn't say much as we moved further into the kitchen.

"That's the perfect top for those pants." The pink floral top with the white pants she matched them up perfectly. She was dressed to impress. "Is Ariana here?" I wondered.

"Yeah. She's around here somewhere," Cristina replied.

Elijah looked our way, "Hey, CJ!" he said. Everyone seemed to call him CJ except me. The gregarious Elijah made his way from behind the counter, looking smart in his teal plead shirt, and sexy with a little chest exposed. Elijah approached and the two joined hands in a fisted handshake. "Glad you could make it, man," Elijah said, Stephanie right behind him beaming.

"Yeah, so am I. And Happy birthday," Cameron patted his back.

"Hey, we forgot the gift in the truck," I suddenly realized.

"Don't worry about it; we have plenty of time for that," said the birthday boy.

"It won't take but a minute to run out and get it. Save me the trouble of forgetting later," Cameron said about to leave.

"Sure, okay." Elijah extended an arm across Cameron's shoulders as they moved along talking.

"I really like that dress on you," Stephanie said.

"And I like that on you—and your hair!"

"Mom did it for me," Stephanie said proudly.

I expected Cristina's input but realized she'd moved clear across the room. I assumed she'd told her already how much she liked her loose-style French braid with a shiny clip in place. It looked picture-perfect, like in a style magazine. And she had on a gorgeous black and white halter dress.

"Cool. I bet Elijah couldn't take his eyes off you when he laid eyes on you," I said, smoothing her hair, making it extra perfect.

"Ye-ah...but I had to ask did he like my dress," Stephanie pouted dissatisfaction.

"Nah, ah-ah. I'm sure he loves the whole package. Otherwise he's a fool."

The atmosphere changed at once when pop music blasted through the speakers.

"Whoa. About time," Cristina said as she and Ariana danced and sang their way over to us.

Snapping my fingers, I rocked over to the punch bowl and scooped up a cupful.

"They're about to start a game of charades,"

Arianna said between lip-synching. "Where did the birthday boy go?" She didn't know he was behind her as she spoke.

"Right behind you," I motioned my head, wondering now what was taking Cameron so long.

"Hey, we're getting ready to start a game of charades," Elijah announced as well. "And, if y'all are interested, we're continuing this party at the Palooza later."

"Ooh," we nodded but none of us expressed interested in going.

"Come on," he beckoned us to follow. We all smiled and followed. Whether we were interested in playing charades or not, we couldn't refuse the birthday boy. We followed him across the room and gathered around others waiting to get the game started. "We're going to play a game or two until the karaoke machine gets here. Then we can really liven up things," Elijah added.

"But why a karaoke machine when we had music?" I whispered to anyone who heard me.

"It wouldn't be a party without the karaoke machine—Elijah's words not mine," Stephanie whispered back.

"Ooh." I began looking around at the gathering. About twenty-five to thirty people scattered throughout the place. Some were off in another room playing pool, some just hung around chatting. But the majority gathered in the center of what I called the "great room," because it was huge and great in my eyes.

With all the seats taken, we had no choice but to stand. All seemed eager about starting the game, and I was getting excited about playing now. It had been awhile since I played charades. It had been awhile since I played any games, now that I thought about it.

"Hey, did you get in touch with that Ebay guy?" Cristina asked, and Stephanie and Ariana sharpened their ears for the answer.

"Ah-ah. Not yet."

"Then what are you going to do?"

"I don't know, Cristina, maybe nothing."

"But 'I don't know' isn't an option, right? So, what you think you might do?"

I sighed, "Come on, not now."

"Okay but think twice about doing it alone. That guy is creepy, and I haven't even met him," she firmly noted.

"And I second that," Ariana agreed. And that was that for now.

It was officially game time. "Hey, I'll be right back," I excused myself wondering what happened to Cameron.

However, I barely moved a foot when the door opened and there he was coming in with the red gift box. I put on an "oh there he is" smile, and then pointed to a tall box beneath a painting that looked to be worth a million bucks. This box was where everyone dropped smaller gifts, and the larger ones stacked around it.

He placed the box on top of another box then came over to join us. "Sorry it took so long. Got a call from my uncle." Then without warning he yelled, "Tiger Woods," putting himself in the game just like that. *Yay!* Our team reacted with a thrilling appreciation for our first win.

And he impressed me. "*You just got here.* How did you get that so fast?"

"Well...you know, easy. When I think golf, naturally Tiger Woods comes to mind," he said with swagger.

I smiled, "Okay Mr. Right-On-Time. Keep that up and the other team won't have a chance."

"I'll see what I can do," he said and winked.

We stood around having so much fun playing the game, as low pop music playing in the background added more spirit to our fun-filled souls. I could have gone on and on playing charades, not doing anything else for as long as the party lasted it was so much fun. But Elijah's dad had arrived with the karaoke machine. And when he blasted the mike, causing a huge stir and distraction, it was definitely time for a game changer.

As we wrapped up the game, a few guys horsed around over who was going first on the karaoke machine. All adults had left as far as I could see. It was time for boys to be boys, I supposed. The clowning escalated into pure entertainment as they made crony faces, cracked funny jokes, did somersaults and other weird things with their bodies, all while trying to get the mike from the one who had it. I was getting a kick out of it. They were the best buffoons I'd seen in a long time. All they were missing was makeup and costumes.

This would have gone on for god knows how long until the one with the mike somehow flipped and landed on his back, and for me, enough was enough.

"That's it y'all, before someone gets hurt." Elijah put down his foot like the adult supervision we needed.

The one in red shirt with spikey hair, Ken, I

heard someone called him, put on a sore look as Elijah beckoned him to hand over the mike.

"Come on now, you can do it," Elijah nurturing him for the task.

It was hilarious. Ken with puckered lips, took teensy-weensy baby steps towards Elijah, then handed him the mike. And we all burst into laughter and applauded; we were amazed at how comical Ken was to the bitter end.

Cameron hugged my neck and I said, "They were so good I would pay to see more."

He chortled, "Yeah, they were pretty good. But the curtain had to come down before someone got hurt."

Elijah had taken control. Now with the mike, he was in the element, like a maestro conducting an orchestra to a peaceful close. "Come on everyone; let's give them a hand for an amazing performance." He then raised the mike at the three clowns.

"What! It was all an act...!" I said, and Elijah's huge smile said it all. And accolades erupted, blowing the roof off as all three of the performers—Percy, Ken, Ryan—lined up and took a bow.

"All right now..." the birthday boy said as our cheering mellowed into steady smiles. "Since chivalry isn't dead and I like to show it, let's let the ladies fight over the mike." All the fellas laughed, including Elijah, and he then kissed the mike. "So-o who's going first?"

"Here, here!" I flexed a pointed finger over Stephanie's head and was tickled pink. The likelihood of Stephanie stepping up to the mike was 99 percent zilch. She had an adorable Muppet singing voice. I had teased her many times about it and yes, I was teasing now.

Anyway, if anyone could encourage her to take the mike, it would be Elijah.

"Nah...ah-ah. Pass the mike to Ariana. You go girl!" Stephanie waved a hand for her to step forward and she Ariana ran up a snatched the mike.

"Wait, hold up!" Stephanie requested the mike back and Ariana handed it to her. "There is something we're forgetting, don't you think?" she said smiling at Elijah.

I was right apparently; Elijah was the one to get her to sing, to sing Happy Birthday that is.

As Stephanie began singing, we all joined in. And Elijah's eyes froze, as if he didn't expect to hear the Happy Birthday song at his own birthday party. He was so humbled, blushing all over the place that he dropped his head and covered his eyes. We were singing Happy Birthday, to him, and he had to stand there and take it like a man.

Afterwards he gave Stephanie a big hug and we went over to cut the cake. Shortly thereafter, Ariana picked up where we'd left off by singing Whitney's *"I Will Always Love You."*

We knew we were in for a treat when she marinated sexy in the lyrics. And she looked fabulous doing it: in a half-strapped, multi-colored dress, the length right above knees, and with her hair in a cute bun.

"A singing private eye...who would've thought," I said to no one in particular.

As she got better and better, I was seeing a side of Ariana I never knew existed. The girl really could sing. And when she finished, we all came together saying, *More, More, More, More...* We wouldn't let her hand the mike to anyone else until she gave us an encore. And she did, just one more song before others took over the karaoke machine.

And from then on there were crazier good performances. A few disastrous ones. And so many hilarious ones in the mix. Every bit of it spelled nothing but *fun, fun, and fun.*

I was so content in having so much fun that my worries were like a thing of the past. It's what Cameron spoke about earlier: being happy and not letting anything deprive me of being happy. I rested my head on his shoulder and, in return, he kissed the top of it.

"I'm glad you asked me to come with you. We probably should do this more often," his warm eyes smiled done on me.

"Yeah. Every chance we get we should take a pause and shut out all the craziness of the world. It feels good..."

Cameron responded not to me but his cellphone. With all the noise, he took the call outside but was back pretty quick. "That was Sebastian," he took my hand and pulled me to the side.

"Sebastian? Really!"

He nodded. "I'm going to the hospital to see him. Something important he needs to talk to me about."

"I...I hope everything's all right."

"I hope so. All I know is that he sounded fine but said it was important that he talked to me. Look, I know this is bad timing, but can you catch a ride with Stephanie?"

"Well, yeah, but...can't this wait? Remember what you said about putting the rest of the world to bed? This time is supposed to be about us." And now you're spoiling things, I also wanted to say.

"I'm sorry, Babe, but this is Sebastian. Please...," he gently kissed my lips. His eyes loaded with regret, and mine held just as much regret. I didn't want him to leave, not now but...

"Okay, go. Go see about Sebastian." What else was I to do? I didn't want to be the villain that came between them, whether it disappointed me so that he was reneging on us. I walked him to the door; one quick kiss, the door opened, and then he was gone.

I didn't hear from him until I got home hours later. Totally exhausted from invigorating chatter, stimulating music, and from a sugar rush I must say: lots of cake, ice cream, punch, you name it. I was tired from having so much fun without Cameron.... The melody from my phone lent sweet music to my ears: *Cameron, finally.* I answered, and in a heartbeat, things changed.

"Pia, don't wait up for me..." His voice came from a deep mortal place, killing me inside. I knew something awful had happened to Sebastian.

If only this... If only that... The pariah of things, I couldn't shut off for a measly night.

Chapter Eleven

The First Episode

I went to sleep thinking about it, I woke up thinking about it, and I knew now what I must do. It was a no-brainer. I needed answers and he said he would give it to me. Therefore, I had to meet with him. If anything, I felt it had become my civic duty and responsibility to do so, because lives were at stake.

Poor Sebastian. Poor, poor Sebastian.

Eleven o'clock I would meet him. I fired up the VW, put it in reverse, and then voices came out of nowhere, stunning me like a taser.

"Going somewhere?" My head jerked to the left and there was Cristina.

"And without us—are you crazy!" Jerked to the right and there's Ariana.

"She gotta be." Back to the left and there's Stephanie.

"Where...where did y'all come from?" I then

glanced through the rearview mirror, and there was Cristina's little blue Chevy blocking the driveway. "You two—weren't you supposed to be somewhere else very important? Don't tell me you cancelled it for this."

"Never mind that," Stephanie interjected. "You were supposed to call me." Looking at her phone, "I'm still waiting for that call, or even a text."

"I'm sorry, okay! I changed my mind. I think it'd be best I do this alone."

"Not cool and you know it, little sister."

I didn't rest time arguing with Stephanie. Frankly, I was in no position to argue and win anything. They were determined not to take "no" for an answer and I didn't have much time to waste.

Stephanie opened the door, "Get out for a minute. We have something to show you."

"Okay, but make it quick," I said getting out.

Cristina remotely popped the trunk of her car, as we move toward it.

And when we got to it, "See, what do you think?" Cristina said as all faces fixed on me to capture my immediate reaction.

"*B-but...what is all this stuff?*" Seeing all these things laid out on a towel in a flat box confused me.

"Well, what does it look like? When I said we were serious about this I meant it. As you can see we're in business," Cristina attested not really saying what the stuff was. But I had a hunch they were Sherlock Holmes gadgets they managed to get their hands on.

She picked up a rectangular device, black. "This disguises your voice. Use it with about any cellphone. Insert this in headset jack and hold the phone to your ear

116

and just talk normal. And it has different voices."

Cristina then picked up another one, a square device with number keys. "This here is a cellphone GPS detector. Get his cellphone number and we can track him up to 100 feet range. And these," she waved a hand over a cap, glasses, another small device, "have built-in DVR. Now this," she pointed to the binoculars, "is top of the line. And this, my dear," picking up a black pen, "has a built-in recorder."

"A recorder?" I was a little surprised.

"Mm-hmm."

"How did you get all of this stuff?" I asked finally.

"Let's just say we have connections," Cristina said proudly.

"Let's just say we have admirers who want to help jumpstart our careers," Ariana appended.

"'To jumpstart your careers'? But you haven't...." *Oh, what the hell,* I decided.

"I know, I know," Stephanie tallied with what I was thinking. "But the point is you need us to watch out for you, whether you think so or not. There's no telling what kind of mess you'd be walking into. So we're going to have your back. Come on, we better get going."

"Okay, but you have to stay out of sight," I said handing the pen back to Cristina.

"*Keep it,*" she said.

"So you can eavesdrop? Do you really think that's necessary?" I questioned.

"It has a tracker on it too," she whispered, someone was passing. I just held on to the gizmo, already deciding what I should do with it.

"Hey?" I said opening the car door. "I almost

117

forgot to tell you. Sebastian took a turn for the worse last night. He slipped back into a coma." We shared a moment of sympathy before driving away in separate cars.

What I didn't tell them was that I felt responsible, not sure how, but I did. All I knew was that I had to meet with Ebay to stop all hell from breaking loose. But then there was the chance I was stone out of my mind, for real this time.

I parked in the parking lot by the jail as I did last time. The gang was nowhere in sight. I saw them last a few streets back, held up by a red light. They should be here soon enough, I told myself. I pressed the key fob locking the door as I walked away from the car.

Looking out for Ebay, I began the short journey over the bridge. It was ten-to-eleven when I arrived in the area where we were to meet. I looked around for him, didn't see him coming, and so decided to take a little stroll up the walkway.

The scenery up and down the river, or just being near the water, I personally could never get enough of. And the exquisite yachts, always a sight to see. The sun was warm. And the humidity moistened my skin like body cream not absorbed into it yet. I was stretching and balling my fingers into a fist, I realized. Nervous, and I supposed I was afraid also. Not afraid of meeting him, but afraid of what I may find out, and consequences, because I was sure it would come with some.

"Pia." His smooth intelligent voice caught me off guard that I winced. "Did I disturb you? You looked far away just now."

"No...not really. I'm just looking forward to finding out why I'm here."

"Is it too late for breakfast?" he asked fingering his ear.

"It's never too late for breakfast, but I'm not hungry."

"Well. I'll get something to drink at least."

"Yeah, sure. I'll be over there," I motioned my head at a bench circling a maple tree.

"Okay," he nodded then headed over to a nearby food stand. I strolled over to the bench. Looking around, I wondered where my Sherlock Holmeses were. They had to of found a perfect spot because I didn't see them anywhere.

Moments later when he joined me, he handed me a full Styrofoam cup and straw. "It's cola. I didn't want to drink alone." He sat sideways to face me; this angle favored the light reflecting shades of brown in his hair. He had on tan shorts with lots of pockets. And a comfortable fitting pullover shirt that softly outlined his toned upper body.

"You shouldn't have," I accepted to be polite, brushing strands of hair out of my face.

"After yesterday I thought you would have some recollection about us," he said in a gentle, nudging way.

"After yesterday I thought I would come here and you shed some light on some things, yes." I removed the wrapping from the straw and slid it through the punctured hole in the lid.

"By all means let me cut to the chase. You insist that you know me. This means that at some point our paths crossed. Believe me...I want nothing more than for you to remember...things. My purpose for being here is to help you the best I can."

"Okay. So this meeting has nothing to do with you but everything to do with me—fine." I sipped cola from the straw as I got my thoughts in order. Cutting to the chase would be fine if only I could without being reckless or offensive. Because it would be hard trying to take back accusations should they turn out to be morbidly wrong. But I had to start somewhere.

"Just tell me about you. Maybe that'll help jog my memory." I thought being perfectly sane was the best way to start.

"But you know me; you may not know it yet."

"Hmm? But I don't, not really. You know this so why would you say that?" I stared at him now. But with his lips on the straw he looked at me puzzled. He let go of the straw and asked, "Do you do that all the time?"

"Do what?"

"Talk to yourself."

I frowned, confused now. "Talk to myself? No, never. I was talking to you just now. You said that I know you... Don't you remember?"

"No, because I didn't. Are you okay?" *This wouldn't be so complicated if I could bend the rules a bit.*

"Uh...yeah...fine..." I stuttered because I heard him, was looking right at him when I heard him. My hearing was fine, and I wasn't going crazy. But he said, *this wouldn't be so complicated if I could bend the rules...,* and his lips didn't move.

"Look, uh...I'm not here to play games. I just need to know what's going on. You show up wherever

I'm at. It's almost like you're following me and—"

Following You? Who was running red lights to keep up yesterday?

There it was again. He spoke but his lips didn't move, and I was in awe thinking, *I didn't run a red light.* Which was beside the point.

"*And, what? You* were saying?" His parts moved now. He gazed at me sipping from the straw.

I sipped a little cola as well, thinking about what was happening between us—that's if he was even aware. I didn't know whether to bring it to his attention or just see how to use it to my advantage. The idea was interesting, except I suspected I was right about him; knew who he was. So how could I read his mind without him knowing? Was he pretending? Or was I for real losing it?

"And...if you are, why?" I concluded.

"I know it appears that way." *But if only you would remember, it would make things easier. Time is precious, and it's running out.*

Again, I heard his mind, and I wondered what he meant.

"You think *my time* isn't valuable?" I uttered, throwing a hint that I was reading his mind.

"Maybe you're afraid of asking the right questions." He surprised me. Was that a confession? Forget about being sensible, it was time to be bold.

"You're not from here, are you? I think you know that I know that much about you. And it's time you tell me where you're from, and, while you're at it, tell me what I have to do with you being here."

He positioned forward, elbows digging in quads, his sentiments striking the concrete. And I sat wondering what his inner voice meant when it said, *'If only you would remember...'* and that *'Time is running out...'*

"The question was good enough for me, whether it's the right one or not. So, if you don't mind...I don't have all day."

He lifted his head precipitously, though not at me, then he straightened his body. "I'm from a place called Massouvia. You, uh, must've heard of it...," he said, gazing at me, but something about how he looked at me made me feel...strange.

"No...I don't," I said.

"Are...ya...ur..." his voice began fading, sounding slurred as my head started spinning that I closed my eyes, covered my face with the palm of my hand. In a few moment I reopened them to get a glimpse of him, though I barely could.

"I don't know what's happening. Did you put something in my drink?" I said but my voice sounded slurred too. Now the feeling was so intense that my head drooped fully in my arms to my lap. Perspiration began pouring out of my face and body.

My eyes got heavy, and then began rolling like a delirious puppet clutched by evil—and my stomach, it felt it might erupt any moment.

Next, there were voices, strident voices that seemed to whoosh me up to a sensation of floating, then the voices disappeared. Now I was floating with images flashing before me. Surreal images of places I'd never seen before. Of castles, cities, landscaping, and a body of blue water where a faint image of a person appeared over it. Who was it? I couldn't see clear enough to tell. But indeed, it was a man, reaching out his hand as he opened his mouth....

"How ya feelin...eelin...eelin...?" His voice caved at my ears. I managed to open my eyes, and through my distorted vision, I saw him, and could feel his hands all over me.

"Nah, nah," I said groggily, trying to shake the hands off. "Get your hands off me!" I mustered enough strength to snap my body up and fling my hands, at Ebay, not at this other blurred figure that was gone now.

"What did you do to me?" I demanded, though sluggishly.

He got up and handed me a wad of napkins, "For you," he said. "You look much better now. I gather this is your first episode?"

I snatched the napkins. "What do you mean my first episode? My first episode of you putting something in my drink, huh? This has gone too far—I know who you are and what you are," I said mopping sickness off my face and neck with the napkins.

"There you go again," he dissented. "Okay...then how 'bout you do me the honors, hmm? If I'm not Ebay then tell me, who I am? Go 'head. Tell me. *I am...*" *Come on. Let me hear you say it.*

As if a gray cloud came down, transported me back in time, and then vanished. I was again on the island, reliving the blob of an ice monster scouring the island—the horror of it. And the frightening reality that we could die, our bodies lost there forever in no man's land. No one knew where to find us; our journey had been top secret. However, luck found us, and we managed to escape. But right before the ferret appeared outside the plane waving, and then, he appeared. Was it because he wanted me to make that connection? So that I would know that he, and the ferret, were one of the same? The big question was, why. What had been his purpose then; what was his purpose now?

"You're...the ferret, and the ghost, and you're," I squared him in the face. "You're an arctic cold-blooded monster...*yeah,*" I scoffed. "And, unfortunately, you know me. You know how I think, what I think. You know me...I think, better than I know myself. Therefore, you know what I have to do."

"Mm." He slid both hands into pants pockets, narrowed his eyes. "Just so we're clear, what is it you think you have to do?"

"Tell the entire world who you really are. Yep," I nodded.

"Oh. And so, you're wondering what I'm going to do about it. Well...nothing. Because, my dear, you won't."

"Yeah? And why won't I?"

"Because you said it yourself, I know you."

"*Why won't I?*" I persisted.

"Because you will only be revealing to the world *who you are.* And that, my dear, would be a grave mistake. You just think about that. But for now, we're done." He sounded serious.

"*Are you kidding me?* You don't get to say something like that and then run off..." I was saying but then... "That. Ring. Where did it come from? I mean, it wasn't on your finger all this time, because I would've noticed it."

I rose to my feet, staring at the ring and before I knew it, grabbed his hand for a closer look. "It's just like

124

that ring," I said softly. And again, what was it about this ring that held me hypnotic?

"It was you at the airport. Wearing those *ridiculous* leather pants. It was you." My eyes grabbed his, "And what exactly did you mean when you said I would be 'revealing who I am'? I know who I am. I'm Pia Wade. I'm Pia Wade!"

He took back his hand, "Sorry, but my time is up." He insisted again on leaving.

I stepped up to him with gritting teeth. "You can't be serious. Leave now when we're just getting started?" Was I afraid? Not one bit. I had been waiting a long time for this moment and I wasn't about to let him get away that easy.

He looked off in the distance, thinking. Then he gazed into my eyes. "Such beautiful, binocular vision," he said in an arcane way. His eyes deflected from me again as if charmed by something in the distance. "Yes, we are," his speech harshened.

I was confused even more by his urgency to leave. And why? Was he stalling for some reason? If so, then why? Whatever his reason, he hadn't done his job in convincing me, and I thought I had better let him know.

"Everyone knows who I am, and I know you're a *fake* trying to fit in. So far, nothing you've said would stop me from letting people know."

"You need more convincing? I don't think I have to convince you that you would do anything to not see anything happen to your brilliant world of people—"

"You say that like you have a grudge against me and the world," I said, but he went on, ignoring me.

"*Instinct,*" he stepped closer. "When you left the

pen in the car without giving it a second thought, that Pia...was instinct. Instinct," he took a hesitating breath, "is an unusual commodity. Without it, you're a cat without whiskers. You won't let go...you can't. We shall meet again."

This person, who became someone else right before my eyes, then turned and walked away, leaving me speechless.

Shortly after, "Pia! Pia!" Stephanie and the gang were running toward me and I was in somewhat of a daze, feeling a little faint.

"What happened? Did he do something to you?" Ariana wore a distressing expression.

Then Stephanie, "Yeah, Pia, you were crouched over like something was wrong. We wanted to move in but didn't want to spoil things." She placed a hand over my forehead. "Did you get sick or something?"

"Aah...well I did, kind of. I think it was something in the drink," I said, still thinking he'd put something in it, though I wasn't sure. I recalled him asking, was it my 'first episode.' What exactly did he mean by that? Did he suspect I would have more?

"You don't look so good; let's sit for a minute." I took Stephanie's advice and sat on the same bench Ebay and I had sat; we all did. Stephanie began rubbing a hand in circles on my back. "Did you find out anything about him?"

"No...not really. Only that he's from a place called Massouvia...something like that. At the time I was starting to feel faint, dizzy...I couldn't grasp all what he was saying."

"That's strange. *The pen*...everything'll be on the

126

pen. *Give it to me.*"

"I-I...don't have it. I left it in the car."

"In the car!" Cristina pounded fist in her thighs and jumped up. "Don't you see how valuable that pen would be right about now? *Damn it, Pia.*"

"I know, and I'm sorry; I just forgot it." I was lying through my teeth. He was right; I left that pen behind on purpose. My negligence disappointed Cristina so much that she paced back and forth with her arms clenched and lips tight.

"*We accomplished nothing. Nothing at all.* But there's going to be a next time, right? When are you seeing him again?" Cristina stopped pacing now.

"I-uh...don't know." Looking at the binoculars hanging off Cristina's neck, reminded me of what Ebay had said, and the way he said it. '...Binocular eyes'—he knew. He they were watching. And what did he mean when his inner voice said, *'If only you would remember'* and that *'Time is running out'?* Running out for what? I couldn't stop wondering.

"Pia, what is it? Why are you looking like that? What is it?" Stephanie sounded worried.

"I...just don't know about all this." I sighed, shook my head. I then looked up at Cristina. "I really messed up. But it'd be okay." I got up then, "Come on...let's go."

"Yeah, let's plan out next move," someone gnarled.

Chapter Twelve
Moping in Tears

I had to break from the girls wanting to plan our next move on Ebay.

One reason was that I wasn't ready for a next move. The other was that I needed to get somewhere, and I couldn't get there fast enough. Even after arriving, I still couldn't get there fast enough. The elevator was taking its good ole time to arrive.

If only you would remember. Time is running out. Those words played in my head and I couldn't turn it off. I wasn't losing my mind, but it surely felt like it.

What was it I have to remember? And how much time did I have to remember it?

Ding. I looked up at the burning green arrow. Finally, it was here.

The doors slid open and a half-dozen people spilled out. I got on with a half-dozen more people who had been waiting about as long I had been waiting. I hit "3" and it lit up; the others hit the floor they wanted. As the doors encapsulated us, my breathing grew with heart-racing anticipation.

When I talked to Cameron last, there hadn't been a change in Sebastian's condition. I hoped this was still the case; that he hadn't gotten worse. Regardless I needed Cameron right now...to be close to him, to support him in any way. Of course I had to tell him about my meeting with Ebay—not just come out and tell him, I would at least play it by ear. Because telling him I met with Ebay behind his back would upset him at first but then he would have to get over it.

Still, the best thing to do was play it by ear.

The elevator doors opened on the third floor; I got off and followed the sign to room 310. When I arrived, I found two empty beds. One made-up with crisp white linen; the other one was the opposite with flowers on a table-tray and extra chairs at its foot.

They had to be around here somewhere, so I headed back up to the nurses' station to get some information.

"I'm looking for the patient in room 310. Sebastian Scott."

"Are you family?"

"Yes," I said, hoping a problem didn't ensue later.

"He's out for tests. He's due back anytime. Other members of the family are in the waiting room. Around the corner, at the very end of the corridor," she gestured.

"Thanks," I said and hurried off.

I slowed down after bending the corner. A couple of women were coming up the corridor. I recognized one of them, the older one: Sebastian's mother. The short,

129

curvy one, I suspected was Sebastian's sister though we had never met. She smiled and said "Hi," her voice soft-spoken. The way she smiled at me, I assumed she knew who I was. "Hi," I spoke back.

"We're going down to the cafeteria," Mrs. Scott said. "If you're looking for CJ he's at the end in the waiting area."

I could see she wasn't up for much chitchat; walking sideways, she didn't exactly stop to talk, making our moment brief. No time for "Hi, you must be..." or "How are you holding up today?" No time to ask about Sebastian. They went on and my eagerness continued onward down the corridor about to surprise Cameron. He didn't have a clue that I was coming.

When I got his text earlier letting me know he was still at the hospital, I didn't bother texting back. I knew that I had to see him and that he was the one person who would understand whether he wanted to or not. Whether he wanted to, he needed to know what was going on so there wouldn't be regrets later.

Again, that would depend on his mood

Voices, intense voices echoing into the corridor prompted my feet to decelerate. Slowly, I approached the entryway and hesitated. Thinking I should check the environment I was about to enter. Or should I say...eavesdrop?

"Just look at you. You're a mess. Are you trying to drain yourself to become comatose, too?" a male voice.

Is that Brian? It surely sounded like Brian.

"You should cancel any plans you have and go home and get some rest."

Yeah, it's Bryan all right.

"I know I look like crap but I'm okay," Cameron scoffed his cousin. "Sebastian is the one that's not okay."

"All right, all right," Brian said. "So, um, how are things with you and Pia?" he asked to change the subject at least.

Thinking this would be the time to show my face, I stepped in the doorway. Neither sensed my presence, though they were looking out the window with their backs to me.

"Brian..." Cameron dropped his head, his hands flat on the windowsill. "...I can't deal with Pia and her speculations right now. I just can't, man."

My bottom lip dropped to the floor, and my heart in a thousand pieces. I couldn't get my feet to move before heads turned and eyes landed on me like headlights on a deer. Only because in that split moment I was debating whether I should make my presence known and pretend I didn't hear him. Or act out how I truly felt about his remark. But I favored neither.

Suddenly I had the urge to get out of here fast before someone got a whiff of my scent like a canine. Responsively my legs began carrying away my slain soul. Fast, I was moving fast now, looking over my shoulder constantly making sure they didn't see me

I got back to the elevator; hit the button many times for the doors to open NOW. But my mind slipped into bypass mode when I saw *EXIT* glaring at me over a door at the end of the hall.

The door open and a nurse came through. And I made it my target as though it was my only way to escape. I downed fast three flights of stairs until I reached the front lobby that I felt I made my escape. And when I got outside, I stopped cold, taking deep breaths as if I had survived a burning building. Then I looked up at glow in the sky, thinking I was right back where I started.

And I was. After getting here as fast as I could, then leaving just as fast, I accomplished nothing at all. I had come full circle in an instant, and in front of me was destination. One I would have to face on my own. A tear streaked down my cheek. I took a finger, gently wiped it away, then another, and another.

As I moped looking up at blue sky, something Mr. Calhoun (my tenth-grade history teacher) had once said came to me. *Sometimes, no matter how difficult, you must take it upon yourself to make a difference. Even if you're not sure, it's the right thing to do. After all, life's about change. And change is ubiquitous: it's constant, and inconstant, all at once.*

That day I'd arrived late to class, so I didn't know what inspired him to say that. Not until later.

By then the entire school was buzzing like locust about the twelfth-grader who'd committed suicide. There was a letter explaining why. She couldn't live without Samuel was what it boiled down to. Samuel, as it turned out, was an art teacher at our school. A situation of unrequited love gone horribly bad rocked the entire school district, and exploded on social media.

By time it aired on the evening news, it was old news. When all had been said and done, or right after the news had broken, the art teacher and the principal were goners.

I figured my history teacher was being poetic. I never understood what "constant and inconstant change" had to do with the girl committing suicide.

Though as I thought about it, the sun came as a perfect analogy, because it appeared every day, and disappeared. Nothing seemed to change, yet, there was change. Like the day I discovered the island, things changed for me *instantly* in a big way, and I learned I wasn't out of my mind. Then again, nothing had changed because there was always the question "why?" And it seemed that I was on the verge of finding out.

I dabbed my dewy eyes dry and headed to the car. *Ferret,* I said to myself. *Ferret.*

Chapter Thirteen

Ring the Separation

Overhearing Cameron dis me must have dulled my memory a little. I completely forgot running into Sebastian's family.

So when Cameron found out I'd been there, he obviously put two and two together. And so over a course of sending many texts—because I refused to answer his calls—Cameron aimed at finding out what happened to me:

You left without letting me know you were here. Did something come up?

Call me as soon as you get this message.

Brian asked about you. He would've loved to see you.

I'm sorry babe. You know I didn't mean it.

But I wouldn't give him the satisfaction via text either. Then about an hour later, my cellphone rang and it's Cameron calling from my back porch. I didn't know he was there at first but answered because I was kind of over being mad.

"Pia?"

"What Cam?" I said looking at him through window. He appeared every bit as drained as Brian expressed earlier, even more so now. Looking at him, I felt partly to blame.

"You're still pissed at me," he said then pressed his forehead against the window. "Come on now, give me a break. I know you think you don't matter but it's not like that. I need you; you need me. That hasn't changed." He began rubbing his forehead.

"I don't want you to feel obligated. Look, you can't give up the competition for your reasons. And I know now what's better for you, for us, for my reasons. You need this, Cam. You admitted it to yourself, and to me, when you said, 'you couldn't deal with me right now.' It's doesn't matter that you didn't know I was there and overheard you. I was in the right place at the right time for a reason. And now I really know you can't deal with me on top of everything else right now."

"If this's how it's going to be, then let's do it the right way. Please, open the door."

I pressed my forehead against the window with cellphone to my ear. "This is crazy," I said, when it dawned on me that we had been talking through the glass door with cellphones at our ears.

I pressed my eyes together, lowered the phone. "You meant what you said, Cam. You can't take it back." Then I unlocked the door, slid it open, and turned my back on him. "You can't take it back," I repeated.

"Why? Because you won't let me? Because you know that in here where it matters most"—he bumped his heart with a fisted hand—"that I didn't mean it. You know me, so why?"

"'Cause... 'cause I'm not sure about things anymore. 'Cause I know how much Sebastian means to you and how much you want to grab hold of that gold medal and make him proud."

And because if I told you about "him" and what he said, it could trigger something awful; that could hurt your chances of winning that trophy. I wanted to say.

And because things were different now that Ebay alluded to the fact that I would do anything to protect my friends, as a threat. I wanted to say that too, yet couldn't bear the thought of anyone wound up hurt because of me. Nor could I bear the thought of dealing with this person without Cameron.

"Make me proud, us both proud. I've never won anything. Well, maybe a few times with those scratch-off tickets. But that's nothing compared to this. This will be huge. A huge win for us both. How can you think about penalizing me for that?" he said.

"That's not what this is all about. Just until the competition is over, okay? It's all I ask. You need space Cam...more than you know. I'll be here when it's all over. I'm not going anywhere, okay? And when that day comes, I promise I'll be there cheering you on. Be there to see you *kiss* that trophy when they hand it to you, because I believe in you. Okay?"

"All that sounds good, but let me get this straight. You're making this a separation like married people?" He contracted his jaws, bobbed and shook his head as though he didn't know whether to laugh or drive a fist through a wall.

He gripped my nape and drew me into his smothering smell of smog and dirty laundry. And as I looked him in the eyes, the tension in his face mingled with the warmth and sympathy I felt for him.

He released his hold on me. "About that Ebay guy, anything new I should know about?" This surprised me.

"Um...no," I frowned, lowered my eyes, didn't know what to think. But he remained unusually quiet. I looked up at him, or up at a pang of suspicion deep within so petrifying that oh so slightly I began shaking my head. *Did he find out, hear something?*

But he surprised me, "You know to come to me for anything right? It doesn't matter what I said before. We're two of a kind, Pia, and don't you ever forget it."

"Yeah," I nodded, now speechless. Why did he have to fit us as "two of a kind" now when I was hell-bent on holding back, and was certain I was doing the right thing?

"I don't want you to forget that. And to prove that I am for real about us, I have something." He dug out of his pocket a small velvet box, black, and opened it. In it was a green stone on a gold band.

"C-Cam, wha—" I choked up, couldn't believe my eyes.

"—It's not what you're thinking. This ring belonged to my mother. And she treasured it. Dad had given it to her. And it would mean a lot to me if...," he brought the ring up to eye level. "Well...will you wear my mother's ring?"

"B-but...but I don't understand...the timing in all."

"The timing?"

"*Well yes*, the timing. And the stone...some kind of emerald is it?" I asked gazing at the ring.

A strange piece of stone it was. And even stranger was that it was like the stone in Ebay's ring. *Too similar*, I repeated to myself as I examined the spiny and exotic details. And the timing, like an unexpected play out of left field, too weird and alarming—I couldn't get over it.

"But this couldn't be a better time, Pia," Cameron ignored my question. He was more concern with my reluctance to wearing it and his purpose for offering it to me. "It's a way for me to prove how much you mean to me. I want to do this...for us. So will you...wear my mother's ring? Please?"

"Cam, it's a beautiful ring, but you don't have to do this. I understand you having to do what you think is right. As I do. The ring won't change anything." I exhaled then turned away.

"You're right, it won't. But for me to accept this so-called separation, you have to agree to wear the ring. I'll feel better knowing that we're on the same page about this." His tone softened, "I don't want to leave here feeling like we have broken up until the competition is over."

He then lifted my hand, slid the ring on the wedded finger, and then gazed into my eyes. "Two weeks, that's all. And all this will be behind us. It'll work out, you'll see."

I then stepped into him, pillowed my head against the drum beating in his chest, as his hugging arms drew me closer.

He covered my hair with soft kisses, then lent soft whispers in my ear that made my body quiver. His hands began kneading up and down my dorsum and across my shoulders. I raised my head and our lips came together like a magnet.

The hungry passion we shared poured into us. So sweet, so loving, and more than I could stand because I knew there would be sacrifices, though I had no clue what it might be.

Then I imagined a long pitch-black tunnel, at the end of it a flicker of light, like a guiding light. And if I got through the darkness to this light, it would mean not only I had made it, but also no more worries. But first I had to get through the darkness, not knowing what lurched within. And I prayed that God be with me.

Our marshy lips lightly brushed apart. "Pia," Cameron uttered a breath of fervency. "I just...I just don't see how this so-call separation will solve anything."

I gently lay my head against his heart. "I know," I conceded softly, never wanting him to let me go.

At some point before going to bed, I sat on a rock on top of a hill, looking over a well-lit city and trees from afar. So quiet and peaceful until suddenly I jumped, something astonishing began to happen.

Right before my eyes, the lit city and the trees broke into pieces and shifted around, and reconnected. Like a jigsaw puzzle falling into place all on its own. Over and over the pieces disconnected, shuffled, and formed the same beautiful picture. And no matter how it amazed me each time, it seemed...natural.

Then suddenly, "Perseaus? Perseaus?" a man called out. What was strange was my ignoring him. "Perseaus?" his voice rang out once more and still I pretended to not hear him. So he then said, "Okay then, have it your way—"

"*What?*" I belted with anger, which snapped me out of the dream.

I opened my eyes, lifted my head. It couldn't have been me in the dream. Because he called me Perseaus, I thought.

I got up from the couch and moved to the bathroom, wondering about Perseaus....

Who was she?

Chapter Fourteen
The Second Episode

I could hear them, scuffling, trying to drown the other out. With my eyes wide-shut, I could see the imagery of dark waters threatening to pull them under. Their voices faint, washed-out, but their calls came through loud and clear:

Cameron: *We're two of a kind. Never forget that. When it's all over things will be fine, you'd see.*

And then Ebay: *You're not who you think you are. You have to remember...remember. Time is running out.*

I rolled over on my side as Ebay's voice gnawed on my brain. *What was it I had to remember?* The island, and the way it met its demise that day popped in my mind. It hadn't been a pretty sight, the glacier creature diminishing it to nothing. Now I was told that time was running out and I had no clue what that meant. I wanted to know, but at the same time, I didn't. But I knew it was a threat to me—to us all—that much I was sure of. The dark waters drowned the voices, if only it were that easy

141

to silence my fears.

I rolled over onto something hard. I opened my eyes and there were diaries strewed across the bed. Last night I was going through them so I could hand them over to Miss Lambert before the deadline I'd promised. "Just get it over with" was what I was thinking. I had gone through most of them. And my plan was to call by tomorrow to let her know they were ready for her to breathe new life into them. News I knew would thrill her to hear, while I still couldn't believe I was letting them go into hands of a stranger. They were like babies. My diaries. Babies I had raised from birth and was about to let go into the world.

But all was different now. I was excited now to see what would become of them. And the anticipation of everything working out for the best felt good as well. But now I felt like a doormat, as Mom would say. My stomach was making a fuss, and an annoying ache monkeyed around in my head. I hadn't eaten a thing since having that drink Ebay gave me yesterday. It was time to do something about that.

I hung my feet off the bed and slipped them into puppy-faced slippers. My pajamas swaddled them when I stood up. I scooted on into the kitchen with fingertips kneading my forehead. And as soon as I opened the refrigerator, disappointment slapped me in the face—*no cereal, no milk*. I could kick my behind back into bed. But the untamed growls in my stomach wouldn't let me do that. They needed calming down and fast. Sausage, eggs, toast, so be it. I grabbed the round-packed maple-flavored sausage, the carton of eggs. Then I bumped the fridge door close with my shoulder and started with breakfast. Times like this I missed Mom the most.

As it turned out, breakfast wasn't all I needed. The growling stopped but emptiness about me remained. I wanted to do something about it. Anything. But how? What? And what was it I had to remember? About what happened the night I went missing? I didn't have a problem remembering that, if only I could. Or about who I was? *But I'm Pia Wade.* My birth certificate was all the proof I needed. And I refused the possibility of being switched at birth; that was a no-no.

So what then?

The ring, on my finger. I studied its striking similarity to the ring on Ebay's finger. I wasn't sure about the timing of one like it on mine now. It was too consequential for it not to be a coincident. But the ring came from Cameron, and he needed me to wear it. As much as I wanted to take it off, I couldn't find it in my heart to do it, because I would only be refusing Cameron.

I got up from the kitchen table, went into the living room and settled down on the sofa. The remote next to me, I picked it up and pressed the power button. The screen lit up on the science channel. The narrator got my attention at once whether God created the universe or not. I had to hear more because if not God created the universe then who or what? I wanted to learn more of what laws of nature had to do with past lives, the hereafter, and angels and demons. I became interested after meeting Nathan Russell on Oprah last year. The island had been and still was one big mystery: Where it came from and where it went?

Moments into the program, my ears started aching, ringing, and a knock came at the door. Rubbing my ears, I got up to answer the door, suspecting it was only Stephanie. I looked through the peephole. *Miss Saunders?* I sighed, put on my best smile then opened the door to greet my next-door neighbor.

"Hi, Precious," she called me. I had to admit it had a nice grandmotherly ring to it, despite the ringing going on in my ears. "How are you this morning?" Her voice echoed this time, ricocheted off the walls and pierced sharply through my ears. "What is it? Are you all right?" There, it happened again, the piercing pain in my ears hearing her voice.

"Uh...yeah, I'm fine, I'm fine." No echo when I spoke, how strange. "It's just that I got this ringing in my ears," I said tapping on my ears, and cringing, expecting her voice to cause me more pain. But was relieved that it wasn't as much this time. Tapping them with my hands seemed to help.

"I stopped by to invite you over for dinner, but I see this isn't a good time for you either."

"No, I should be fine...." I tried telling her, but she wasn't buying it.

"You don't look much like company. Try a few drops of peroxide in each ear to see if that'd help, and I'll check on you later, and bring you a plate."

I smiled, "Thank you," I said, and then she left. I closed the door and reclaimed my position in front of the TV. All I wanted was to lie down, melt away into a deep sleep, and wake up cured from whatever this was.

However, before I put my feet up, my cellphone

started ringing, way in the kitchen. Which was too far since I didn't want to get back up to get it. But I did.

"Pia." My sensitive ears detected acute concern in her voice. "Honey, are you all right?"

"I'm fine, Mom. Why wouldn't I be?" I asked, though Mom's maternal instinct never ceased to amaze me. A hundred miles away and yet it was as if she were here doting over me, analyzing lines of worry and pain in my forehead. As if, her fingertips were here smoothing away the throbbing at my temple. Hundreds of miles away, yet nothing in my voice I thought sent the message that I was having a difficult day—unless. Yes, of course, it was Miss Saunders. She didn't waste any time contacting Mom. I went on and told her Miss Saunders had stopped by, and that I could have an ear infection but not to worry. By no means did I want her to worry over nothing.

However, for the next two days, it would take all of me to keep that up.

Suddenly I felt faint, feverish, and right as I collapsed on the sofa, his face flashed before me.

Monday

I was worse the next day. All I wanted to do was lie between sheets on a plump pillow.

I woke up with a case of severe nausea, thought for sure I would throw up. I had taken Tums and two tablespoons of the pink stuff. It was all I had. Now I was in and out of the bathroom; making progress I supposed. The nausea turned from gut-wrenching pain to a delicate cramp. Which was a teaser suspecting it would reap havoc on me again at any moment.

I still had ringing in my ear, but the echoing was gone. My eyes but were a different story. As I lay on my back, they rolled around in my head as if they were trying to break free, then they stopped, like "what's the use?" I opened and closed them again, and it was the same thing: rolling until they got tired and stopped. Strange, my eyes had never behaved this way before. If that wasn't enough, when I got up my head would pound, my stomach would sink, and my legs would buckle. This was strange too, because if I kept my helpless body in bed, I didn't feel so sick.

My closed eyelids began fluttering. And then, as if they grew wings, they soared over hills and hills; hills painted in multi-layers of red, green, and yellow. I was in an odyssey of a sort, seeing spectacular places. Now at a statue, a Buddha statue of pure gold, posed atop a staircase monument. Lines of trees flanked the square that extended below the monument; my eyes in the center, gazed up at the statue. Then in a flash I was dipping over another mountain. And down below were hundreds of pink flamingoes flocking in the water. At once they took flight to the sky, and the feeling of being swept along in their migration was wondrous.

What was this? I opened my eyes wondering this but was compelled to continue the journey, hoping I'd find out, so I closed them back. Because I hadn't experienced sickness, visions quite like this before. When I opened my eyes, it stopped, closed them it went on. I didn't know why, but I thought I was seeing someone else's memories and my body powerless because of it. Possessed, was I? Or were the visions starting again, only different this time? After all what'd happened....

Again, I wondered what he meant by *my first episode.* As I wondered had he truly put something in my drink. As I thought about it, I recalled having a vision that day. So, it had been that day the visions started.

My first episode, what exactly did he mean?

All day I was in and out of sleep and traveled the world while awake. Later in the night, I went on what seemed like a safari, riding the back of an elephant. Voices were all around me. I wasn't alone, though I couldn't confirm it visually. Only voices I heard, never saw faces.

And when it all ceased, I was in a dark, quiet place.

Tuesday

More of the same rolled into the next day with no sign of letting up. I clung to the bed still, only getting up when necessary.

Today, I travelled through time. Days turned into nights, weeks, into months. Leaves turned into brilliant colors then fell to the ground. Then a spontaneous winter blew in and blanketed it with beautiful white crystals. As time charged on flowers bloomed and trees grew tall. It all was so fascinating, though I didn't understand why. But I hoped that would change as it ran its course.

Soon I came to a phase of nothingness but refused to open my eyes. This phase was like a film with nothing on it; I had no doubt it would resume though. And I was right. There I was staring up at a translucent staircase, escalating high above the clouds. As I marveled my appreciation of the site, something interesting, I began rising. Not the real, physical me (though it felt like it), but me in whatever this was—rising and feeling the atmosphere. The warmth of the sun against my skin, and the breeze. It reminded me of an out-of-body experience I used to have, but not like this. This was something different.

Without warning a breeze collected me and whooshed off, moving so fast to orbit the world in a day. I was still travelling through time, forward in time, had to be. Right before my eyes streets rolled out like dominoes collapsing all over the place. Then at once buildings sprouted up from the ground. An entire city right before my eyes. And when night fell on it, like someone flicked the switch, festive lights were everywhere. *As a celebration for building a city in a day?* The idea crossed my mind because of the laughter, coming from somewhere. Laughter without faces I was dying to see.

But time was swift in moving me along; now I feasted my eyes on a treehouse in a humongous tree springing out of a forest. It had windows, and a staircase spiraled all the way to the top. For some reason it didn't seem imaginary. That I had seen something like it before, in a magazine, I was thinking. Yet, with the scenery rapidly changing, my pondering collapsed, only to form anew on something else.

In a pit of a mountainous forest, I stood now on a frozen lake, huge snowflakes the size of my hand falling from the sky. My body shivered as I held out a hand to catch one. One, two, three perfect snowflakes landed in my hand. Then suddenly snowflakes began swirling around me, gradually lifting me. I smiled with delight. The snowflakes were so beautiful and playful, whirling like on a merry-go-round as more flakes hopped aboard. The more flakes the faster it went that I grew afraid of being buried alive in a mountain of snow. I tried opening

149

my eyes to snap out of it, and to make sure this wasn't real and that where I was, was where I was supposed to be—*Home.*

I tried hard to open them, but then I heard voices. The same voices from earlier. And before I knew it, the snow had vanished. I got excited. "Who are you! Thanks for helping me!" I craved for interaction, because they had to know I was there. But as their voices drifted away, "Wait, come back!" my voice sought them. Perhaps they didn't after all.

The sky changed rapidly, from a clear blue sky to ranges of color designs like an artist running a magic paint brush through the sky till the end of time. As time raced on, the fascinating places flashing before me seemed endless too. Until I came to a moment like a feather drifting in the wind, where again there were voices. The same voices, of course with no faces, but I could see them, curling and streaking limpidly across the sky like animated wind. Like translucent souls as they were dazzling me. Airy and pristine were the voices.

"*This is glorious,*" the woman said to him. "*The Bagan bash is starting soon. Will you join me for a little while at least?*"

I couldn't help giving it another shot. "Hey, hi. I'm here, and I agree, this is glorious. Can you hear me?"

Their voices drifted away, and it just didn't seem fair...so sad to hear them go. Ignoring me just for spite, I couldn't imagine them doing that.

I opened my eyes thinking. *He said time was*

150

running out. Said that I had to remember [something] before it did. But what? Could it be what the visions were about? I pondered and pondered.

And what weighed on me the most, were the voices without faces.

Chapter Fifteen

Memory Lane

A fairy must have sprinkled me with pixie dust before I opened my eyes this morning. It was gone: the headache, the sick stomach, the ringing in my ears. I was like brand-new through and through, that I had to pinch myself to make sure I wasn't dreaming. After being cooped up in the house for days, it felt like the best day of my life. And for that I wanted to run wild, breathe fresh air, and feel it for real against my skin.

I hopped into my VW, stuck the key in and started the engine. In moments I was on my way. To nowhere in particular, just getting out of the house, *because this was the best day of my life.* I began meditating that, realizing that it was a lie. It wasn't like all my problems had vanished. Something crucial was about to happen; I could feel it.

In wonder, I just drove and drove, my eyes straight ahead on the road, oblivious to anything else around me at times. So much on my mind that didn't make sense. Yet, time was running out and I had no clue what that meant. Also, I hadn't had a vision in over a year, and now suddenly, I was. In the dream he called her Perseaus. Who was she? And what did she have to do with me? I wanted answers and I wanted it NOW.

I got up this morning feeling this was the best day of my life. In an oxymoron kind a way it was. I woke up feeling better than ever before, on this gorgeous day, *alive*. And I was crazy to get out in it. But on the flip-side, hungry for answers, yet afraid of what I might find.

I was afraid, yes, so afraid indeed.

Where am I? My voice blew gently through my mind. I glanced at the clock; digits glowed 10:45. I'd been driving for over an hour, and nothing looked familiar, which meant I had no clue where I was. But it appeared I was driving in circles. Passing the same buildings, the same area of trees and bushes, the same everything—even the people started looking familiar. Not familiar, familiar. I knew no one personally. But the jogger with a happy-face printed on her T-shirt, I was certain I'd passed a few blocks back. And the woman walking four Pomeranians, how could I forget seeing her? Not only that, this area was starting to feel like déjà vu. And strange, there were no street signs.

I drove to the next intersection and still, no street sign. I glared up through the windshield, up at tall glass buildings that set off the feeling of being in a maze. Or a dream. But no, I couldn't be dreaming. A car behind me started blowing.

No, I wasn't dreaming.

I sped through the now-green light. My curiosity growing, I still looked for some sign of where I was.

Deeper I drove into this conundrum, making turns here and there, still baffled that I saw not one street sign. Until finally I came to a shaded area, which offered a sense of relief, only because it was different, and, there was a street sign.

Hmm, Memory Lane. I didn't give the street name much thought but decided I would turn on it. Right then I made a right turn. The trees in this area were tall with huge trunks and branches...oak trees they were. I knew because we had oak trees in our yard in Texas.

I looked at the mileage but couldn't get the reading I wanted. If only I had thought to reset the trip mileage. I came to a four-way stop intersection, I drew a deep breath, let it out, and drew in another as I waited my turn. Then I continued up Memory Lane for about a mile, enjoying the scenery and the feel of a nice community with large trees protecting it. But I was beginning to wonder why this was the only street I saw with a name. But that changed. I ran into a street marking the end of Memory Lane. A grassy median divided this street. And the name was...To-Memory Avenue? Of course that was strange to me, considering everything else.

The only way I could turn was right. Hearing the music, I didn't hesitate. About a block up the car gradually came to a stop along a curb lined with meters. Meters lined the street on both sides of the median. I had the urge to stop but wasn't sure why. I knew I should be trying to find my way back home. But here I was at a park, beholden to check it out.

I dug out quarters from a slot in the console for the meter, got out and powered locked the doors. I looked the area over before moving. Through some trees was a city skyline in the distance, but not in the direction I had come though. And I wondered again where was I, as I admired the huge trees around me. Tall, leafy trees, none were palm trees, like unique walls enclosing the area from the world.

I walked up to the meter, fed it coins, then paused as curiosity spoke to me. *How was it I'd never seen this part of town before? And why did I bother to stop here?* Gazing off into the park, I had not one reason. No more than it was easy to stop and see what this place was all about.

I moved pass the black iron fence surrounding the park. People everywhere and music filled the air. At the entrance people sat on concrete benches. Some like donuts with trees in the center, and just off the path to my right was a memorial monument. I moved ahead then meandered through one of the connecting walkways in the park, seeing all that my eyes could see. And there was a lot to see for the park was huge. Across the way to my left was a lake, people in it kayaking. And off from the lake was a bandstand, and off from it were a couple of two-story buildings. Each of the buildings had green verandas. And as I bent the corner, I saw there were red verandas on the backside of the buildings.

It was in this area the music came from. Enthusiastic kids joined by people dressed in fancy costumes, like the *Cat in a hat, Sponge Bob, and Cinderella*, danced around in a circle. I watched for a moment, smiling. In this section was also a tree. It had a twisted trunk that sprouted out at the top like real trees with leaves. An aluminum tree it was, raining down on giggling kids so full of joy. Next to it was more water

155

jetting up from the ground. A playground, food stands, and a variety of shops were here, too.

This was more than a park. The buildings with verandas were a place for learning, from art to kayaking to Zumba. Impressive, I thought. And then I overheard someone say the park had a movie screen, I thought that impressive, too. I made my way around to the bandstand, and noticed men hanging a banner that read Flutist Zone. "Mmm. *Flutist Zone...,*" I repeated softly, trying to figure why it seemed so familiar. But it only bugged me; as usual, nothing came to mind.

A flute started playing from somewhere. I looked around for where it could be coming from, but it seemed to be coming from everywhere. Turning, still trying to see where it was coming from —and then it stopped. *Flutist Zone,* it whispered to me—and that was enough! I shook it out of my head and went ahead on my exploratory journey.

Coming toward me was a woman, not too old, wearing jeans, a white top, and dark shades. I didn't know where I was and thought now was time to find out.

"Excuse me? I haven't seen a sign anywhere; can you tell me where I'm at?"

"Well everyone knows Discovery Oak Park," she said then spread a thin smile. "Are you new to Opa-locka?"

"Well, yes, I am. I got lost and found this place. It's really nice here," I looked off. "Well, thanks for your help," I said, not wanting to take up much of her time.

The woman nodded and moved on.

Opa-locka? I had heard of it but wasn't sure where it was, though obviously not too far away from home.

After a while I came upon a small area of groves and gardens. An area dedicated to individuals, which was so lovely, it felt like a Garden of Eden, and so unreal, like a dream—I didn't know why. Lost and confused, I knew for sure, and I knew I should be trying to find my way back. But there was something about this place, and the day was young. Honestly, I couldn't help myself.

I arrived at one of the exits, way on the other side from where I'd parked. Just beyond the fence was a red-white-blue art monument about thirty-feet high. I went past the fence to get a closer look, and realized the structure was actually three structures, created with tubes of odd shapes. I examined the art and the tallest one looked to me like a giraffe missing its pointed ears. I couldn't quite make out the other two, but they looked like a couple of starved elephants with tall legs and truncated trunks. Between one elephant and the giraffe, it looked to be a face of a monkey with huge eyes. And between the giraffe and the other elephant, the face of a hippo stood out. As I continued examining the figures, I saw what looked like a zebra, with stripes running up the neck. No stripes anywhere else. It was interesting to see so many things in the monuments.

I began running my fingertips over it, knocked on it a few times trying to figure out if it was hollow. It was hard to tell if it was hollow or not, but I was sure the frame was metal. The art had me fully intrigued that I looked for a placard to learn more about it. Moving around with my back bent, I noticed a pair of legs in jeans.

My eyes glided up the legs, then held for a moment on a brown belt, with a navy blue striped shirt tucked beneath it. My eyes then crawled up to crossed arms and instantly froze on that all-familiar ring. Right then I covered the green stone on my finger, turned it and clutched it in the palm of my hand, not knowing why. All I knew was that I didn't want him to see it. And as my eyes met with the stoic look in his, they narrowed viciously.

"What are you doing here?" I resumed an upright position and continued searching for a placard.

"Monument Au Fantome," he said.

I turned, "Huh?"

"The sculptures...Monument Au Fantome. French...it means imaginary city. Fascinating work by Dubuffet...," he went on.

"*What are you doing here?*" I cut him off.

"Just thought I'd help out...save you time."

"Save me time on what?"

"On what this is. The Monument Au Fantome. You seemed quite drawn to it. There is one like it in France, Africa, too. The figures in the monuments, reminds you of a safari, wouldn't you say?" He took a pause. "So, have you ever been interested in art of this caliber before?"

I thought strange he asked. My answer was no, though I kept it to myself because I was asking the questions. "What are you doing, stalking me? Or are you here to pick up where we left off?"

"Not stalking you...but...I am here because you're trying to remember...some things. And though it's not much I can do, I want you to remember. Believe me. But it's all up to you. Everything's in your hands...all up to you...," his voice trailed off.

"I was kidnapped five years ago in my sleep. Was it you? I don't know because I can't remember anything about that night. I was missing for fourteen hours and I remember nothing at all. I would give anything to remember." I stared at him, "But you know. Don't you?"

"I may know something about it. But if you're asking if I kidnapped you, then no, I didn't."

"Then what do you know?"

"That if that night hadn't happened I wouldn't be here now."

"B-but...but that was over five years ago. Why now?" I said, and then something else came to me. "The other time when you appeared as a ferret, a ghost, and then as human, like now. You're really Ferret. You won't admit it, but I know. Why are you here now?"

"For reasons you are yet to remember, understand. Reasons I can't explain. Not now. But in time, things change."

"Then you are useless to me. No help at all."

He nodded his head slightly and began looking around. "All of this...this entire scene...the park here, the buildings over yonder. Your drive here. Have you given any thought to why you are here? That maybe you've been here before?" He walked over to a nearby tree, pulled off a leaf, and then waved it. "This is alive, you are alive. Life is a wonderful thing isn't it?"

Thinking he should lower his voice, I moved closer to him.

"Don't worry," he said. I expected him to elaborate but he didn't.

"Living is life. To not live is to die," I said, as he crushed the leaf in his hand. "And this is my life; it's all

I've got, and I need to make the most of it." He now opened his hand and the leaf fell to the ground. "And...I don't remember any other life," I felt compelled to say.

"If you could would you want to?" he asked with a trace of something different about his face. Sadness, I believed it was.

I wasn't sure how I should respond to that; I felt as though it was a trick question. But then, I wanted to see where it would lead. "If it would help me remember what happened the night I went missing, then, maybe."

He nodded. "Yes, I agree. How can you remember anything about past lives if you can't remember anything about that day?"

"Right."

"All this," he spread his hands, "this place, the people—everything—is just an illusion. Of a memory embedded up here," he pointed to his head, "of another time and place."

"What do you mean...?" I stopped midsentence, thinking about the places I saw in the visions. I'd thought then I was seeing it all through someone else's eyes. On my drive here, I thought about too: how it felt like déjà vu, and how strange there were no street signs, except when....

All you must do is remember, and all your concerns would be answered. I want you to remember. I need you to remember.

"W-Why? Why do you need me to remember?" I couldn't pretend this time.

And he looked surprised.

"Sometimes I can read your mind. That...surprises you?"

"Not really. It's complicated, but, I'm hoping

160

you'll come to understand."

"Wait. You expect me to believe you didn't know I was reading your mind? That's crap. I know what you're been doing. You've been putting thoughts in my head, wanting me to believe I was reading your mind. And why would you do that? Just tell me why you're here, because I'm not causing any of this. I didn't bring you here!"

"That's where you're wrong. I'm here because of you, because you summoned me."

My body shook nervously. "No. How did I do that? *I didn't.* You're trying to take over my mind, fill it with stuff I know nothing about. Like the other day...I was sick for two whole days after seeing you. Sick like I had never been before. And today, I'm better, but somehow...I ended up here. And behold, here you are.

"So, don't for a minute insinuate that all this is my doing. My life was fine until that night, when everything changed." I turned away and grabbed a breath. "You say I summoned you. Okay, well, I summoned you because I desperately need answers. So give them to me. Now, get it over with. What do you want from me?" Tears in my eyes, I looked to see if we had attracted an audience. "You say all of this is just an illusion, then it shouldn't matter who hears us," I sneered, though what good it did.

"It doesn't matter if you believe," he said. Whatever that was supposed to mean.

"Yeah, right." Wiping away tears, I stormed across the grass to a nearby bench.

He came behind me and eased down next to

me.

"So?" I said looking straight ahead with my arms folded.

"I...I can't do what you want. Not now. But, there is something I can do that may help as things unfold. That's if you will allow me."

I turned to him. He had his hand out requesting mine. "What do you need with my hand?" I rejected. I wouldn't dare, couldn't give him the hand clutching the stone. But that wasn't my only reason—I didn't trust him.

"It's Cameron," he said, shaking his head.

"*Cameron?* What does he have to do with anything?"

"He's...what's holding you back."

"Humph," I hopped up and began backing away. "I knew it. You're after Cameron. Why? Why do you want to hurt him? What does he have to do with anything? Except..." I didn't know what I was thinking.

"I'm not trying to hurt your friend."

"I don't believe you. You...you stay away from him, *and from me*." I turned and picked up pace, couldn't get away fast enough.

If only you'd remember, before time runs out. Soon you'll know everything. Soon it'll be all over.

I could hear it, his mind, chasing me. No matter how fast I moved and the distance I put between us, his mind was there, chasing me down.

It'd be over soon. It'd be over soon. It'd be over soon.

I summon you to disappear, I said back and started running. And I couldn't run fast enough.

If only distance could end it all.

162

Chapter Sixteen
Ball of Confusion

"This is a switch: me riding shotgun with you behind the wheel."

"I know. And it's 'bout time," Stephanie said beaming with pride. Her mother finally got a new SUV, and making good on her promise, Stephanie now sported the Celica, a beautiful royal blue and it was like new itself.

"I'm glad you're over that nasty stomach flu...," she said. I had told everyone I had stomach flu to keep them away. For all I knew I could have had it; I certainly had the symptoms. But the visions, and the dreams, that was something entirely different. "You know, sometimes I think...." Stephanie carried on as we headed for DSW for shoe shopping.

I smiled at what she was talking about, as I slipped away thinking about what occurred earlier today at the park with Ebay. Then that name Perseaus popped in my mind, as it had many times, especially since the dream. *Did he know someone by that name?*

Yeah, he put it in my head! Like how ferret magically entered my mind that day. Perseaus...and the voices....

"What are you thinking about over there?" Stephanie interrupted my thoughts.

It took me a moment, and then I asked, "Do you ever wonder about past lives? Like who you were in another life?"

"Well I...I have thought about it. Especially after everything that happened with you last year. But not lately though. Why do you ask?"

"Because...I saw him again."

"Saw who, when?"

"Ebay, who else? I saw him today at a park...in...Opa-locka," I grimaced, not sure I pronounced it right, and because I felt like something was off.

"Really? What time was this?"

"What time what?"

"What time did you see him?"

"Oh, um...about eleven-thirty," I said, remembering 10:45 glaring back at me when I'd checked the time before arriving at the park. "Yeah, it was around that time," I affirmed, still with that feeling that something was off.

"You saw him, meaning you just happened to run into him at the park, right?"

"Yeah, right."

"Well then, how did you get there?"

I gave her a knock-knock-is-anybody-at-home look.

"Don't look at me like that. What's gotten into you? Your car was right there in the driveway around that time."

"No, you must have the time mixed up."

"I don't think so. Your car was in the driveway this morning when Mom and I left to go pick up her car at ten. And it was still in the driveway when I got back. About noon." She looked at me and came back adamant. "I know what I saw and I'm certain of the time, cross my heart. Your car was home in the driveway, Pia. I even called you when I got back. Look."

She quickly reached for her phone, and while keeping her eyes on the road, managed to pull up her recent calls menu. "See, 12:13pm? We talked, you were at home, don't you remember?" She waited for me to say something or at least admit that she was right.

To be sure, I picked up my phone in my lap and checked. And there it was, proof. I couldn't believe it. How could I've been in two places at once? Unless....

"He didn't pick me up, believe me; I didn't lie about that. And I didn't hitch a ride with someone else. I drove myself...but...I don't know...it had to of been a dream. Are you absolutely sure—yes, of course you are. But, it all being a dream...." I had a tough time with that sinking in.

"That real, huh?"

"Yes, strange because I was there—I mean," I shook my head. "I remember getting in the car and driving there, because I did but I...I don't remember driving back. I remember running to the car, and when I got in it, I started it up and drove away. From that point, I don't remember driving back. How can I not remember the drive back? From the time I left the park till the time I got the call from you, is a total blank."

"What you're saying, is that you don't know what

165

you were doing right before I called?"

"All I remember the phone ringing and I picked it up from the table and answered it."

"The table, not the nightstand?"

"Yeah. The kitchen table. *Wait.* I remember standing, looking out the kitchen window right when you called. That's it. That's all I remember."

"Pia, I hate to say this, but maybe you had a weird vision, so real that you think you left the house and went to Opa-locka of all places. Why Opa-locka, have you been there before?"

"No. Not that I know of. But he claimed that I have, claimed that I created the place from my memory." I looked at Stephanie and chuckled.

"Weird. What was the name of the park?"

"Discovery Oak Park. And the park is huge, Steph. It's a recreational-type park. And there's so much to do there..." I went on telling Stephanie about the park as she pulled into the strip center where DSW was.

Stephanie parked the car and quickly responded to a text she had gotten. Then without my knowing checked out that park.

"Pia, there isn't a park by that name in this area, which means you couldn't have gone there. See here?"

I refused, shaking my head. "I believe you. He said it was from my memory, but I have no memory of it so how could that be? A sick vision, had to be. The visions are back, Steph, but different this time."

My cellphone started ringing. It was Cameron; I just let the phone ring.

Pia glanced over and saw who was calling. "Pia, you probably should answer that and let CJ know what's going on."

"I know but, Cam and I are separated," I made a face and Stephanie goggled. "I know how that sounds but that's how things are right now. All screwed up."

"I'll say. Does this have anything to do with Ebay?"

I exhaled, lightly shaking my head.

"Well, what's going on with you and CJ?" she asked.

"We both agreed to separate until after the skateboarding contest. And just now he broke our agreement."

Stephanie released a noisy sigh. "Now who came up with that brilliant idea? You know something, Pia, I never would have thought I'd be taking CJ's side on anything. A separation? Now what's that all about?"

"Not that it's any of your business but rather than us breaking up, *we* decided to separate. Look," I said before she could get a word out, "he's under pressure; I'm under pressure. It's for the best for both of us. We both agreed."

"But that was your CJ calling. What if he's calling about something important?"

"Then he'll leave a message!" I said at Stephanie glaring an intoxicating expression. And I glared back thinking, *you didn't hear a word I just said.* But of course, she didn't. She showed me her feeling of disappointment regardless. I felt a strain creeping up the back of my neck and I began massaging the area. Stephanie then shut off the engine and cracked open the door.

"I can't believe you sometimes," she said grudgingly. "It doesn't do me any good; it doesn't do

167

anyone any good," she mumbled opening the door. She got out, closed it, started walking then stopped, "*Are you coming?*" she said to get me to budge.

"Yeah. I'll be in in a minute," I yelled back. And she went on without me, as I needed time to process things, because my world was speeding off its axle, again.

This morning I got up, got in the car, and left. And I got lost and ended up at that park. How did I not do that? It seemed too real not to have happened. My clothes, I looked down at them. The charcoal gray Levi's and silver-gray top, the same exact things I had on at the park. *And what else?* I tried hard trying to piece this together.

Then feeling the stone in my palm, it dawned on me that I had turned it so he wouldn't see it. I was starting to see a pattern here, revealing that some things happened for sure. I got out of the car, and fumbled with the ring, thinking about Cameron, as I approached the store. The ring was Cameron's, and his life, it felt like in the palm of my hand. And somehow, I had to protect it.

Because, whether I took the drive this morning or not, I perceived a very important message. That somehow Cameron was interfering with his plan. And that, however very unusual, that the rings were somehow connected, and that Cameron was totally in the dark about it. And as for what it was I had to remember, and if I didn't remember in time, that it would be consequences. And I feared what the consequences may be.

As I approached the double glass doors of the shoe store, so did a woman and a girl. Gypsies, I noted my mind. They wore long peasant skirts and beaded jewelry. The woman had on large hoop earrings, and a colorful scarf tied to one side around her head. The little girl had a printed headband around hers. Each had hair cascading off their shoulders. The woman held the door open for me. I smiled, "Thank you," I said.

I entered, then paused near the entrance looking around for Stephanie. The gypsies had moved off to the left of the store. Looking off in that direction, my attention stalled on the little girl. I couldn't help seeing her eyes pent on me. *Yes, on me:* I confirmed after a quick glance over my shoulder. Curious, bewitching eyes—then again, she could be, or it seemed, she was looking straight through me.

Could be she was a dreamer, a fantasizer, and today she chose me to fantasize on. Either way, *I've had my share of weirdness over the last few days,* I said to myself. And I certainly didn't need a strange little girl adding to it.

I started moving through one of the long aisles of shoes to get to the back of the store. I didn't see Stephanie anywhere, so I suspected she was in the small narrow room in back. It also had aisles of shoes, except the aisles were way shorter. This area stocked hefty-discounted shoes.

"Hey, what do you think of these?" Stephanie said as soon as she spotted me. She was strutting around in red stilettoes, the same pigment in the shorts she had on. And the heals really made her bare legs look long and bony. But prancing around in the stilettoes was just for fun. We both knew she wasn't about to buy heals that high. She would break those bony legs for sure.

"Those are to die for. But be careful. Remember they have a way of knocking you off your feet," I mocked her words as she continued prancing around in the shoes.

Stephanie grimaced, primping in front of the mirror, then gazed through the mirror at me with my arms folded. "Are you going to just stand there and watch me?" she said. In other words, you're not going to shop for shoes?

My lips hissed. "Take your time. I'll be over here," and I moved over to the yellow vinyl seats against the wall, sighed as I sat down. I rested my head against the wall and closed my eyes. Everything around me just faded away, except his voice; I wasn't surprised.

If only you knew what it would mean to remember, a gift it would be....

My eyes began to flutter as my mind grew agitated from the thought of him in it. *But a gift?* This was new; I never considered any part of all this a gift.

"Are you okay?"

My eyes flew open to the unique accent. And there, standing before me, the little girl. My mind stuttered before finding the words to speak, seeing that it was the strange little girl who was watching me earlier. "Well, yes, I'm fine," I said finally. She then moved and peeped sneakily around the corner.

"Playing hide-and-seek with your mom?" I asked.

"Oh, no...just making sure she's not looking for me."

I couldn't get over her accent. She looked like a gypsy, but her accent had...I want to say...a Jamaican twang to it.

She settled down next to me. "I'm Geena. What's your name?"

"Well, hi, Geena. I'm Pia." I graced little Ms.

Secretive with a curious smile. "How old are you?" I wondered.

"Ten. And I'm a palm reader. I can read yours. Now, if you like."

I cocked my head, raised my brows; I was amazed to say the least. "This should be interesting. Well sure, why not," I agreed, wondering if she approached people at random all the time. That's what she was doing earlier, pegging my palm as her next subject, I thought.

In her whimsical eyes, I could see her eagerness to do this. I smirked as I extended my hand to see what was in store for my future. I smiled up at Stephanie when she suddenly appeared. Her eyes were surprised, but it was easy to see what was taking place. I then landed my attention back on the reading at hand.

As her eyes rolled over my palm, she lowered them for a closer look. She became still, as frowns around the eyes intensified. She closed her eyes, and then her head flinched like an electric shock. Rubbing fingertips in my palm, she resumed. She was so intense I didn't want to interrupt this unusual reading, though I sensed something was wrong. *What do you see?* I repeated once or twice to myself until I blurted it. "What do you see?"

"Quiet please," she instructed curtly, and I wanted right then to yank my hand away but didn't. I let her have it her way for a few moments longer. Or until I decided that this was a stranger I was giving in to, and that I had let this *bull* go on long enough. I was about to yank my hand when—

"Geena!" The woman startled us both.

Geena jumped up and hurried over to the woman

171

with a distinct accent like her own.

"What did I tell you!" the woman scolded.

"Mommy, I know, b-but, but it's true…"

They both looked my way, as to confirm what the girl was trying to say, and a trace of horror in their faces horrified me. As I was about to question them the woman said, "I'm sorry, forgive my daughter," and grabbed the girl's hand, pulling her away.

"But Mommy, it's true. We have to…" The mother wagged a finger. "But Mommy, she doesn't have much time…we have to…before it's too late…" The girl was whispering but not low enough for my ear.

I started moving toward them. "Excuse me? But what is it you saw? Please, tell me."

"Silence!" the mother said to the child. Then turned to me, "I'm so sorry for my daughter. We don't mean you no harm. My daughter…she knows better. Forgive her. Please, we must go now. God bless you." The mother then hauled the girl away like a scared cat.

Stunned, I stalked every inch of their movement. It took all of me to not chase them down and demand the results of my reading. And I did, take a few steps after them, feeling that my life depended on catching them. But my feet stopped cold to Stephanie's voice coming up behind me.

"Pia? Pia? What was that all about?"

"Nothing, nothing." I turned to her, raised a calm, forbidding hand. "She read my palm but left without telling me what she saw, that's all."

"What! It looked like it was much more than that. Why wouldn't she give you the reading?"

"I don't know why but her mother wouldn't let

her," I sighed. "I don't know Steph. But this is turning out to be one crazy day. And I need to get out of here. Are you about done?"

"Almost."

I followed her to another aisle. "Oh...I forgot to tell you. We have a dinner date with Ms. Saunders."

She looked at me lopsided. "And when did you arrange this?"

"This. Morning. Before I..." I trailed off looking at Stephanie. I could see she was thinking the same thing I was thinking.

"Before you left this morning," Stephanie completed my thought. "But you didn't—okay, okay, we'll check it out with Ms. Saunders."

"Yeah." I closed my eyes as the little girl's voice began scrolling through my mind like a lyrical banner. *She doesn't have much time....*

I couldn't get it out of my head.

Was I dying?

Chapter Seventeen

Human Shackles

Fact: Driving to Opa-locka where I met Ebay yesterday hadn't really happened. But my making dinner arrangements with Ms. Saunders had.

Now I was more confused over what happened yesterday than I was over what happened days before. Because after making dinner arrangements with Ms. Saunders, I remembered getting in the car and leaving. I thought for sure Ms. Saunders would have confirmed that, but she didn't.

I was careful approaching her on this matter though, not wanting to lead on that something was wrong. But she couldn't corroborate my story, which was odd, because she'd been right there in the yard when I left.

Now I was more determined than ever.

"I've been in the dark for far too long and today...," I'd grumbled getting out of the bed this morning, grumbled while eating a bowl of cheerios and while getting dressed. And my grumbling fired up even more when I cranked up the VW. I'd been up half the night deciding what to do next, and what I had to say wasn't going to fall on death ears. If that meant making a scene then so be it.

And why would it have to come to that anyway? It shouldn't have to, I thought as I arrived at my destination.

As I entered he was standing behind the counter with his head in a book. Immediately he looked up, but a girl with a couple of items approaching him averted his attention. My eyes darted around the bookstore because he wasn't who I was looking for anyway. Another clerk was in the back assisting one of the few shoppers in the store, but he had no resemblance of the person I was looking for either. The salesperson at the register handed the girl her purchase. He was now free so I promptly approached.

"Hi. I'm looking for Ebay. Is he working today?"

"Ebay? I don't know anyone by that name that works here," he said undoubtedly.

"You have to be mistaken. He was here the other day when I picked up my book." I set my eyes on his nametag, clipped on the collar of his navy-blue shirt. Ebay didn't have on a nametag that day, I recalled. I would have noticed.

"I've been here a week now, and I believe I've met everyone that works here. I told the other girl who was in here not long ago looking for the same person."

"Someone else was here looking for him? Will you describe her?"

"Well, um...she was about so high"—about my height he gestured—"wearing a sleeveless top, bluish...black shorts...," he was saying until someone approached the counter. "I'll be right with you," he said to the customer. "Look, I'm not sure if I should be telling you this so...."

"Yeah, I understand. Thanks anyway." I then left the store, hightailing to the car with the skatepark on the brain. He could be there.

When I arrived at the head of the aisle I'd parked the car, I noticed a black car blocking me in. And standing in front of it, facing me head-on with crossed arms was...*shit*...someone obviously one-step ahead of me. And she stood bodaciously, this person wearing a blue tank top, black shorts. The bookstore clerk had described her to a tee. Inching forward, I was close enough to see Cristina behind the wheel. It was her car after all and I assumed Ariana was in the car, too.

"Great mines think alike, huh?" Stephanie wore an aura of proudness all too well. And I wasn't pleased one bit.

"What do you think you doing? You shouldn't be here."

"If I shouldn't be here then you shouldn't be here either. You know how it is. You know how it's going to be from here-on-out." Oh, she was bodacious all right.

"And I'm telling you it won't work like that." *Because he's not going to deal with anyone but me,* I said to myself.

"You say that. We tried to find out something about him, but with no last name, we ran into a brick wall. No one seems to know his last name, where he lives—nothing. Did you find out anything about him?"

"Uh, you've been doing this behind my back the

176

whole time?"

She gave me a "what do you think?" look then said, "No one got a memo that we were off the case."

"Okay. Well I'm giving it to you now. You're off the case." Then I brushed past her. "Move the car, Christina!" I pressed the key fob, unlocking the car door.

"Nope. I'm not letting you go without us."

"Back off Steph. I mean it. Look, I appreciate you wanting to help but you're fired—"

"No, Pia. If I have to tell your parents to get you straight about this then I will."

"Oh really? And what exactly would you tell them? Huh? Na-thing...nothing because you have nothing that'd make sense. You would just ruin things for me and have them worried sick. So I had another incident, that doesn't mean anything." Of course I didn't think that. "I could be losing my mind, you said so yourself. Listen, this whole thing could blow over like before."

"And?"

"And so I made a mistake involving you, and you need to stay out of it and let me deal with this and my parents."

"You need us, Pia, and you got us. If we find out there's nothing to this, then we all could breathe a sigh of relief. Stop trying to push us away. You need someone, especially since you got Cameron out of the loop on this ridiculous separation you came up with. You're being irrational, don't you see?

"Now, we know he's not here. And since the competition is coming up soon, he's probably at the skatepark. So...what do you say?"

"I really don't like that you've been sneaking

behind my back. You could've told me what you were planning. And now I wonder—have you thought for one second that y'all going behind my back could be the reason for what's happened...?"

Her eyes widened. "Nice try," she chuckled. "You're not getting rid of us that easy. So what are you going to do?"

My next move was going to the skatepark, but I expected to go alone. "Uhhh," I brooded up at the sky. Then glared at Stephanie and imagined smacking her upside the head. "Yeah, all right," I croaked giving in to being hauled away by human shackles on a bandwagon that I had to get rid of, one way or another.

"I have a feeling this is going to be a waste a time," I said as Stephanie opened the passenger-side door. Hunching forward I climbed into the backseat. I wanted to say why I thought it would be a waste of time, which was because he could spot us coming a mile away, but I knew it would only go in one ear and out the other. They were too determined to hear anything that would put a damper on their pursuit. Even though they were hindering my plan, I had to play along to keep Stephanie's mouth shut. I couldn't risk her going to my parents. Not now.

Ebay's car wasn't in the parking lot when we arrived. A sign he may not be inside and that we had made a blank trip. A very good sign, I hoped.

A red truck was missing from the lot also: Cameron's. I sighed a big relief for that too. I missed

Cameron, but I wasn't ready to see him yet. As for Ebay, I wanted to see him on my own terms: alone. Otherwise I would never get the answers I needed.

Suddenly Cristina whipped between two parked cars then shoved the gearshift into park, really caught me by surprise. I thought for sure I was on my way back to fetch my car left back at the school.

"What are you doing, Cristina, he's not here?" I said.

"I think we should go in to make sure," Cristina uttered tersely.

"You're going about this all wrong," I exhausted.

"Don't you want to at least know that we didn't come all this way for nothing? I know I would. So...who's going in with me?"

"I'm going with you," Ariana spoke.

"Me too," Stephanie said, then looked back at me with twisted lips, waiting on me to answer. "We don't have to be seen together. You can come in after us if you want," Stephanie said; the first reasonable gesture I could agree on if I was in a cooperative mood.

"No...y'all just go with my blessings," I said.

"And if he's in there?" Stephanie twisted her body a little more over the seat to look me in the eyes as Cristina tried to look back as best she could.

If he's in there then what...? I took a moment to think. But then I decided to turn the question on them. "What are you going to do if he's in there? You came all this way...for what?"

Stephanie spewed anger, "We came here to have your back because you're too dense right now to have your own. You know, you seem to be forgetting something: that you asked for this...yeah...us, *everything*—remember? When you turned down Harvard to come here?"

And there it was. Under the circumstances it was a perfect time for her to bring it up, especially after that *fantasy* trip I took to the park yesterday.

So now she said it and she was right. If I had gone to Harvard, anywhere but here, I probably would've been better off, but still I wouldn't have had—couldn't have had—peace of mind, always wondering *what if* and *why*. But the *why* was out there, reaching deep inside me, nagging me to see it, feel it, and hear it. Nagging me to remember it.

Nagging me to remember before time ran out.

My god, maybe I should've stayed away.

"What do you suggest we do? Leave? When he could be in there?" Stephanie's voice treated with patience now.

"I think we should think this through. Nothing you have done so far has gotten us closer to finding out who he is. With no last name you couldn't get his record at the school. But I'm starting to think there isn't a record. Today we found out that no one at the bookstore has heard of him, even though he was there the day I picked up my book. Even still we saw him that day on campus, tailed him...and remember how crazy things got? And the air balloon that crashed...?" I went in deep thought, reflecting on the plane with that banner, *I love you Perseaus.*

"Yeah, it was. But what exactly are you thinking?" Ariana chimed in.

I looked at all of them. "I think we need to

address the elephant in the room."

"What about it?" Cristina encouraged.

"I don't think you see how serious this thing is. Maybe you think because we got off the island safely and because no one else could really confirm that we were on the island that you think it didn't really happen. And you're not the only ones to think that. But I'm telling you it really did happen. It wasn't a fantasy. We could have died on that island and no one would never have known.

"It's like you're blind to how serious this can be. And I'm just putting it out there before things get out of hand and before...it's too late. Because I know you wouldn't want to go through anything like that...not in a million years."

With the elephant addressed things got quiet. I hoped I'd gotten through to them and it seemed so. But then Ariana reached beneath her shirt revealing a medallion with a cat's eye. "We all have one," she said. "We got it yesterday, and what it does is ward off evil." Christina and Stephanie revealed theirs around their necks. "And we got one for you too," Ariana concluded.

Shaking my head, I could just die crying, laughing in madness. "No, no, no. It's seems you have thought this through so just have it your way. I'm just glad you got some kind of protection. And it looks scary enough that it might work...." I said, not knowing what more I could say at this point.

"Look, we're not fools so don't worry, okay?" Ariana said trying to mend things a bit.

"Yep. And what we need to do now is get his tag number and see who it's registered to. He can't be driving around here with fake plates. And, if he's in there, we should wait around to see what car he gets in," Stephanie said.

"Yeah, if only we'd gotten it the first time. Well I'm going in to see if he's in there," Cristina nodded.

"Okay, do that. I still say he's not in there but if he is...just leave it to me to decide what to do next. If he's not, then getting his tag number is our best way—the first chance we get. And something else: promise that you'd never approach him. *Promise me.*"

"Okay, we promise...." they said simultaneously.

"Okay, the boss lady has spoken," Cristina cracked open the door, ready to go.

Cristina and Stephanie got out and went inside and were back before I missed them. They confirmed what I already knew: he wasn't inside. I then began thinking, he wouldn't hurt them, because they were never his target, but Cameron, that was a different story. And why?

I needed to find him. For once and for all, I needed to know why.

Chapter Eighteen
On the Run

For now, I wasn't worried about Stephanie ratting me out to my parents. "Things are going to be fine, don't worry," she said with her head hanging out the window as they pulled off. I thought she was being dropped off with me, but she'd hopped back in the car.

"Sure. See you later," I waved them off wondering what they were up to. I unlocked the door and entered the house. They were so sneaky I bet they'd be somewhere out there watching the house to see if I leave, I thought. They may have even put a tracking device on the car also. They were so in to this I couldn't put anything past them.

Even so, they would be right to think I had something up, because I did. It was time I put matters back in my hands. To do that I had to move forward with caution, no more of them being one or two steps ahead of me.

I hung around the house for about a half hour then made my move. Out the backdoor where no one would see me, it had always been a way for me to escape. I made my way down the stairs leading to the beach. Looking over shoulders constantly, my unwelcomed shadows would be on my tail in a heartbeat by now if they were on to me. But they weren't.

I hit the beach shore trudging through the sand going south. I glanced over my shoulder. *So far so good.* What a relief not a soul was behind me. And the few random faces I came upon as I advanced up the shore, were like invisible to me because they didn't have the power to stop me.

I was feeling relaxed now. A stroll on the beach was divine like that. I began reexamining my purpose for wanting to get away. To be alone, yes. To outsmart them, this too. But I wanted to better that, and he was the only one to help me.

He'd said, 'I knew where to find him.' And where might that be? Certainly not at the bookstore. And he wasn't at the skatepark, though I was pleased with that: too many familiar faces hung out there.

Up ahead was a figure standing by the shoreline. *An illusion,* I thought to myself for no particular reason. Just that it could be because how could I be certain about anything these days? For that reason, among others, I needed answers. *Where was he?*

I made a slow 360-degree turn now, walking backwards for only a moment as I did, as I again double-checked to see if I was being followed. Not far was a couple of people trekking down the sandy slope near the poly-level resorts. They didn't look like anyone I knew, so the coast was still clear.

As I got back on a forward path, my phone began ringing. I dug it out of pocket and saw that it was Stephanie calling. "Oh no, they must be on to me," I whispered to myself, then pressed the button sending her straight to voicemail.

Next Cameron's picture popped up on the screen, he was calling too. "Not now, Cam. I promise I'll call you back," I whispered to his picture, promising him, or rather myself.

When his face disappeared on the phone, I set the ringer on mute, but something told me to turn it off completely, so I did. No ringing or vibrating phone to interfere with any message I might receive telepathically; this crossed my mind. With the phone I stuffed my hands in my pockets, then filled my lungs with the ocean-scented breeze as I tramped farther up the shoreline.

The same figure was still in place, facing the ocean. But someone else had landed between us, who seemed to have appeared out of nowhere. But then he could have come off the hill during my brief distraction. Suddenly he was moving hurriedly, but then his stride turned into a jog and then to a sprint. As he got closer, I realized coming toward me was the one person I had hoped to see. But something was wrong. What was the hurry? I looked behind me and saw someone in the distance running this way.

When Ebay got to me, he grabbed my hand at once. "Come on! You're being followed."

"What!" I glanced over my shoulder. Stephanie, Ariana, and Cristina, I expected to see three girl figures together but no, not them. But whoever that man was in the distance, he was gaining on us fast, so I trusted my hand in his as we fled.

He moved like a locomotive hauling carts, or one cart, me. And with sandals on my feet I was stumbling trying to keep up. "Do you know that guy? And why on earth would he be after me?" I heaved.

"My hunch...to see what you're up to, and from the looks of it, he has something else in mind and that can't be good."

"But why would this person be after me? I don't understand."

"I know you don't, but you will...."

Whoever this man was, he was like a dark shadow—wearing a black cap, black shirt, gray pants—and he wasn't letting up. All the more reason we had to keep moving.

"Where are we going?" I huffed as we darted up hill; my feet sinking in the grainy, it felt like new sand just laid. At the top, we cut through a line of shrubs, stepping in a bed mulch as we did. We then leaped off a curb arriving at a cul de sac. A couple of buildings were in this area: a small gift shop and a café. Also, there were three cars parked on the street. I didn't realize one was his car until lights flashed via his remote, when he pressed it to unlock the doors. He got to the car first and opened the passenger-side door.

"Wait a minute—" I stopped alongside the car, not sure if I should get in.

"You're want answers, right? We don't have time." He looked off in the direction we'd just come, seeing if the man had caught up to us

He hadn't yet, and this was my chance to get

answers. I sank into the black leather seat as I got in. He slammed the door shut and quickly rounded the front end to get to the driver's side. He got in and fired up the engine. As the car pulled off, I turned to look out the back window, thinking this person should come through the bushes at any moment. And when he didn't, I wondered where was he...what was taking him so long. The car bent the corner, and my wondering took a quantum leap.

"Maybe he gave up. Maybe he wasn't after me after all," I said.

He shook his head. "Trust me. He was after you. And no, he won't give up that easily."

"Then I'm in danger? Who was that man and what does he want with me?"

"It's...complicated. But you're safe now, try not to worry."

"Try not to worry? Now that's complicated. You know what else is complicated? You knowing he was after me and you showing up in the nick of time to help me get away. And you know something else is complicated? Not knowing what the hell is going on!" I took a breather, giving him an opening to start making sense of things.

"Yeah, I know," was all he offered.

"I saw you yesterday, at a park. Did you see me?" I was duplicitous somewhat, I know.

"If you saw me then you know I was there."

"Okay...so...what you are saying is that you were there?"

"I'm saying if you saw me, how could I not be there. I'm saying it's your reality, and your reality isn't necessarily mine.

"Look, all sorts of things will come at you, when you're not prepared for it, but you have to grasp the experience, learn from it and in time, see it for what it really is. As I said before, there are things you must remember. It appears you're trying to do that. Sometimes you will draw from, say...the spirit of your subconscious. Which can boggle things if you don't know what's stored there. It can be the same thing when you draw from the future."

"What...what do you mean by that?"

"Tapping into your psychic ability...seeing the past, and the future."

"Okay...so you didn't see me at the park? is kinda what I'm hearing. Or, you're refusing to admit it." I wouldn't let all that talk sidetrack me.

He gave a pondering stare, "Yeah, maybe you're right."

"Okay, fine," I nodded, realizing he wasn't going to give me a direct answer, and that for some reason that topic was off limits. So I moved on.

"Something else happened yesterday that bothers me. At the shoe store I met a girl, a gypsy girl, and she was a palm reader. She came up to me and offered to read my palm. She was the strangest little girl, but polite, so I agreed.

"During the reading, she saw something. I don't know what, but it scared her, and me, not knowing what it was she saw. Her mother rushed her away, wouldn't let her tell me. They couldn't get out of the store fast enough to get away from me. And it's been bothering me ever since, wondering what she saw. But the little girl kept saying, 'I didn't have much time.'" I looked at him, hoping he had something straightforward to offer this time.

"I see why that would bother you. But it could be nothing but a coincidence." He looked at me, his dark eyes thoughtful. "There are humans who have remnants of the supernatural, like the seers or palm readers. I say 'remnants' because they don't possess full range of their capabilities. But they are the real deal; they come about their gift naturally. Kind of like how what you're experiencing came 'unnaturally' to you. And I say that because I know that's how you feel about it."

I was boiling inside now. "So that's it? I'm so fed up with you not being straight with me. And if that's how it's going to be then stop the car right now." I grabbed the door handle. "Stop right now or I'll open the door and jump out."

"Are you serious? Stop the car right now?" He shined disbelieving eyes, but then they grew dim; it seemed he'd decided not to take me seriously. He made no effort to slow down, nor was he checking the mirrors for an opportunity to pull over.

"I mean it!" I clamored still gripping the door handle.

"Yeah you probably would do something crazy like that; anything to show how stubborn you can be." He looked at me with gritty teeth.

"Why are you looking at me like that?"

"Because I can't believe you!" this came out of his mouth. But this, *and dammit because I know you and you're austere as ever,* came from his mind. Yeah, I was reading it again. And should I make him aware that I was? Could he right now read my thoughts? If so, he didn't act like it.

Suddenly he stopped, raised both hands off the steering wheel. "There you go. You satisfied now?"

Looking ahead I realized that all the cars had stopped. Farther ahead the drawbridge was rising. You could even hear the horn of an oncoming boat. My urge to get out, I didn't know where it went. For the moment, I just sat quietly, rubbing both hands up and down my arms. I wasn't sure now what I wanted to do, whether to get out, start walking, or stay. Did he arrange for the bridge to go up? Did he...? I didn't know what or how to think about being in his company, and alone with him at that. No one knew where I was.

And yet, nothing was stopping me from leaving now. Nothing.

"You wonder about so much. What happened that night that started this chain reaction of something unbeknownst to you. But you know at some point it all must come to an end. And it will, soon. That's why I'm here. To help in any way I can to see you through this. But there's only so much I can do. But Pia, to remember—*everything*—is a gift. *A gift,*" he stressed with a nod. "And there's nothing I want more than for you to remember." He then drew quiet as his eyes turned away and wandered out the window.

Calmly I asked, "What is it you can do...right now to help me?"

"Right past the bridge is a marina, lots of people...." he said, leaving a blank for me to fill in, and make up my mind.

Chapter Nineteen

When Hands Join

A boat show was going on at the marina, with some of the fanciest boats you could ever feast your eyes on, and with price tags out of this world. Most of the people in the area were at the event. We admired the setting as we breezed through, not thinking for a moment that we should hang around for the free hotdogs and stuff. No. There was so much I needed to know and had no time for delay.

"Over there is a perfect spot," I pointed in direction of a park along the bay with an empty bench. It was pretty much vacant with everyone up by the boat show. Off the bank were swaying boats in the water.

We walked at a steady pace and soon we were at the spot. Then I stole a moment, quietly looking off into the water, all sorts of thoughts running through my mind.

He stood beside me. "You don't know where to begin, do you?"

"It's...it's hard to prioritize. You can't tell me what

happened the night all of this started. So yes, it's hard. So much has happened; so much is going on now...and I'm afraid."

"I know, I know. It would help a great deal if you remembered...what's important. I know you're tired of hearing me say that."

"Yeah, you keep saying that, not telling me exactly what it is I have to remember. Why can't you just tell me, just make it easy on me? Am I going to die, is that it?" I shuddered after saying it. But I wouldn't unsay it, I had to let it out. It had been on my mind since the palm reading. And he was the one person I could say it to.

Looking up at the sky, he asked, "How does all of this space of life and death make you feel?" as though the question was essential.

"I...hmm...don't understand. It sounds like a trick question. Why do you ask?"

He inflated his jaws then drained it sharply. "Look, I'm sorry. That was insensitive of me."

"But why would that matter? Here, and now?" I moved over to the concrete bench and sat.

"You're right, it doesn't matter." He settled down beside me.

"Then why don't you just stop dancing around my questions? You must know what's going to happen next. Like how you knew my friends were watching and that I left the pen-recorder in the seat of the car. You're not fooling me. You can read minds, and somehow, I can sometimes read yours. But you still won't admit it."

"Can you imagine what that'd be like hearing minds yakking all the time? And what would you do about it if you could?"

192

"Mm," I grunted. "I suppose there are many things you could do about it but I'm talking about just one mind. You know, it's like I'm not getting anywhere with you. Will you at least tell me about the gypsy girl? What did she see that got her so upset?" I stared into his dark eyes. "Because, if it wasn't death...." I gave him enough time to respond then scoffed and turned away. He was relentless—no help at all by leaving it all on me to figure things out. And for that I kept at it:

"Remember when I got sick the other day, and you asked, 'was it my first episode?'"

"Yes, I remember."

"Well, I got worse, was sick for two whole days. It was strange because, if I stayed in bed I didn't feel that sick. And I lay there traveling the world, seeing strange places in visions. But it was like seeing these places through someone else's eyes. And there were voices, of a man and woman. But I never saw their faces." I turned to capture his reaction, as I fumbled with the ring I'd been hiding from him the whole time. I couldn't explain it...just instinct.

He looked content, interested in this particularly. But did he elaborate? No. He said nothing at all.

"You're no help at all. What are you going to do, just sit here for however long it takes me to remember? Stop pretending you don't have a clue of what I'm talking about. Because it's been you from day one: the night I went missing to that day on the island. And you're here now." I bit down on my lip, nodding with infuriating eyes.

"I know, it's complicated. Especially when it seems like you're talking to a wall. But I'm here to help...right now. From a perspective, it will be my gift to

193

you. Insight that'll help you better understand. Hopefully, it'd be what you need for a breakthrough. I hope so, because...it would mean more than you would ever imagine, if you remembered. But for this to work you must be sure you're ready. Are you?"

"Um...I think so...yes," I hesitated, curious of what exactly I was agreeing to.

He then held out his left hand, "May I?"

My hand. I stared at his hand trancelike. "Things get boggled...when drawn from the future," I said as I looked up at him. "Like what's happening now...which is...the future. This is what you were talking about. Because..." *Because I wanted to see you, I left the house hoping to see you, that my subconscious placed you in that scene...at the park....* I closed my eyes—if only closing them would shut off my thoughts, because I couldn't believe what I was thinking. I couldn't believe how I was analyzing this new reality of things in a way to understand...me.

"Tell me, why are you here?" I asked abruptly, the same question I'd asked at the park. I had to test him, hear him say exactly what he'd said then.

He licked his bottom lip, thirsty for my exact meaning, as his squinted eyes swam the depths of my mind for the answer. But he already knew the answer, I just knew.

Looking him straight in the eyes, I repeated the question with my mind: *Why. Are. You. Here?* Hoping that he would prove my theory once and for all. That whether it was an illusion or not, he was there with me at the park. *Come on, what did you say to me when I asked that question? You said...?* I waited a moment, still no answer, and then I went on hoping he was reading my mind. Because how could he not be? *I know you hear me; you have to, and you will. So tell me, you are here because, what?*

His mouth gapped as if the words were about to spill. But it didn't, and I grew impatient, and I asked again aloud, "Tell me, why are you here?"

"Because, you summoned me." Finally, there it was.

"*I summoned you*, yes, it's what you'd said at the park. It really did happen. I mean, how can you know if you weren't there?"

"Because that's the honest truth. Isn't that what you wanted, the truth?" With his head tilted, he gazed at me with warm and sincere eyes. "I'm here to help...one step at a time. Are you ready?" he turned over his hand.

I nodded, "Yeah. Just what can I expect when we join hands?"

"Don't worry, this won't hurt, trust me. However, this is a delicate matter. And it's not at my will to force it on you. You have to accept it totally, otherwise it won't work. So, shall we?" he extended his hand this time.

I placed my hand in his. Right then shards of light showered down on me and levitating before me a surreal image of Cameron. Then I got a shock to my hand and I yanked loose from his, and right then we snapped out of it.

"Whoa! What was that!" I began kneading my hand. From the expression on his face, he was as stunned as I was. "Has this ever happened before?"

"Yes, but not with me. This is an example of what I was trying to explain, when I said you have to be in total acceptance for it to work. You are truly devoted to him...more than I realized," he shot me a painstaking grin.

"Yes, but...?"

"I believe you really want to do this. But adverse emotions interfere with the process. That's what we experienced just now."

"Meaning...Cameron." I recalled him saying in the illusion that he was holding me back. "Look...I really want to do this."

"We'll try again. But first, take time to relax." He put a hand over my stacked hands, "Just relax...and breathe. Release the tension. Clear your mind...calm your emotions." He freed his hand from mine as they relaxed apart in my lap. "Come in tune with your spirit. Release the guilt, and relax. No rush...just take your time...and relax..." his voice faded away, leaving it all to me.

Cameron, the image of him moments ago, entered my mind and I tried harder, I needed this to work. *Take your time, relax in your spirit,* I could hear his mind telling me. I focused on my breathing. Even amounts of air in lungs I drew in, holding it to the count of five, then releasing it slowly, very slowly. It felt like I was letting my heart go, my heart being Cameron. But never would I do that. *Never,* I imagined him hearing me, right there in my thoughts.

A few moments later I opened my eyes. I was as ready as I would ever be. I placed my hand in his, and....

Chapter Twenty
Island, the *Island*

And ready I was. Instantly we were in a forest of nothing but trees, that looked and felt like 3-D; the area whooshed silently, like underwater. Then my head winced to the sound of running water, to the sound of all of nature coming to life, like, the sound of a jungle.

A rainforest, Ebay tapped into my senses.

My eyes peered over my shoulder, and there to my surprise was a log cabin with a thatched roof. Then I looked up when a tunnel of sunlight broke through the trees directly on us. And before I knew it we were rising in this tunnel of light, rising like the trees endlessly in the sky.

"Where are we going?" I asked with my neck craning, and with my eyes in wonder of what's above.

"This is a wait-and-see. Hopefully it will all come back to you."

I turned to him after that, and was surprised to see him, *Ferret,* translucent. Yes, Ferret. He hadn't confirmed it, but I knew. And he was translucent, I could see right through him. I then waved a hand across my vision, realizing that I, too, was translucent. Our bodies, I imagined them parked on the bench like statues, unbothered, unnoticed, while our souls passed through an element so fascinating.

High above the trees our ascent slowed above the clouds. Something was coming toward us and coming fast, like a fireball with a flaming tail. Quite honestly, the fireball was the color of her hair, and she and her male companion were coming toward us on a flying carpet. *Wow.* I couldn't believe my eyes. But they were moving too fast and unyielding from a course headed straight toward us. My heart fluttered, and my spirit quailed for fear that any moment we would collide. Did they even see us? And if we didn't move would they pass right through us? We were like invisible. But then swiftly they swooped down and disappeared in the cloud.

"What was that?" I exclaimed, recovering from shell shock.

"Make-believe...just make-believe," he said, surprising me. But I didn't question him, for a huge, ominous shadow appeared in the distance. Transfiguring and becoming to be what looked like, more 'make-believe'? Had to be, I supposed as this sensation of a city materialized right before my eyes.

First the grounds rolled out like carpet, revealing a marble surface, and then one building at a time, a city magically formed on top of it. Except this wasn't your typical city with streets, neighborhoods..., but a place like city hall, absent a city to govern. And this place was about the size of football field. Five golden buildings stood out, sparkling like diamonds. One on each corner of the block. And the fifth one, the grandest of them all, set in the center, and it had four trees situated on all four corners of it. And over this building, somehow a dome hung freely.

"But I don't understand. Why are you showing me this?" I said finally.

"Why?" He let the question hang for a few. "Nothing about it comes to mind? Nothing at all?"

"No...it doesn't," I hesitated, focusing a moment on the business-like square. "The building in the middle, with the dome, reminds me of the white house." I then turned to him, and realize we were no longer invisible. "But, that's not what you hoped to hear. I'm sorry, but I don't have a clue what I'm looking at and what it has to do with me," I emitted with anxiety.

"I know how you feel, and it's perfectly natural. As natural as willing anything you wish into existence. Like a city on top of the world. And one beneath the sea. Anywhere your spirit desires. Remember this?" he said, and then magically—

We were on a white horse, galloping across the blue sky on a ribbon of clouds, and that city, it was now fading away. But ahead off in the distance, another shadow was forming. Slowly coming to focus at the peak of this shadow was something eerie and jagged. My arms clung tighter around his waist, and my head pressed against his back as fear pricked the depths of my soul. As this place in the shadow became known to me, this place in all its glory and conviction, forever etched in my brain, I began extinguishing my fear. *I shouldn't be afraid. I'm not afraid. I should be anything but...afraid.*

"Remember?" he asked as we sailed over the island. "Remember how natural it felt to you seeing it? Because you knew it had to be real (when you see, you believe), even when you're the only one to see it. You couldn't understand how that was, but you couldn't and wouldn't let that stop you from believing. And that itself fueled the flames for you to prove it. Not just to yourself, but to others also. *And you did.* But all isn't done...yet. You don't understand why, but it's why you summoned me. To understand is to remember, Pia. And just know that you're trying."

"If only you could tell me, because, if I don't...what then?"

"Try not to think about it," he recommended, as we came upon the jagged cliff.

The lord of the land, I'd called it the first time I saw it, because it looked like the island's ruler. But as it turned out, *The Lord of the land* had been nothing but a helpless attraction, because it, and the entire island, fell prey to that horrible ice monster. It as much had swallowed the entire island, and then, itself, disappeared. But what did it matter now? Here it was, as beautiful as ever.

Like roads in the mountains, we curved around bouldery edges at the speed of an incredibly fast racehorse. Fitting, since we were on a horse, keeping an uncompromising distance from the edge. We dipped into a terrain rich with colorful vegetation; a botanical garden came to mind. Then suddenly, we were in a dark tunnel, which didn't feel so spooky passing through; that glimmer of light at the end seemed promising. We came out in a downward swoop, swooping through and around pine trees...all kinds of pine trees. A pine tree farm in an area of rolling hills—what else?

Seeing the island like this, close-up and from some many different angles, seeing it in all its glory, was unbelievable, my orbs in total awe. It was like seeing it again for the first time, only this time in paradise. I say paradise, because on that black, fateful day, it'd died and sunk beneath the sea, and because we barely made it off ourselves...alive. Which reminded me, *why what happened that day happened at all?*

"It was you that day on the island...you, the ice monster. But why...why did you run us off the island like that?" My voice was wispy for some reason.

His was also. "You're wrong. It's more complicated than that. It had every bit to do with you trying to remember; I won't say anymore. But yes, it was me outside the plane before it took off. And yes, I turned into an ice sculpture and rose up to the plane in the air. I frightened you; sorry about that. I was just showing off my anger.

"You made it that far, *that far,* and you didn't even remember me, the one key factor to remembering. After what you achieved that day, I thought for sure you would have...but you didn't. Hopefully it'd be different this time around, because, there won't be..." his words faded.

"How things work is what you need to understand. Especially the malfunctions as it pertains to you and your situation. As I've said before, to understand comes with the luxury of remembering. You have to, there's no other way. It's how the system works in our world."

Malfunctions? System? "So...I'm part of the

201

system?" I said aloud.

"Yes, but that's it for now," he said sternly.

"Sure...if you say so. Over there!" I said as something grabbed my attention.

"Where?"

"Over there, is that what I think it is?" I asked pointing to my left.

Rounding the top of a hill, he followed my point to a bridge, linking two majestic peaks. And we were upon it in moments for a clearer view. It had to be about 300 feet high. Then again, it could have been much higher. I didn't exactly know what 300 feet would look like.

The horse dove to a much lower elevation and we glided under it; down below was water. One thing I always wondered was how they build bridges across huge lakes, wide rivers, which seemed impossible. So, a bridge this high over water seemed impossible also, and it probably was. Only could I imagine a crossing so high, though I didn't have to, I could very well be imagining this now. Imagining everything.

Moments after passing the bridge, we came face to face with soaring granite cliffs, its peaks dome-shaped with a reddish glow. The horse nickered, surprising me, because it had been quiet the whole time. It circled a platform overlooking *the* perfect panorama view then landed us on it.

I freed my arms from his torso I'd been hugging for dear life, as my eyes darted across another spectacular view, drinking it all in. The island was so beautiful and had so much more to offer than I had ever imagined. As I gazed over his shoulder at the mountains reddish glowing tips, it crossed my mind that I had seen those tips somewhere before. I pondered for a moment trying to recall where I'd seen it.

"It was a tremendous breakthrough the day you arrived here," Ebay said as if his mind was wandering. He was gazing off at the mountains as well.

"Yes," I responded reflectively. "You know, it's something about this particular spot. It reminds me of a place. I'm not sure where, though." I continued pondering then grew frustrated and hissed, "This isn't working, I can't seem to remember a thing."

"But you're trying, though it's not always about trying. It's about perceiving what's natural. I know it's confusing, trying to understand a primitive nature you know nothing about, but have a sense of because you're—"

"Trying to remember," I took the words out of his mouth.

"Yes. And before all of this is done with, you will begin to understand why I'm here, and not someone else," he said as we magically stood face-to-face now. Our chauffeuring white horse vanished in thin air.

I swirled around to get a full view of the flat mountaintop we stood on that felt like the center of the universe. And as I swirled my pondering began to pay off.

"I think I know this place now. Or rather, what it reminds me of...here in this spot, facing those mountains. And right over there," I said, pointing at the birdbath, "yes...I remember there was a wedding ceremony going on, and I remember thinking the reddish glow over the mountain was such a beautiful backdrop for the ceremony. I remember because I had my camera and took a picture. I was at The Glacier Point at Yosemite

National Park. In California. That's what the glow on the mountains reminds me of. I suppose in some ways your world is much like mine." I paused, thinking that I may be toying with his sense of hope, though not intentionally of course.

I went on, "Don't you see? I remembered that because it happened in a period of my life that I could remember. And...and I didn't have to remember it like my life depended on it, even though I struggled trying to remember just now. It seems all of this is fogging up my memory. But the point is I remembered, and I'm not at all sorry for remembering that and not something else. But...I can see that you are." My tone turned sympathetic, seeing a hint of letdown in his face. It suspended me for a moment, and then I finished speaking my mind.

"I want a normal life; if everything about this would just go away. You know, someday I want to get married. Drive off into the sunset, and then maybe, have a couple of kids...live happily ever after. And if not that then that's okay—because you see, life isn't perfect; it's not meant to be perfect. There's always going to be ups and downs, things not going your way and it's okay with me. But what you propose isn't okay. It shouldn't be like this. If something needs fixing, then it should be fixed without involving me. This is insane, don't you get it? Your system sucks!"

"Of course, I get it! But it doesn't change a thing, and for that I'm sorry. I'm truly sorry."

"I don't care that you're sorry! What if I don't remember this time too? What then?" I cried out, practically in tears.

"I know, I know," he drew me into his arms.

"Believe me, if I could undo everything, leave you forever, I would. Believe me…I'm not here at my own freewill."

I pulled away. "But you're here because I summoned you."

Dismay saturated his visage. "Yep. But even that's not your fault. No one is really to blame here. It's just that things go wrong that can't easily be fixed sometimes. What's happened to you is one of those things. The first sign that something had gone wrong was the night you vanished."

"About that night I disappeared—"

Suddenly there were gleeful voices coming from somewhere. And now with a spark of optimism on his face, he said, "It's time."

And before I could say anything, the island vanished from beneath us and we were in a free fall back to earth. A weightless, feather-like free fall it became when Ebay (Ferret) put the brakes on gravity, to relax what little fear showing on my face. However, the voices, I could still hear them. Voices without faces, where were they coming from? I looked across the blue sky, and saw no streaking souls. I looked down, and it troubled me to see a bottomless sky. Trouble me to see no end in sight. Yet we were falling and there were voices. Again, where were they coming from? And why no faces?

Falling, I didn't know how to feel.

Falling, why no bottom, as if we had gone as far as outer space?

Falling, *oh where oh where was earth?* The vast blue sky was an eternity.

Falling, and still…no end in sight.

Chapter Twenty-One

Them, Him, and Me

The bottom was in view, *finally*. Trees, nothing but trees, that looked like a field of bushes all bunched together. *The rainforest,* I minded. We were going back the way we came.

'It's time,' he'd said. Time for what, I wondered what I had put off asking and couldn't wait to find out.

Time for what?

Maybe he would answer me. If not, I knew I would soon find out.

Through the tunnel of light, we penetrated the atmosphere of the rainforest and surprisingly landed in a tree, overlooking the log cabin from before. The leaves and branches camouflaged us. But I suspected our presence was invisible anyway as voices exited the cabin. And the moment I saw her fiery red hair (in a French-braid hanging down her back), I knew they were the couple we had seen on the flying carpet. They both wore light fabrics in shades of white. She, a peasant skirt, crop top; he, short sleeve shirt, jockey-style pants tucked in tall black boots. His dark hair pulled back in a ponytail.

"It was their voices.... Who are they?" I whispered, though I suspected they couldn't hear me.

"Two people in love, but in love with entirely different things that will tear them worlds apart," Ferret said drearily as we became full-fledged eavesdroppers.

"I want to spend all the time I have left with you. I want us to visit all our favorite places," the young woman said as she wrapped thin arms around her lover's neck then landed kisses on his lips.

"If that's what you want, then so be it," the young man cast his promise lovingly. *"You know, my love, it won't be the same without you. No matter how much this means to you, I have to at least try to sway you in seeing things my way."*

"Or the reverse...me persuading you to go with me."

"No...I've gone that route many times already and never again, it's not worth it. All we could ever want is right here."

"You can say that. But, how can I? All I know is what it's like here, in this world."

"Why don't you trust me?" His tone insisted.

"But I do, I do, you know I do. But...but it's not as simple as trust, and love, because I do so much. It's just that I must find things out for myself—live it for myself. The two worlds are different; there's no question about it. We are here—and I know what you're thinking. But we don't know how it's even possible—we just exist it seems...for one purpose.

"But they, they are born into their world, and then grow and change over a period of life. They feel real pain, shed real tears—and blood, real blood runs through

their veins. We are none of that. We're all spirit through and through. Our bodies, not real. We relish in the illusion because magic comes natural to us."

"And you love it. Though now, I'm not so sure. Has that much changed, you no longer appreciate our nature?"

"No, that's not it at all. But even you can't deny how magnificent creatures, humans are. They will the power of imagination, bringing things to life like magic. Like magic, creating machines that fly, fly like birds, far beyond this planet. My dear, you have to admit we don't have such capability—we're stuck here for dear life. And if it weren't for them and their world, we wouldn't have a purpose."

"You're talking silly. There will always be a place for us and our cause." He then looked up then continued, "Don't you believe? Believe in the masters of the universe? Believe that there are other worlds out there somewhere? Believe...that we are forever, and that we were meant to be together." He then drew her into him. "If you go, we may never be together like this ever again. Because even if I decided to, you know there's no guarantee we would end up together. Doesn't that bother you at all?"

"Don't, don't." She pulled away, showing a longing expression. "I understand why you choose to stay, and I accept that I will miss you dearly."

"Except, you won't...not really."

"You know what I mean." Looking into his eyes, she took his hand. She then gazed off into the forest, like she was looking for something but then said, "Listen to that. It's calling us. We should take that walk through the

208

waterfall now." Right as she made the gesture, a white, glittery walkway stretching off into the forest appeared at their feet. She yanked at his hand, and began swinging it. *"Come on, let's go."*

"Perseaus, wait."

"Perseaus?" I turned to Ferret. "Who is she?" But he didn't have to say a word. I was coming to realize that I knew the answer already. Knew that she was me...me. "But, no...s-she...me, no, it can't be...no...," I stammered, couldn't get it out. Because I couldn't accept it.

But looking at Ferret, the sure look in his eyes, his shallow nod, spoke volumes that I had to accept what was right in front of me. It all seemed to add up now, make sense. The voices in the visions, they had to be hers, and his. *The voices without faces*—yes, it made perfect sense.

I quickly returned my focus on the scene playing out before me. Thinking that once upon a time her eyes were my eyes and my hair was flaming red and I, strikingly beautiful. Suddenly it all made sense and felt perfectly right, even though it felt surreal, and real, and unreal all at once. This person I once was, was in love, but with whom? I was anxious for him to turn my way so that I could see his face.

"What is it?" she (Perseaus) urged him to speak. But instead he delivered a kiss on her cheek, then looked her in the eyes. Studying her and wondering should he say what he was about to say; I tended to read his mind.

"What is it?" Perseaus asked again, as both her hands held his.

He then offered his arm, and she at once wrapped her arm around his. He then led the way up a glowing walkway into the forest.

We held our positions in the tree, watching them move through the rainforest, like watching a movie and enjoying every moment of it. Even the part when they went through a shimmery wall of water, a waterfall, and arrived on the other side of it bone dry. "Not a single drop of water touched them," I whispered to Ferret.

"That's life," he whispered back. At that moment I realized the limitless possibility of his world hadn't really sunk in. Otherwise, the idea of them walking through water without getting wet wouldn't have amazed me. All the same, it did.

They were now in a cave with a candlelight glow, but there weren't candles as far as I could see. Nothing visible to substantiate the artificial glow. The walls in the cave was amazingly beautiful, draped in various shades of white paint. From their artistry of affection, I assumed. The soothing sound of the waterfall imported a romantic feel.

But something else was going on here, more than what met the eyes. Even their steps leading up to this exact moment now felt special. He cupped his hands at the sides of her waist. *Cupping my waist,* the notion penetrated me. And then it hit me. All this time wondering who was this person Perseaus was in love with, it suddenly dawned on me that it was he all along. I couldn't believe it—I mean, *how could I not see it?*

"It's. You," I enunciated. I turned to him and looking back at me was his undeniable truth. I turned back, not wanting to miss a moment of...us.

And then, for the first time, I could see his face, as if he knew right when I figured it out. As if it was

210

meant for me to see it in that exact moment. His eyes soared over Perseaus and landed directly on me, as if...he knew I was there. As if he knew what I was thinking in this moment sitting next to him in the tree, though he couldn't possibly know....

"It's you," I repeated. "All this time it was you. And he looks this way as he knows we're here," I muttered, looking at him in the cave, wondering if it was possible.

"What is it?" Perseaus looked in my direction now, curious of what caught her lover's eye. And since he couldn't be looking at me, I was curious also.

He put on a smile then turned to her, and then he looked back in our direction. Clearly, he was teasing her, building her up for a surprise he then magically produced. A beautiful white three-tiered birdbath, standing about four feet. Water cascaded through spouted edges from one level to the next.

Perseaus stood with a confused, dazzled smile, gazing back and forth, from him to the birdbath. He placed a hand on the small of her back, and they moved forward, ceremoniously. Halfway there, an ivory pillow materialized on top of the birdbath; something atop glittered. But...something was wrong; a pang of anxiety began creeping up my spine as they drew closer; growing more intense by the second....

It's the ring, on the pillow...the ring.

The anxiety so intense, *the ring*...I didn't know what was happening, but I wanted to SCREAM.

Chapter Twenty-Two
The Ring in Truth

Suddenly I was overlooking the channel with boats sailing through. In my periphery was a birdbath in the grass. I noticed it not sure if it had been there all along.

Feeling as I had just awakened from a dream, I slowly turned my head and came face to face with his bewildering stare. "What happened?" I asked.

"You screamed, and so, here we are."

"I remember wanting to scream but I don't remember doing it. Things got confusing all of a sudden...." I was trying to understand why.

"It was the ring, Pia. You couldn't bear the significance of it...and what it meant."

"But I don't understand why," I said as a cue for him to explain.

"Seeing the ring on the birdbath was starting to dredge up memories. About things that happened...things you regretted, and never forgave yourself for. I believe it's what's blocking you from remembering. You were so adamant, more devoted to becoming a human that

212

nothing else mattered. As you saw, not even my love for you, or our love for each other, was enough to get you to stay."

"The ring, it was much like the one you're wearing. And the setup, was it a proposal?"

"It was a proposal of reconciliation, to reconsider me, us. By accepting the ring, you pledge your devotion to our world. That means you would give up talk about leaving and becoming human, not permanently though...only for a time not less than six months.

"You see, once the ring is on your finger...well, I'm not sure if I should be telling you this. But, once the ring is on your finger, you get this upmost feeling of pride that it becomes hard for most to give it up. It was the only hope I had left of saving us, and what we had together."

"Sounds like brainwashing in a way." I got up and mused over that, moved around in circles...feeling oddly sympathetic. "But it wasn't because of you; it was because I wanted to experience this world. That's what Perseaus said." I stopped forming circles and exhaled.

"But I just don't know...I wish I could remember everything about the world I came from. So that I can understand why I chose this world over it. But the magic, walking through water without getting wet, transforming into a human anytime you want, is so cool. To be able to do the things you showed me is like the perfect gift to have. But it's much more to it than that, is it?"

"Mm-hmm...more than you can imagine."

I settled back down on the bench. "When you said to Perseaus that you couldn't risk not remembering, what exactly did you mean?"

"Let me make clear that Massouvia is a place of a

213

world also called Massouvia. And to go there, when your mortal life ends, you must remember that you came from there. I, for one, treasure the gift of remembering."

"You're saying you lived...how many times and remembered?"

"Several times, dating back as far as the 15th century. I was Richard Gavin then, a theorist and philosopher who advocated the mean justified the end. But, there's a huge gap from that time to when I was George Ripley living in Europe during the 18th century. It wasn't until the mid-20th century did I start remembering every time."

I scoffed, "Wow. You're a very old soul. So, what happens when you don't remember?"

"Well, there are several possibilities. First, you're transported by light to the cycle of 'Wait and See'. Where it's decided what life form your soul will undergo next. Most of the time the choice is up to you but could be decided for you.

"You see, it's in the transitional period you learn whether you'll be born again or reincarnated in another form. Like animals...mermaids," he smiled jokingly. "But most souls decide to be born again, and it's granted most of the time. Don't get me wrong. By no means do we play god, but...at times souls are lost in the channel. Or taken off our hands, I should say. It's then when gods of the universe intervene. Where they go or what happens to them varies.

"Massouvia, you can say, is at the head governing the system, and it's not perfect. Sometimes souls slip through the cracks during the transitional phase and run free until caught. Ghosts you'd call them. And then there are those given a pass to enter our world." He squared me in the eyes. "You, Perseaus, were new to the territory." He stopped, suspecting I would respond.

"So...what you're saying is that you, the world you're from...collect, manage souls...kinda like morticians?"

He nodded. "Yes, you can say that."

"And, is that what I—"

"Yes, exactly that. It's Massouvia's life work, always been."

"And, to go back there I would have to remember. You know," I covered my mouth, shaking my head, "I'm so blown away by all this that all sorts of questions clogging up my brain right now. And on top of that, I feel like I know too much and it's so overwhelming that I'm afraid of it."

"I understand. It is a lot to take in."

My thoughts narrowed into one channel as I eyed his ring. The first time I saw it...never would I have imagined it a symbol of a world I once lived in. I fumbled with the stone beneath my curled fingers. What a coincidence that the stones were identical, I thought.

"You wear the ring; so obvious you're committed to Massouvia. Have you made up your mind, I mean, are you committed, *forever*?" Because forever is such a very long time, I thought as an afterthought.

"I-I...I waited...in devastation till that final moment, when all hope was lost. It was hard, painful. But once the doors of the birthing chamber closed, there's no turning back. No turning back, no sudden change of mind, you were gone, Perseaus, gone... You had made your choice. I wanted to go after you—it took all the power in me not to because I couldn't. You know why. As for '*forever*'...yes...yes."

I looked off, playing with the stone still. "I know how that must've hurt you. But that was a lifetime ago. You can't still be bothered by that...."

"Some things never change. But like I said before, I wouldn't be here if I didn't have to be."

"Then why are you here?" I delivered the words from my pang of fear. He gave a gloomy look in return. "C'mon, you can't be serious, after all what you've revealed to me? Which is nothing when I still don't understand why all this is happening to me in the first place. Take me...take me out of my misery, or just tell me, get it over with because I can't take it anymore!"

I got up, stuffed hands in back pockets of my pants, paced back and forth. "I'm afraid of where this is leading. If you are back for me—I'm serious, just do it, take me!"

"You don't want that. You need to calm down. Will you please stop pacing? You're driving me crazy."

"Me, driving you crazy?" I shoved the ring in his face. "You see? You must've known that I was wearing a ring with the same kind of stone in your ring? And the same stone in the ring you were proposing to me with?"

He stared up at me, then lowered his eyes on the stone. "It's a moldavite...the rarest of its kind. Its origin is of the cosmos," he informed. And he must've known what I would ask next.

"Rare, that it is," I nodded. "And it makes you wonder, wouldn't you say?"

I drew the ring to my chest. "Don't you think it's a coincidence how similar the stones are? So similar that

216

they could have been cut from the same, cosmic stone?" No, what am I thinking? I thought to myself, vaguely shaking my head. "Cut from the same stone, but that can't be possible because—because I got this ring from Cameron. But...." Agitated, I began rubbing my forehead, then I tucked my other hand under my elbow and began pacing all over again. "But you know already he gave me the ring, don't you?" I concluded with something finally.

"And yet all this time you've been trying to hide it from me. Why? Don't you even know!" He paused briefly. "Isn't it obvious?" his tone softened.

"The first time I saw your ring, at the airport, it was something about it. It was weird because I didn't know what it was, and it bugged me trying to make a connection. But, had I recognized you, I would've known why it had a weird effect on me. But I would never have imagined you proposing to me with a ring like it...never."

I eased down next to him. "Why I hid it from you, is because I sensed it meant something special to you— and I didn't want you to think...whatever."

I sensed his feelings hadn't changed, even after all this time with us living worlds apart.

He refused to admit it, but if he had come for me, to rekindle lost love, wouldn't it break all laws of the universe? Cause a kind of chain reaction that would spin the world off its axis? A sure disaster could occur—and it was, brewing, with the rings at the center of it all. And Cameron, somehow caught up in the middle too.

I looked off in direction of the boat show. *Had anyone noticed us, wondered what was going on with us,* I wondered.

"Don't worry. They're closed off from us." I got

my answer, along with a reminder that he'd said something similar in the illusion at the park.

"What...what would happen if you told me everything?" I couldn't give up. Hell-bent on beating my head against the wall, I supposed.

"I can't, Pia—"

"But you could show we had a relationship?"

"Yes. But you will understand why when the time comes."

"But in the meantime, I have to remember whatever it is I have to remember, because (how can I forget), time is running out. It all sounds like a bunch of crap to me!"

"I know how hard this is for you. But there is a consolation to this. If you haven't figured this thing out yourself when the time comes, then it'd be up to me to explain things. I can't say when that'll be; but it won't be until then."

"'When the time comes,'" I repeated, thinking how dreadful it sounded. "Okay, but until then, I want you to do one thing. Stay away from me until that time comes. That's not asking too much is it?"

"No, except it might be a bit of a problem, considering I'm in the skateboarding competition."

"*You gotta be kidding me.* Why does that matter to you?"

He chuckled. "Well, back in my heyday, I was a champion skateboarder. And I just want to see if I still got it."

"'Heyday? Still got it?' Funny, this new revelation," I said thinking about the time. And how worried-crazy everyone must be by now wondering where

218

I was. Immediately I got out my phone, pressed the button. When it didn't light up I remembered I'd turned it off. So I powered it up, and in moments a galore of voice and texted messages screamed at me. I bounced to my feet. "I better get back; the cavalry is out looking for me."

As we began moving toward the car, I sent Stephanie a quick text letting her know I was okay. I then scrolled to the three messages from Cameron.

The first one: *I'm on my way to see you.*

The second one: *Don't do this, please, just open the door.*

The third one: *What's going on, why did you run from me? And who's that you with? Call me, I need to know you're okay.*

Oh my god.... "You bastard! You say this isn't about *us.* So why did you pretend some pervert was after me when you knew all along it was *Cameron?*"

"Now wait a minute! I was trying to protect your interest."

"Liar!"

"*Shhh,* lower your voice."

"*Shhh?* Now didn't you just say we were shut off from everyone?"

"Listen! I gave you what you wanted: some answers. His interference would have only delayed things. That's not what you wanted, don't you see?"

"You say that, but I know there's more to this than what you're saying. And it has as much to do with Cameron as it does me. He's the real reason you're in the competition. The real reason you showed your face.

"After all this time, it seems to me you would do anything to try to win me back. And I wonder—no,

219

believe, that you'd do anything to succeed. Even if it means hurting Cameron in the process."

"You're wrong, Pia; that's not it at all."

"Then tell me why you're here, *Ferret*."

He exhaled. "Sorry, no can do."

"Then just take me now; I'll do anything you want. You know me...my mind, my soul. No one knows me like you do or loves me like you do—right? So why not just get this over with?"

He gripped my shoulders. "It's not that *simple*."

"Yeah? Withdraw from the competition," I yanked his hands off me then backed off. "Withdraw, it's that simple. *Please?*" I begged, nearly in tears now. "Just do it for me."

He rested both hands on his hip. It seemed he was thinking about it, but, "I can't do that," he said. "I can't."

"You can't, or you won't? Hmm? Not even for me?"

His jaws constricted as his eyes looked over me. *Not even for you, Perseaus,* his mind answered.

"You're the devil." I brushed his arm as I quickly moved past him. In a quick motion he grabbed me. "Let me go!" He let go and I kept walking, wanting to get as far away as I could.

"I hope for everyone's sake that you keep this to yourself," he said after me.

I turned around. "There you go again. And what if I don't?" I said, walking backwards. "You showed up here like you're all high and mighty, pretending to be sworn in secrecy just so—for what? Oh yeah, you can't tell me. It's all a game and I'm sick and tired of it. Just stay away from me and better yet, go back where you came from."

"You know I can't do that. You're so close and we've accomplished so much..."

"Ha," I threw a hand then gave him my back.

His voice surged, repeating the same-ole thing. I could even feel it bouncing off my back. If I could catch it, throw it back, I would. But then I didn't want to give him satisfaction, by showing I wasn't done with him—because I was...so done with him. As surely as I was aiming to get as far away for him as I could.

I came upon a street curb, cars flying by. I dropped my head, closed my eyes as I started rubbing the back of my neck. It felt like something creeping up it, doing something to the circulation to my brain. A bit extreme I thought, but my face and my neck got sweaty, and I, woozy, like in any moment I could pass out.

Horns started blaring. *What's going on?* I could barely open my eyes to see. But as I did through blurred vision, all I saw was the face of a big-rig coming at me.

Chapter Twenty-Three
We Stick Together

It wasn't your time.

My eyes opened to his whispery voice. I rose, wondering what happened and how I ended up here, at home, and in bed of all places. And I wasn't alone. I could hear footsteps moving through the house.

"Hey, you're up, it's about time." Cameron appeared in the doorway.

"Cameron? Wha-what are you doing here?"

"If only you knew how worried-sick I've been...you not returning my calls, my messages. The backdoor was open, so I let myself in. Come to find out you were here the whole time...napping," he made a tough face. "You looked so peaceful I didn't want to bother you. I thought I'd hang around, you know, in case you needed me for something, and to make sure you're okay. You have no idea how worried we were, thinking something'd happened to you. Hey, why are you looking at me like that? Is something wrong?"

"Umph. Cam, how long have you been here?"

"Mmm...say, forty-five minutes, an hour."

"You finding me here, in bed, seems odd, don't you think? Especially after the messages you sent."

"Messages? I'm not following," he squinted his eyes.

I began looking around for my purse, hoping I didn't lose it with my phone. I spotted it and my shoes lined neatly on the floor by the nightstand. I gravitated over the edge of the bed reaching for it. I opened my purse, took out my phone, checked to see if the messages I knew he'd sent were still there. It hadn't been just another dream; I needed to be right this time. No, I needed to be certain with proof. And there it was, proof. Now I was curious: *Why didn't he clear it from my phone?*

"I didn't know it was you—" I stopped midstream, giving more thought to what I was about to say. Should I really get into this with Cameron? He thought I was here the entire time; everyone else had to think the same thing. I could leave it like that; no one would ever know, except me. However, I wasn't sure if that was the right thing to do. Why didn't he erase the messages from my phone? I questioned now. Did he want me to know that it wasn't a dream? Had I gotten sick in front of a big-rig, and he stepped in and saved me? Or had he designed it to look as if nothing happened, so I wouldn't have to explain myself, to Cameron especially? *How thoughtful....*

"Pia? Pia?"

I gazed up at Cameron.

"What do you mean you didn't know it was me?"

223

I gazed at Cameron, wondering should I or shouldn't I. It took me a few moments, and then my mouth formed a gap. "You were trying to catch me. But he made me believe I was being followed and in danger. I ran off with him not knowing it was you."

"Wait a minute. When I lost you, I came straight back here. Stephanie and the others were here the whole time waiting for you to show up. You couldn't have gotten pass them without them seeing you."

Don't. His voice whispered.

Oh, but I want to, I communicated back, though now I was debating whether I should go on.

"Pia, talk to me," Cameron encouraged me to go on.

I decided to continue. "I wasn't here, Cam. As I was saying, I thought someone was really after me. He tricked me; I didn't realize until I got your messages. Anyway, his car was just over the hill. We went up to the marina by the bridge. Stop looking at me like that. I'm not crazy, far from it. Who was it you thought you were chasing if it wasn't me?" I looked down at my clothes. "My clothes...don't you recognize them, the colors at least?" I held out my arms. The green pants, white-yellow-green plaid top—hadn't he been close enough to see...?

"Yeah, but..." he scratched his head, "how is it possible, you being in two places at once—because that's what I'm hearing? And if what you're telling me really happened, then how did you get home?"

I swayed my head. "I don't know. The last thing I remember was a big-rig coming at me." I rose from the edge of the bed, "But, I have a theory."

After freshening up and slipping on something more comfortable, I curled up next to Cameron on the sofa. I had already given him my theory on how I got home. Which was Ferret had dialed back the clock and delivered me home to my bed to avoid what would have been fatal. Because no way would I have survived that big-rig had he not did what he did. I had come very close to being a goner. The thought of that was too much to bear.

But that was only one theory. My other theories: He was offering a way for me to deceive Cameron and the others. And I could have. Easily. Or he was showing me how easy he could take my life if he wanted to. It would explain why I'd been on the verge of passing out then, while now I was perfectly fine. But what was confusing, was why he would go out of his way to show what he could do to me, because I wasn't a fool...he had to know that. This I scratched my head on; it didn't make sense. What was clear though, he wanted me to remember everything.

Regardless, I was alive and breathing. No one was hurt and I wanted to keep it that way. For that reason, I was reluctant to finish telling Cameron what took place at the marina, but no way was he about to let me off the hook that easy. I had pushed the rock-solid ball down the hill and there was no way I could see myself getting in the way to try and stop it. Not while my heart was telling me that Cameron was in the middle of this somehow. And deserved to know.

"I want you to know I've always been there for you, though it probably didn't seem like it. But, Cam...all I want is to protect you. And it's been tough, keeping you in the dark about things, and I hated it. But...I don't know, maybe this isn't—"

"Uh-uh, don't do that. You can't brush this off no more than I can stand back and pretend I didn't hear what you have told me already—and you know that. Come on, get it out. I'm all ears and I'm not going anywhere. Okay?"

I smiled up at him, said, "Okay," then rested my head against the rhythm in his chest. "I just love you; can't bear the thought of anything happening to you."

He planted kisses on my hair. "I know. I love you, too."

I got teary-eyed as I began. "He calls me Perseaus. He calls me Perseaus because that was my name, when I lived in another lifetime, in a world different from this one."

Cameron chuckled, lifted his back. "Are you serious?"

"Unbelievable, I know," I said, blinking away tears. "It was hard for me to swallow at first too. But it's true. I wouldn't be telling you this if I didn't believe it myself."

"Pia, come on now. I can't believe you're falling for this bull."

"I'm in a place where I have to believe something. How can I not? And you?" I gazed at him and kept going. "He's from this world called Massouvia. Today he showed me it."

"And how did he do that?"

"By joining hands. When we joined hands, our spirits instantly were in a rainforest. Then we elevated to the sky through this light. He showed me this place in the sky, hoping I would remember it, but I didn't. I said he showed me his world, but he didn't exactly. Not how we would show our world to outsiders...or aliens. What he showed me was what his world was about: the spirit and magic. All about magic. Life...how you want it. Want a city in the sky, will it, and right before your eyes you have it. Want to travel the world on a flying carpet—no problem, you can do that too. Anything you want you can have, because what's in the mind is real, and what's real is tangible.

"That's the fun and amazing part about his world. And you know what else? In his world, they collect souls after death, and kinda help them along in their next life...something like that." I stopped, assuming he'd say something.

But he only let out a crummy sigh. "Go on, I'm listening," he said.

"I saw the island again. Yes, *the* island," I responded to his raised eyebrows. "And we rode a white horse across the sky to get to it. He took me there hoping it would jar my memory about living in his world. And when that didn't work he made the island disappear. And we ended up back in the rainforest, in a tree eavesdropping."

"This is too bizarre," he butted in.

"Yes, it is, but not really. Remember the how the island formed right before your eyes? That was bizarre. I will never forget the look on your face.... You can't disbelieve that happened no matter how hard you want to disbelieve this."

He leaned forward with folded hands, gazing down at the floor. And I began running my hand up and down his back.

"No...I can't. But it's not about that. I just don't buy his reason for taking you to this place. I...I should have listened to you when you told me he'd come on to you. These people you eavesdropped on," he looked me in the eyes, "were they from this world?"

"Yes, but," I faltered, expecting his reaction to what I was about to spring on him. "It's just that...I don't want to lose you over this."

"And why would you think that?" He straightened up and wrapped arms around me.

"Because...you might not like what I'm about to tell you," I emitted softly.

"Maybe not. But know I will fight for you with all I got if that's what it takes," he surprised me.

"And I, too, for you," I said, then eased on the topic of Perseaus. "I looked nothing like I do now, and I had long, fiery-red hair. My body, not much different I would say. And I seemed wild, full of life, and my voice, it was soft like an angel. *No, no listen....*" I insisted on telling him about my then-person and my reason for leaving that world with no interruptions. Even though there wasn't much to tell, I knew very little. But when there was nothing left to tell, except for the part about my relationship with Ferret—I couldn't...I couldn't bring myself to tell him.

I began stroking his hand gently. "I think I understand why this ring was special to your mother," I said looking down at it. "It's a rare stone, from the cosmos. A moldavite, he said it is. I thought it was some kind of emerald at first."

"It looks like an emerald, but no, it's a moldavite."

"I'd never heard of it until today."

"It's also a natural birthstone. For birthdays from April 20th to May 20th. And from my understanding, it's the only natural birthstone not for a specific month, like July is the ruby and so on. And I don't know why that is. Just so happen my mother's birthday was May 3rd, so she had two birthstones: the moldavite and the emerald."

"Tell me more. The stone is so interesting I feel there's so much more about it."

"That's because it is. It's used for many things, mostly for spiritual connection. Mom liked it because of its connection to the Holy Grail, having to do with the life and death of Christ. The Holy Grail was made with this kind of stone.

"Talk about rare. The stone is also star-born. It's from a meteorite that fell to earth millions of years ago, and believe to have energy to communicate with extraterrestrials. Yep, imagine that," he nodded to my amazement. "Do you think it communicates with extraterrestrials?"

"I-I..." I put on a thinking face, "I don't know if I do or not. Do you? And what about your parents, you think they did?"

"That is something to think about. What I know about the ring I learned from my parents. But...I don't know. I never saw them trying to communicate with it." He then brought my hand up to examine the ring more closely. "It looks...brainy to me," he chuckled. "You know, it gets me thinking about my parents...and their disappearance...." Gazing at it, he went into deep thought.

"Yeah, me too." We both mulled over the stone a few moments longer. Then I beckoned his attention, "Cameron?" And he turned to me. "There's more I need to tell you about today."

"Yeah, okay," he nodded.

"About Perseaus. I really felt a connection with her. I mean, like it was me in the scene, living it for real in that moment. He could've caused me to feel that way, but I don't think so. What I'm trying to say is that Perseaus and Ferret entered this cave beneath the waterfall, and it was set up for this special occasion. You see, Ebay, or Ferret, proposed to me then. But I didn't see the actual proposal play out, because something inside me snapped. He said I screamed, and when I did it broke the connection and we were back sitting on the bench."

"So, you two were..." he began but then scoffed. "Why am I not surprised. This dude's really pulling punches," he said to himself mostly. "You say you screamed, right when he was about to do the deed, why?"

"I think because I knew what he was about to do. The ring...when I saw it...I don't know...just instinct I guess. The ring had a stone just like this one, just like the one on Ebay's finger too."

Cameron became quiet, his head turned to me, but his eyes not exactly on me.

"I don't blame you for wanting to close your mind on all this, Cam. But I'm telling you this because I didn't want to keep it from you. But...but I hate thinking that I've made a mistake. And I'm sorry if—"

"Nah, that's not it. It's that I can't see you two ever being an item. And, I can't see him working with God. He's not godly. What he's doing is filling your head with garbage. The way I see it, he's nothing but an alien aiming to steal my girl."

"I understand why you would think that. But why would he want to do that if he wasn't telling the truth? And let's assume that he is. Wouldn't that make me...an alien too?"

"No! Never! You're human, all skin and bone, flesh, and blood. Never think anything but.... What I'm trying to spell out here, is that you can't take him at his word, believing he and his kind are a band of guardian angels looking over us," he said, wiping sweat from his forehead with the back of his hand.

"I'll go turn on the air conditioner," I hopped up, went to the back and did just that.

"Thanks," he said as I settled back down on the sofa.

"I'm worried about this, Cam. Because this is about you as much as it's about me. Don't you think it's odd that he's in the competition, hmm? He's in it for a reason and it has to do with you. I don't know what or why. But I think he wants to hurt you somehow. And we have to do something."

"Like what?"

"Like getting the word out. Exposing him for what he really is to the entire universe."

Cameron chuckled. "The universe is a mighty huge place," he said, being ironic.

"The world then! Is that small enough? My point is that we go to the local news with this, so it'd go viral around the globe. We have to do something. We shouldn't go at this alone like we did with the island. Not this time."

"No-no-no. We can't do that, it would be a big mistake. We can't involve anyone; it's the best way to deal with him. Starting now, Stephanie and the gang are out. We have to be smart going forward, more importantly, careful." He then whispered, "What if he's eavesdropping on us now, hmm? And you know what he's capable of. We can't do anything that'd piss him off." He began looking around then, even up at the ceiling when he yelled, "Did you hear that you ungodly creature?"

"What do you think you're doing? Turning superman on me?"

"No, but I refuse to go down lying down. Listen, you believe all that stuff, so I can't fault him for having a beef with me. I mean, after all, I got his girl, right?"

I scoffed, couldn't believe how deranged he sounded. "So you believe all that 'bull' now? Great!"

"He's after you, this I know. Look, what am I supposed to do? Be a little more sympathetic to this creature, hmm? Keep an open mind? You tell me. But get this: I won't be afraid of this creep."

"Look, I like the idea of not pissing him off. It's a damn-good, perfectly-sane one. And, I can't bear losing you over this." Staring at the ring, I thought aloud, "Cam, how 'bout I take the ring off, just until—"

"No, that's out of the question. If I had my father's ring, I would be wearing it. I'm thinking there's something to this ring. When you said you were reluctant to let him see the ring, you weren't sure why. Yet, somehow in that moment, the 'why' came to you when you screamed. And when you did, look what happened. It threw things out of whack. To me that says power. Don't you see? That power had to come from somewhere. The ring...think about it."

"Mmm. When our hands joined the first time, you appeared in an image, then we got a shock that broke the connection. He said because I was too tense and needed to relax. But...I don't know. It's something to think about."

"This is fate again at work, it has to be. You were meant to have the ring, Pia."

I nodded, "Hmm, that could be, due to the timing of it all. You, giving me a ring, just like his, in the midst of all this. Yeah, it's the timing, and I know how much you believe in fate. But Cam, why did you—?"

"Why did I choose this particular ring to give to you?"

"*Well, yes.*" I was amazed that he took the words right out of my mouth.

"Mom had always said it helps bring harmony and peace to marital relationships. And since we were having problems, well, I thought it was right. Aside from the ring, I think the love we have for each other is our best weapon against him, and only if we stick together. I strongly believe that. No matter what, we have to stick together," he delivered with his eyes, making sure I understood.

Because no power is greater than love crossed my mind.

Then he said, "Because no power is greater than love."

"What! I can't believe it. If I didn't know better I'd say you're reading my mind, though you did just now. You know something, the other day," I began, thinking I'd tell him about the gypsies. But for some reason I changed my mind, and instead, asked about Sebastian.

"He's still in a coma but holding his own," he replied, then tilted his head in a questionable fashion. "But that's not what was on your mind; you wanted to say something else."

"Yes, but—" A knock came at the door.

"It's probably no one but Stephanie," Cameron said.

"You're probably right," I grimaced. Curious, I pondered if he knew what I was about to say.

We both got up and went to the door.

"Remember, we really should keep this between us," Cameron reminded me.

And I gave a face that showed no sign that I agreed or disagreed. I thought I would let my mind speak for me.

We opened the door to Stephanie and Elijah smooching. And strutting up the walkway was Ariana and Christina with boxes of pizza and other stuff.

"It's party time," I said.

Cameron and I gave way for them all to course through the door straight into the kitchen. And as everyone flocked around the kitchen table, Stephanie pulled me off into the bedroom and closed the door.

"Don't you know you scared the hell out of us? You didn't answer the door and our text messages, so we thought something was wrong. But all that time you were here dead to the world. Some nap! Well anyhow, when

CJ showed up I told him I thought you snuck out to meet Ebay. Sorry about that, but I thought you could be in trouble."

"Don't worry about it. But you and Elijah, is it what I think it is? Finally?" I had never seen them mouth-to-mouth like that with such passion and longevity. I had to know what's changed. Stephanie had insisted their relationship was strictly platonic, which was unusual to me with their on-again, off-again relationship. I didn't know what that was all about.

"Yes, finally!" she radiated ecstasy. "But what about you and CJ?" She was quick to change the subject. "He must have said something to you about Ebay. What did you tell him? Everything I hope."

"I'm done with Ebay," I shook my head. "Hunting him down like we've been doing is crazy. So our little investigation is over. Here on out, I'm going to wait for him to make a move. And who knows, he probably won't. Understood?"

"I take it that you and CJ had a meeting of the minds. So yeah, I'm cool with that."

"Thanks." I gave her a quick kiss on the cheek, and we left the room to join the others.

This day still had a few hours of daylight left. Cameron and I stood against the counter eating the last of the pizza. Our guest—live, carefree, and innocent—had taken over the table in a stimulating game of Taboo. If only they knew the stuff weighing on my mind. So much was at stake, though I wasn't sure what that was exactly. Cameron and I turned to each other and had a momentary meeting of the minds; just that, no words exchanged. And the meeting adjourned as we turned to everyone else having so much fun. We were just here as nonparticipants. Kind of like on the outside looking in, our minds high in the balance, wondering what the future would bring.

Chapter Twenty-Four

White Nightgown

Time closed in on what was coming.

For instance, the skateboarding competition to begin in a few days, and things were heating up. It was now the talk of the town with it on radio and television, and you couldn't go anywhere without seeing flyers about it.

I underestimated how important the event was because all the attention it was getting surprised me, and because my mind had been on other things, and still was.

Still, it had me nervous. Had me dying for it to be over and done with so I could focus on other things. Like walking the halls of City College as a new freshman. I wanted the new phase of my life to have a smooth transition. But it wouldn't, not until this thing with Ferret came to past. Time, slowly but surely, closed in on that also.

Cameron was at the park getting in some practice-time before work. This morning Stephanie got a surprise visit from her dad, and so she was who-knew-where now. I'd turned down an opportunity to "just hang out and do whatever" with Cristina and Ariana. I didn't feel much like anything today. So I was home alone with a book and it wasn't helping any. A few chapters in and it still didn't have me hooked that I slammed it shut. Now what was on the back of my mind had my undivided attention.

About past lives and reincarnation. I wondered where Cameron stood on the subject, and once again grew curious why he had seen the visions and no one else. Could he had once lived in that world, and like me, couldn't remember? Could it be that Cameron and Ebay crossed paths in another lifetime? If so, had they been rivals? Ebay would likely know the answer but he wouldn't tell. Scary it was thinking about it all.

As scary as last night.

I got off the sofa, moved to the window as I mulled over last night. There had been a click, like a key unlocking a door, that awakened me. When I opened my eyes, there was my life flashing before me. I blinked my eyes, but still, it was there. I reached for Cameron, he was there next to me, so it couldn't have been a dream. Then it stopped, but I sensed more to come when I heard whimpering. What appeared next, a dim room with rolls of pews and a long aisle in the center leading up to a coffin. Two figures stood over it. *The gypsies,* I gasped. "Mommy...why couldn't we...?" the little girl whimpered. Then the sound of a heavy *click* and they quickly turned. And by the looks on their faces, it was as if they had seen a ghost.

So I wondered now, as I had last night following

the vision, who did they see. Was it me?

Was it really? Because it was the weirdest thing, seeing it all with my eyes open. Who was in the coffin? It had to have been someone they knew. Not me, but just the same, could it have been?

No-no, that couldn't be, because I was here, and because "It wasn't my time," I whispered to myself. Those very words I repeated last night, like counting sheep, until I'd finally drifted to sleep.

As days slid by, one thing was constant, me wondering about a dream I'd had the night before, and this day was no different.

Out back on the screened porch, I gazed at leaves on the ancient willow tree dancing in the wind. It'd been a while since I last added something to my diary. Stretched out on a lounger with it on my lap, I had the good attention of doing so before I got another headache. Why I was having them of a sudden, and dizziness (stress perhaps), I wasn't sure.

My eyes tired so I closed them, reflecting on a dream I had last night. In it was a supermoon at the edge of the darkness, and I was tiptoeing through this place, wondering where I was. A voice pierced through the darkness, stopping me in my tracks. A man's voice and it said, *"My forever sweetheart, won't you carry me home..."* Then light, the size of marbles, rained down from the sky. Then the voice again, *"My forever sweetheart, won't you carry me home..."*

"Where are you? Let me see you," I cried out,

tiptoeing, feeling my way through. No matter how bright the moon, nothing but darkness. "Where are you?" I repeated.

A window with light appeared. Weird, because it was a window attached to nothing it seemed, and the person in it was Ferret.

"Who's there?" A stern voice panted through the pitch-darkness, startled me.

Suddenly a spotlight came on overhead, revealing two husky men. "Well look what we have here. She's just a child," one with a beard said. The other one, younger but looked as mean as hell, said, "How in the devil did you get yourself here?" Then they both lunged at me, but I was too quick.

I ran...ran as fast as I could deep into the night. How I managed to get away...? I didn't know, but somehow, I came into daylight and found myself on a cliff overlooking a beach. My white nightgown billowing up in the wind, I gathered the sides to prevent it from escaping over my head. I was alone, or so I thought. Someone had grabbed me from behind, and right then all lights in the universe went out.

I picked up my diary but began thinking. *He said I made it to the island and didn't remember a thing.* For whatever reason, I concentrated on that, and then it came to me. *The nightgown I had on in the dream, it's what I had on the night I disappeared.*

Chapter Twenty-Five
Confrontation

To remember meant understanding, and understanding was the one thing I didn't have.

My mind bounced back and forth from the dream to the stark reality of where we were. In the skatepark parking lot, and I wasn't at bit excited about going in. But Cameron, he wouldn't have me be anywhere else, insisting we stick together. And I agreed, yes, we had to stick together. No matter what, nothing could turn Cameron away, anyway. Not now. He had long awaited this day, had expected so much, and now, at last... *The* big day, *the* grand finale of all the practice-time he'd put in preparing for, yes, it finally was here.

So here we were, in the packed parking lot of Wave Skatepark in Miami. Cameron backed the truck in, shifted the gear in park then killed the engine. "I lost you a few miles back. You want to talk before going in?" He relaxed as he asked.

I'll be so glad when it's all over, I wanted to say, but that went without saying.

A Celica whipped between parked cars; I noticed because I could not believe my eyes. As I waited for them to get out to be sure, I responded to Cameron. "I don't think I want the dreams to stop. The gown I had on in the dream and those men saying I was just a little girl, I can't stop thinking about it. And I know it's not enough as far as me remembering, but it's something. Everything...is so different now, not like before. Well, guess who's here," I abruptly changed the subject seeing it was them.

He followed my gaze. "*Surprise-surprise.* You didn't expect them, I gather?"

"Nope," I said. We then got out and moved to the front of the truck, and waited as they approached, me with my arms crossed.

I smiled. "You gotta be kidding me. What are you guys doing here?"

"Can you believe we talked ourselves out of going in the mall? We drove there and turned around," Cristina uttered.

"Yeah. We couldn't miss this for the world—I mean, all the action is here—so *yay,* here we are. We'll just go to the mall later," Ariana added.

"Hilarious," I chuckled. "You made it to the mall then changed your mind? I invited you, but *nooo, ah-ah, you were going to the mall. No way would you waste your time on this.* That's what you said. So what really changed your mind about coming here?" I looked them all in the eyes, one by one.

"Oh, c'mon, aren't you glad to see us? We're

here for you—and you too, CJ," said Stephanie jovially, as the others grinned from cheek to cheek.

"Ah, whatever," I said to the sky as we moved toward the entrance. Their already-made-up minds had arrived for whatever reason. There was no use discussing it further though I still wondered what changed their minds. In their laughing eyes, I could see that these sneaky private eyes were keeping something from me.

We entered the lobby packed crazy with more people I'd ever seen, and they seemed to just be hanging around. "Hey, CJ, you not hitting the pit today?" A skateboarder, wearing a gold cross around his neck and t-shirt with cut out sleeves, hollered at Cameron, letting him know he was missing his gear.

"Wait here, I'll be right back," Cameron said as he left to run back out to the truck to retrieve his skateboard.

"Look, there's Mark and James," Ariana said waving at a couple of ordinary guys who waved back. They were among a group of people making their way into the park.

"Who are they?" I asked.

"They're just friends of relatives," Ariana tone nonchalant.

I began looking around, still amazed by the number of people in the lobby alone. A lot more than I had expected, giving the event wouldn't start for a few hours yet. This was a highly expected event that's the reason. It was all over the news, everywhere. But I couldn't stand it. Being here had me so unhinged that I had to unhinge myself.

"Oh, there's Memphis." Cristina waved to

someone else I had never met.

As if it stopped, my mind was at it again. All these people, I couldn't understand why they made me feel even more like something may happen. Because I couldn't help myself that's why. Couldn't help feeling that a storm was coming, and the current atmosphere was just the calm before the storm. Somehow, I had to get hold of myself, but under the circumstances it was tricky.

"Why is everybody here?" I couldn't believe I didn't have better control of my mind. Cristina, Stephanie—all of them—gave me a hard what-do-you-mean look. "Stop looking at me like that," I said. "I mean it's still early, that's all. We have a good four hours before the show starts."

"I know; they're here just like us. Clearly everyone's excited about this competition. You know, we overheard some girls talking about it at the mall, like it was something you didn't want to miss. And it got us to thinking about you-know-who, so we put the brakes on shopping and came straight here," Cristina explained.

"Yeah, but...," I hesitated.

"But what, Pia?" Stephanie with crossed arms a chided me with her eyes. "What are you so uptight about? It's all about the competition and the dreamers looking to score big. That's all it is, right?"

I turned away, then turned back, "*Yes.*" And she stared as she was thinking in the clouds. I suspected I knew what she was thinking: that Ebay had more to do with this than I cared to admit. As far as I was concerned—everything—this whole fiasco was all about him and Cameron. And me, though for dissimilar reasons I believed. That in the end, nothing else would

244

matter. But *the end*, it sounded so final. If only I knew what was coming.

"I'm just a little jittery. I probably should've stayed home," I spoke to Stephanie's now-troubling expression.

"Are you feeling sick again?"

I shrugged, "No, I hope not."

A few days ago, I saw the doctor. Mom had set the appointment and insisted that I kept it. The doctor had run tests and found nothing that concerned him. Just the same, he prescribed something to help with my symptoms, including something for the headaches. The following day I was better. But now, I didn't know, maybe I was sick with the jitters. And I had a sudden case of chills. With crossed arms I ran my hands up and down my arms. As I melted away the chills, I moved around taking in the growing excitement, as if I was looking for someone specific, and may as well have been. Because Cameron—*Where was he? What was taking him so long?*

Was I psychic? Doors behind me opened and there he was coming in with his partner Dax. The two were in a serious conversation. I could tell by the seriousness in their faces, by how they motioned their hands, mostly. It prevented me anyhow from interrupting. And had me wondering what they were talking about and was it more important than the fact they would compete against each other in a while. Still that didn't hamper the fact that they were partners, no matter who won.

Patiently I waited to get Cameron to myself as Stephanie and the others chatted without me. Cameron approached as soon as his conversation with Dax was over.

"Hey, sorry it took so long." He then looked over

245

the lobby. "Boy, it's crazy in here. Kind of early but I'm not surprised."

"Yeah, crazy," I said, surprised how he at once addressed what was troubling me not knowing he was. I didn't get how he was connecting with me like never before. Was he even aware? If so, he was cool about it. I didn't want to believe he was. Yet it was different, strange, and I didn't know what to think, because it was sudden, and felt far more coincidental.

We both turned to doors opening to more people entering the park. As they headed inside the park, I noticed the lobby had thinned out some.

"How are you feeling? You think you can hang?" he asked.

"I'm fine, Cam...but, I don't know."

He drew me into him. "I know, I know. You feel like today is when it all hits the fan, and that's because it is; this is it. And you need to chill out and believe that in the end, fate will be on our side. Don't worry. If we stick together, we'll be okay, you'll see." He kissed my forehead. "Just try not to worry, Babe."

Stephanie stepped into our moment. "We better go and get seats before they're all gone," she suggested.

Cameron nodded, "Go 'head, I'll see you in there." He touched my lips lightly in a kiss, but I wasn't quite ready to leave him

"I'll catch up with you in a minute," I decided, and they went on without me. "I wanted to ask about Sebastian. How is he? Is he still in a coma?" I thought this might be what he and Dax were talking about.

"It's touch and go right now. He came out of the coma but slipped back in. But don't worry. He'll pull

246

through; I just know."

"If you say so," I nodded a distressing nod. "Well, I'll see you in there. And try not to use up all your energy in practice. You can't get any better than you are now in so little time." I craned my neck for a quick kiss. "Love ya."

I stepped out of his hug, looked off toward the other end of the lobby and saw a group of people headed this way. Among them, front and center, was Ebay and his partner in crime (I had the urge to call him). Winston, however, was his name, and he had his arm hanging around a girl's neck. The others, young boys, tagging behind them, I wondered were they all together. "*The man...,*" one boy's Spanish accent landed in sharp ears. On second thought, maybe they weren't all together, that the boys following them, could be they were fans. Ebay had built a repetition for himself with that skateboard he carried.

Back to his partner in crime, I realized the only time I saw him was here. Never alone. Always with Ebay. *Why was that?* I bridled for a sec because I had more pressing matters on my mind. Like the strange look in Cameron's face as he watched them draw near, bothered me.

The girl with them, I focused more on her now. One thing I noticed was how attractive she was, but something about her eyes. A shade of pink highlighted the shades of her enormous eyes, and the lashes traced with a dark eyeliner—this I would soon spot as prominent features when she got close enough for me to see. But it wasn't her glamorous eyes, not right away, that got my attention. It was the way she used them—sizing you up, slicing you up—that made people notice and wonder. Like a runway model in a way, only the way she flaunted herself was bitchy and spooky. Something else, for an odd reason I thought I knew her or had seen her somewhere. As always, I despised trying to figure out whether I knew someone. As much as I despised hearing Ebay's voice in my head now, telling me *I had to remember,* that I could whack myself upside the head to get him out of it.

I stared up at Cameron. His face miserably distorted that I could see him mounting in a rage.

"Cam, what is it? Do you know her?" I sensed that he did.

His shaky head gave me a quick glance, and he muttered, "After all this time...I can't believe it."

"Believe what?"

"Celine," someone next to me whispered. I whipped my head around to see this person then back to Cameron. I took Cam's hand in mine and stared at them staring at us as they moved closer.

"You know her. Who is she to you?" My strained voice commanded.

He looked me in the eyes. "She's someone I once knew, a close friend but...but it's been years since I've seen her. One day she was just gone. More like vanished—the whole family. No one knew where they went or why, nothing; it was one big mystery. Now after all this time, here she is. And with them of all people." He bit his bottom lip. "I have to warn her, Pia. She doesn't have a clue what she's up against."

Fearful, I clinched his arm with both hands. "No wait."

In my periphery, I saw they'd stopped. Curious, I turned to see why, and saw the entrance to the arena blocked. In fact, all the doors were blocked. I also realized a lot more people now than it was a moment ago, and they had us surrounded in a way that felt daunting. Where did they come from? I wondered. As if they came out of the woodwork to besiege us like a bunch of kids expecting a good fight. I gazed at Ebay, shifted the gaze to Cameron, and from the cold, antagonistic look in both their eyes, it appeared a fight was imminent.

"Celine. It's me, Cam. You haven't forgotten me, your friend, have you? It's nice to see you. What a surprise! Where have you been all this time?" Cameron stepped forward, but my grip around his arm grew firmer.

"Pia? Let me do this...," he said as I stared at animating lips, not wanting to accept the whispering passing through them. "It'll be okay, you'll see. Can I have a word with you?" he went back to talking to her, Celine.

Winston stepped forward. "If you haven't noticed, we're over here minding our own business. You really should listen to the little lady there."

"What I notice is you sticking your nose in where it doesn't belong. She's not your property. You know that, right?"

Winston shot a vexing grin then hung his body lopsidedly as he popped knuckles in his right hand and then his left.

I wished Cameron didn't have to do this. Something about this was off, way off. I understood Cameron's concern about her being in their company, but I wasn't sure this was the time to discuss it with her.

"Celine?" Even so, he wasn't backing down. "You must know how surprise I am to see you. It's been a long time. My god, where have you been all this time?" Cameron glanced over the crowd, then came back to her. "I would like to think we're still friends. And as a friend, can I have a moment of your time...*alone?*" He trained his eyes on both Ebay and Winston. Uneasy how this would pan out, I put on a brave face, and hoped this would end without anyone throwing punches. Though it wouldn't hurt if Celine stepped in and played nice, I thought too.

"Look, you heard the man. Are you looking for trouble?" Ebay chimed in this time.

"Nah," Cameron said.

"Then a word of advice: if you don't want trouble then don't start trouble," Ebay underlined.

Murmurs dispersed through the anxious bunch of people. Everyone, including me, was waiting in suspense because this could escalate at any moment. Because I knew Cameron, I knew he was up for the challenge, and knew he wouldn't back off if his life depended on it. Everything about this scene wasn't doing anything if not charging him up to the max, and I didn't know how to deal with it. But for now, I seemed to find solace from the many people around us.

"Me...looking for trouble?" Cameron snapped back. "Now why would you think that? Huh? All I'm asking is a moment with an old friend. Whom I haven't seen...since forever."

Celine rolled her eyes, then opened her mouth as she was about to say something but in that split-second, thought otherwise. Or was it the cat that caught her tongue? that cat being Ebay. Or did she intend for her enormous eyes to do the talking for her? Apparently not. She seemed to have found her voice.

"We have nothing to talk about." The way she said it, like "that's it, end of discussion".

"You have nothing to say to an old friend? No hello, longtime-no-see, how you been doing...nothing?" Cameron paused, then took on a different approach. "Celine, look, you know nothing about these people you're with. Believe me, they're just using you." Then I couldn't believe it!

She got up in Cam's face—too bold, too close. "Get this through you thick head—I don't care what you think. And, I have nothing to say to you. Not now, not ever." She said what little she had to say then withdrew herself. She could be one tough-cookie if she wanted to, I'd gathered that much already. But why was she like that with Cam?

"I don't get it. Have I done something I'm not aware of? We have always been cool. The last time I saw you we were cool. So where is this coming from?"

Celine's eyes rolled down then she turned her head.

"Look, I'm sure everybody is wondering what happened to you, not just me. Are you pissed off at everybody? I mean, how personal can this be?"

Cameron's remark stirred the crowd, and I thought for sure someone would speak up in his defense. At least then she would cut the crap, I hoped. Because I trusted Cameron in what he suggested. He couldn't have been her only friend wondering what happened to her. Even the person next to me knew who she was. But amidst the muffled sound of commotion in the crowd, no one spoke up. And how odd that was. So very odd.

"I've been around. And as you can see, I'm perfectly fine. And I don't want to talk about where I've been, you know, play catch up. Maybe we can get together later and talk, or not. I really don't have the time. But what I need right now is for you to *back off.*"

"We need to talk now, Celine." Cameron grabbed her by the arm.

"Cam, don't," I said as she yanked loose furiously.

"Don't you touch me," she spewed. "I'm not that naive girl you once knew, your pushover...*your...girlfriend,*" she scowled, rolled her eyes at me. By now I was furious, looking dead at Ebay, screaming in my head, *Girlfriend! Girlfriend!* She then jabbed a finger in Cam's chest, "Are you insane? What you think you have to say to me is irrelevant."

I stepped between them and fired back. "That's enough! All he's trying to do is help you, but never mind that now because you're irrelevant."

"Pia?" Cameron moved me back.

"Just let her go, Cam, just let her go. She's not worth it. You need to stop this. What's gotten in to you?"

"Look, Babe. I'm not the perpetrator here."

"Oh, but you kinda are right now. Don't you see?"

"Listen, please..." He buttoned up, drew a breath, exhaled. Looking in his eyes, I couldn't stand seeing how much he wanted to get through to her but couldn't.

I shot Ebay a venomous regard. "This is your fault, stirring up all this confusion!" I turned back to Cameron. "He's just using her to get at you, at us. That's what this is all about. He staged all of this...even all these people...everything; it's all him. Think about it. He's goading you with her, trying to make it look like you're jealous. And you know why," I whispered. Then I looked at Celine. "Cam is right. He's just using you, but you obviously can't see it, but it's true."

"Using her?" Ebay stormed forth, motioning Celine out of the way. "Looks to me you're trying to drive a wedge in something that has nothing to do with you. Now you heard the lady. She's made herself clear that she wants nothing to do with you." He spat the words in Cameron's face, probably not intentionally. But it didn't matter.

Because in a raging heartbeat Cameron shoved him into the crowd that dispersed every which way to get out of the way. Ebay charged back like a bull, but Cameron was so swift to move. Like a ninja, he thrust Ebay to the floor with his foot and Ebay went sliding across the floor klutzy-like. That it looked like an invisible force dragging him. Or like a movie running in slow motion. So weird. And startling. I couldn't believe my eyes. And then all of a sudden—

Chapter Twenty-Six
Oh no, not Again

Things. Were. Different.

One moment we were in an atmosphere filled with commotion, and the next, we were in this quiet, dreamlike place. Yes, we were still in the lobby at the skatepark...yes but...

Oh my god. It was happening again.

As I turned in a full circle, everyone became statues like in a wax museum. I couldn't believe my eyes, couldn't believe it was happening to me again. But it was, right now and why?

The first time it happened, last year while on a bus headed to the mall. But this time it was different. This time I wasn't also turned to a statue. Not like before when only my eyes moved and saw the world at a standstill and, for the first time, saw Ferret as a ghost. That's one thing! The other, the space was hazy, reminded me of a dead zone, and I wasn't the only one not grounded like a piece of art.

Ebay's back collided into the wall as their fighting continued. He quickly sprang to his feet, his body revitalized with the heroic strength of a superhero. But the cagey, nervous look now wearing in his face, as something just spooked him, I found confusing. He was the one with all the power and usually he had no problem showing it with his arrogance. But now...the panicky look in his face couldn't be a good sign. In my eyes a time bomb was about to explode, and I had to do something. Anything!

"Stop this at once!" I moved between them. "Why are you doing this? Will you please stop before you do something you'll regret?" My heart begged. Yet, the panic in his eyes, I couldn't figure; I mean he was the reason for this happening. Not Cameron, and certainly not me. Now he... seeming to be afraid of Cameron, what was wrong with this picture?

Cameron moved around slowly, his body positioned like a boxer, ready to defend itself. I turned back to Ebay. He was motionless by default, I would say. Still, the tension of something's not right in his face, and I sensed him backing off. Which was complicated, because I sensed him on the verge of attacking, too.

Then I did a double take when I saw Cameron exuding the confidence I'd expected to see in Ebay. Standing tall with his hand on his hips, his smiling eyes glared at Ebay. You would think he was ready for anything and had total control of this situation. Again, what was wrong with this picture? Had Cameron gone completely mad?

"Cam?" I said, about to address my immediate

concern when I cried out, "*No-o-o.*"

My cry shattered through the hazy cocoon of still madness as the Cameron I did not recognize tore through it charging at Ebay. I got in his path trying to stop him but went stumbling to the floor dodging his swinging forearm. I craned my head up to the ceiling, cried out to be heard by anyone. "Help! Help! Help!" But in this place of purgatory, my cry went unanswered.

All I could do was watch, *scream*, as Cameron rammed his head into Ebay's stomach. As Ebay flipped over him, made a swift turn in midair and delivered an uppercut to Cameron's chin. Blood spat out on impact. "Stop," I belted out a horrific cry.

The situation seemed it would progress to no end with no one around to stop it. And before I knew it, Cameron had Ebay pressed to the ground by the full weight of his body. For as long as a referee counting down at a wrestling match I imagined. Because Ebay knocked him off, sending him sailing into a wall of our lifeless audience.

Cameron hit it, and like a ball hitting it at an angle, he bounced off sailing upward, then dropped to his feet with a bounce. *What?* I couldn't believe it. He landed perfectly on his feet like a cat. But how?

How did he do that? My eyes amplified to the mix of craziness and confusion happening in front of them. My Cameron in rare performance like a superhero, wasn't my Cameron at all. How was it even possible, he holding his own against the almighty Ferret? But Cam took another blow to his jaw—and another. Spitting blood, he was hurt. Yet he swung at Ebay but missed. His head drooped. Staggering backwards and frontwards, he was running out of steam.

Ebay preyed on his condition, kicking him to the floor, stabbing him in the back with his knee when he came down on him, smashing his face on the floor.

Cameron grunted, "You punk. This the best you got?" He began wiggling, trying to free himself, and heaving so bad I thought he would pass out.

"This is it, see?" I said. "He doesn't have any fight left in him," and he's still in one piece, *thank goodness.* "So it's over, okay? All's well that ends well." I hoped for it to be that simple.

However, hope was crazier than I thought, and wasn't ready to give up the fight just yet. Because in all that heaving, Cameron somehow pulled Hercules muscles out of thin air. Before I knew it Ebay was tumbling across the floor. No matter how incredible— Cameron sprung to his feet in acrobatic style, and in a swift-leg motion, struck his legs like bowling pins. His legs spread-eagled, but Ebay wouldn't let that get the best of him. How Cam was able to contend with him in the first place baffled me. Besides, Ebay didn't hit the floor. He rose midair showing off a sci-fi ninja move. A cat, the move reminded me of, in human form of course, with many more vicious tricks in its meow.

But the wearing on his face now, like a new rage of determination, elevated the terror inside me. His mouth curled gapingly as he ripped through space, but whatever he was saying, I couldn't make out. The language was foreign to my ears.

He got to Cameron and immediately put him in a chokehold, twisted his arm around his back. Cameron struggled as a ferocious lion to get loose. Ebay had him good and he wasn't budging a bit to Cam's struggle. Cameron resulted to kicking, digging nails in the arm wrapped around him. To no avail, not even that worked. Ebay appeared immune to feeling anything now.

In moments, Cameron again showed signs of losing steam. Was it over, finally? Wishful thinking it turned out to be because he did it again. He flipped Ebay over his shoulder but Ebay clung to him and they both went rolling around like a tire.

But Cam's attempt changed nothing, after a few spins and he was back on his feet in a chokehold.

"That was stimulating. I really enjoyed it. Let's see what stimulating maneuvers you come up with next," Ebay snickered.

"Okay enough, already! Haven't this been stimulating enough—and for what?" I released a stiff sigh. "I can't take anymore of this. Let him go, and now!" I demanded.

He gritted teeth, strengthened his grip around Cameron's neck, striking me with pain, the same pain reflecting at me through Cameron.

"C'mon...let him go. What do I have to do, beg? Because that's exactly what I'm doing."

Still, as stubborn as ever, his arm gradually cut into Cameron's throat. His eyes bulged more with every relentless pressure Ebay applied. Poor Cameron, he continued to try to free himself.

I took a step, attempting something, I didn't know what.

"Don't come any closer. I assure, you'd regret it," he groaned, dragging Cameron back a few steps.

The white in Cameron's eyes was now bloodshot.

Ebay tightened his grip a notch and his eyes rolled up in his head. Cameron was giving in to his restraint though he still held a grip on Ebay with his free arm. However not for long, his hand flopped to his side. His body so weak, his eyes dizzy and his mind paralyzed, he was fighting to remain conscious. Once more he lifted his left hand to clench the arm of his strangler, only to be stifled with more pain to show disapproval.

"This isn't you, *I know*, you don't mean to do this. For once, what is it you want? I would do anything, please," I expressed through blinding tears. "If I ever meant anything to you, then how could you...? You must know this would only rip my heart out."

"You keep thinking this is all about you. But you don't know the half of it," he shot back angrily.

"Then make me understand." I then thought about the ring. Wondering where, in all its luster, the magic we needed to help us through this.

"'Make you understand'? I'll let Cammy boy here do the honors. Come on, Cammy boy, explain it to her."

"Cam, what is he talking about?"

"P-ia...," Cameron could barely speak, his voice withering for dear life. "I don't know, ah, what he's talking about. It's a trick. I-I...promise you. The ring. The ring, Pia...the ring. The power's in...the ring."

I stared into Ebay's wicked eyes and then looked down at nervous fingers fumbling with the ring. If I asked the ring to help us out of this situation, how exactly? I bridled as much with such passion, then prayed for it to lend me power to get us out of this mess. But nothing was happening I could see. So I had to rely on somehow convincing Ebay to give up on this madness.

"I don't know what this is all about, but I'm giving you a choice. Kill him then you might as well kill me, too. Let him leave and it's all forgiven. Deep down, you don't want to hurt me, I know. So...please," I said in the gentlest of kindness. As I investigated Cameron's eyes, I began wondering why was he stalling, why hadn't he done the deed already.

Well that's it! Why hadn't he done Cameron in already? I devoted every ounce of my brain thinking about that, until it came to me, somewhat of an answer.

"Don't, I mean it, stay back," Ebay said as I approached, slow and easy.

"You won't do it, you can't." I continued moving forward when suddenly he turned into a gigantic ferret and roared as he lunged at me. I screamed, fell back into the wall of human statues, trying to avoid getting my head bit off. When he parted with the grizzly side of him, I quickly got to my feet. Yet nothing had changed; Cameron still at his mercy.

"You won't say much. Why are you doing this...?" I wailed in tears. "Is it about revenge?" I wondered again had they been rivals in another lifetime and now was his chance to settle the score. That would make sense, except, Cameron wasn't in the know. I mean, how could he be? Cameron had said he was trying to trick us. Said that the power was in the ring.

"Revenge?" Ebay chuckled mockingly.

I thumbed the ring, swelling with emotion. I'd had just about enough of this and was seriously wondering about the ring having powers. "You are deeply disturbed, because this isn't you," I said as I pondered about the ring.

"How can you? You can't know what you don't remember."

"Yeah, suppose you're right. But what I do know...is that your thoughts too deep to be expressed, and too strong to be suppressed. So it's easier to take the coward's way out. Even in your world there must be a penalty for breaking a golden rule, such as murder."

I couldn't believe the words I had spoken. And the tone in which I'd spoken them, as a powerful ruler. Where did it come from? *The ring. Had Cameron been right all along?*

Ebay eyes narrowed, his head and arm moving nervously as he stared at me; his breathing seemed labored. He couldn't believe the words I spoke either, I could tell.

I went on, "Look around you. At all you have done in the heat of the moment. Is this an act of honor that would rip great rewards from the parliament? You may undo the carnage set in your mind. Not yet is your harm fatal. So, here's your chance to undo it. And you will! Because to do injustice is more disgraceful than to suffer it. Isn't that right, Ferret?" my voice raised saying his name.

Wow. The power I felt in saying those words, supernatural, and yes, by the ruthful shadow on Ferret's face now, the words had a powerful effect on him.

I stepped forward then stopped when images flashed before my eyes. Only for a split second and it was gone. I didn't give it much thought. Much like the dreams and visions I'd had in days passed, it wasn't a solid clue about anything.

Slowly, I continued to move closer. With every

step I made, Ebay pulled Cameron back two.

"I'm warning you; don't take another step," he said.

I stayed put, glaring at the bluish-gray flush in Cameron's face. Ferret only spared him the slightest of breath to remain conscious. And seeing his body weak, his eyes dizzy, his mind paralyzed, tormented me so.

"You don't understand. You can't begin to understand," Ebay added after a few moments.

I took another step, and when I thought he would do the unthinkable, a got an impulse to say, "He that will not when he may, he shall not when he will," and then suddenly...

"Hey! If you two don't straighten up, you both will be disqualified," a man said. We were back to when the fight started, back to when Cameron thrust Ebay to the floor. He was getting up off the floor as the man instructed them to stop. Things were back to normal, us surrounded by a live, eruptive audience. Yes, things were back to normal, but different, too. How I viewed things moving into the competition, different now.

"You boys got that?" The man bringing the disturbance to order stood over six-feet tall. And both Cameron and Ebay responded to him with a quiet nod. The man took them at their nod and went on about his business.

Meanwhile, we all wore perplexing expressions staring at one another. Neither of us spoke. Neither of us had the words to speak. Words were far behind in the moments passed, trying to catch up to us in the present. Keeping our cool and our mouths shut deemed appropriate for the moment. I was puzzled by what really happened...who or what brought us back. *Was it you?* I intensified my stare on Ebay. *Did you really have a change of heart? That's what I thought;* I frowned when I got no response from him.

If not him then who (what) intervened?

Was it God? The master of Massouvia? Or was it...the ring?

Ebay was the first to break the mode. He turned, walked away, his comrades in toll.

Cameron and I held our positions watching them. Then our orbs met, visiting the secret between us that we knew we would revisit many times over. I couldn't help wondering about him though. How he'd garnered such amazing strength to contend with Ebay. But I couldn't tackle the subject, not now. I needed time to recover, get some air.

Or was I afraid...? Or did I just want the suspense to last a few moments longer?

Cam took my hand, "Come on. Let's go get some air."

I gawked nervously into his eyes. "Yeah...air." Then I looked over my shoulder as Ferret's voice came to me.

No matter how much I love you, nothing I do help you remember. It's him, Perseaus; he's why you can't remember.

Famous last words. It's only a trick, you trying to tear us apart. I turned away as Cam pushed open the door. *Just a trick...trying to tear us apart.*

No matter how confused I was, I needed to believe that....

Chapter Twenty-Seven
Let the Games Begin

They're good. Every one of them. But what they didn't know, they're in a bowl with sharks. The kind of sharks they could never know existed, and therefore, could never see coming. Even with eyes opened...not in a million years. They'd be eaten alive and not even know it. Oh, but they're good. So damn good. But just not good enough.

In a brooding cocoon, focusing on those below in the bowl, I wasn't fitting in well amidst a crammed stadium. To sit back and relax and just go with the flow, at the moment, was impossible. And once things really got heated up, what mess I'd be in then remained to be seen. Not that it would matter, I wasn't going anywhere, anyway. I had no choice but be here.

"I know you're nervous about this. But will you try to loosen up some? You're missing the fun of it all. Just think good thoughts, feel the excitement." Stephanie and her words of encouragement. In this case they were easier said than done.

If only things were normal.

Meanwhile, I shrank back in my shell. *The little gold fishes were so good, but, not good enough.* In the bowl with hungry sharks, they didn't have a chance, and no, it didn't seem fair at all. I knew it would come down to one of two potential winners. And their names just lit up in gold lights on the scoreboard, along with six other competitors.

Flynn? I never knew Ebay's last name but there it was, on the board. "An imposter is who he is," I mumbled to myself. *And Churchill?* There I had it, Winston's last name, too. It seemed too random. But I wondered, could it be that he was *the* Winston Churchill in a formal life? And the contest, why did he enter? Ferret had given his reason but Winston—I would love to hear his story. If at all interesting as I thought.

They were clearing the bowl now. My eyes followed Cameron, as I recalled the conversation we had earlier. I had asked about his unusual power with Ebay and how he think that was. In responding, he'd appeared as confused as I was.

"I want to say that it was the ring, but, I don't know," he'd said.

"You don't think it was the ring?"

"Yes—I mean, well, not at first. It's when you put all your energy on the ring was when it worked its magic. Because it was then something strange was going on with him. A weird tremor in his body...a bulging tremor. Like his soul, or something, trying to get out." The frown on his face, intense. "Whether it's what gave me power, I like to think so, but, I don't know."

"It's strange, because, not once did he appear threatened by the ring. Yet, what you're saying is that it could have been something else."

"What I'm saying..." He'd taken a long moment thinking about it, then said, "Fate, Pia. Whatever it was, it had to do with the power of fate. As for the ring...don't ever, ever take it off."

"May I have your attention?" a man on a loudspeaker pierced through the stadium of eagerly awaiting fans. "The moment has come to reveal the mystery man dedicated to putting this event in motion just for you...." Some hoped the surprise would be that the X games or Vans was sponsoring the event, but the announcer said a mystery man, singular, meaning one person. Not a conglomerate, singular, with members around the world. So, who was this mystery man?

The announcer continued. "Ladies and gentlemen, please give a warm welcome to the one and only, Bruce Hawk." Instantly the arena went wild applauding. Except me, I had no clue who this person was, though got swept up in the excitement, anyway. I grinned in disbelief at Stephanie, Cristina, and Ariana; they also so thrilled by this Hawk person I felt left out even more

As I paid attention to the announcer, I learned Bruce Hawk was Florida-grown, here in Miami, and had won many medals and traveled the world. Had lived for a while overseas and was back to start his own skateboarding company and was seeking good talent to sponsor. And why not jumpstart the business by sponsoring this event? "So, without further ado...," the announcer said now and handed Bruce Hawk the mic.

"Hi everyone, and welcome to the Best Tricks Competition. Each contestant will be rated on four runs. And the one with the highest-accumulative score, the numero uno, will win the gold medal and five big ones. And that's not all, our numero uno will also receive an invitation to compete in the Regional Championship, *and the finalists*—yeah, that's right! We're going to shake things up in here now that— Now hear this. *Now that the X Games is here, and that means this event is going live. Yeah, baby!*"

With that the audience rose in a crazy frenzy over the game-changer. *The X Games?* Here? And now? The crowd was still going nuts: bouncing on their feet, clapping and waving their hands, crying out all the cheer and joy they could muster up together. There was no way for Bruce to get another word in if his life depended on it. So he gave the audience its moment and when it died down, he continued.

"Yeah, I feel ya! The X Games right here at Wave Skatepark!" he blasted more excitement for the fans to eat up. And they were about to erupt again but he was quick at holding the floor. "*Now-now-now*, as I was saying, there will be not one winner but three. The two finalists will win one thousand dollars and...."

Bruce went on a few moments longer with details about the event, then he put the mic to rest, leaving us all excited and eager for the competition to begin shortly.

"Thanks for inviting us, Pia. I knew this would turn out better than going to the mall," Cristina all excited, and Stephanie, "Yep, and it hasn't even started yet," she just as excited.

"Yeah, right," shaking my head, I chuckled. Thought about Cameron then smiled to myself. Wherever he was, I knew how ecstatic he must be.

He, in the X games? It was a dream-come-true. And I didn't want to jinx it, but I couldn't overlook that he was up against an immortal who may or may not play fair. Then too, Cameron himself was unpredictable. How he got the power to handle Ferret for as long as he had was baffling. He'd as much insinuated it could've been something else other than the ring. The question: How had he come about such strength? Could it reembody him and hand him the trophy?

Yes...yes it could. I slipped back in my cocoon, imagining Ebay and Cameron as sharks, and the others, as pretty little gold fish with no chance of winning.

"Hey! Look, look!" Excited Ariana, turned in her seat, was looking up at the entrance. We turned and saw the door held open, and my eyes popped.

"Oh, my god. But how...?" I choked up as he entered, and on his own two feet. Not someone who looked like him, it was actually him. My stare watered in happiness, because he was an example of hope, hope in this exact moment, teaching me once again that anything's possible. Seeing him, Sebastian, right here and now, was like seeing Almighty himself.

A couple of men escorted him to his seat. "Look, it's Sebastian...," the whispering spread like poetry casting a spell on all picking up the sensation. Before long everyone was on their feet, transfixed on him. Then at once everyone lavished him in a standing ovation, so heartwarming you could feel the spirit of white doves soaring through the roof.

The clapping, nothing but clapping, lasting for inexhaustible moments, was so moving, tears of bliss glistened in my eyes. Sebastian bowed graciously and waved to all. His presence, so amazing and unbelievable. This morning he was in a coma, and now.... Well, the announcement about the X Games didn't hold a candle to Sebastian being here to see it. He was the most precious prize anyone could hope for.

The acclamation diminished. I looked around for Cameron, hoping he wasn't missing out, and he wasn't. I spotted him with the other contestants, including Ferret and Winston, contributing to the ongoing praise for his dear friend.

He got nerves, I thought. Because I still had my doubts about how Sebastian ended up in the hospital, I couldn't exonerate Ferret. Now that Sebastian was here I believed he was all the strength Cameron needed. This new turn of events made me feel, without a doubt, that God was on our side. The ring, and its connection, I wasn't sure of, but this moment I attributed all to God.

The event jumped off by introducing the first contestant. He slapped a black cap on his curly blonde hair and then dipped into the bowl with speed and focus. He skated up a wall, slid the edge of it then dipped back into the bowl. Piece a cake, off to a good start, I thought as he went on with his performance. This contender, I hadn't met personally but had seen around a few times. Like most of the skaters, his attire was typical, dark pants, a T-shirt, his, white. No question he was good, but it wasn't saying much. They all had what it took, came highly skilled, and were interesting to watch. He wrapped up his performance in the 45-second timeframe allowed, setting the bar for the next one to come on stage. He exited the bowl wearing an accomplished expression as the audience applauded.

The next one came out donning a red cap, dark loose pants coming down to his knees. He was slim, average height like the skater before him. And he wasn't messing around. He came out and tackled the eight-foot wall like a monster wave. At the top, and as if the wave was crashing, his grabbed the end of the board and spun and spun. "Holy moly! We got our first 540 spin!" the announcer heralded, and the crowd stormed with cheers and applauses. The skater continued hacking the bowl, sailing up and down the walls, skating on the landing part outside of the bowl. All over the bowl he was before completing his performance.

As another one came out for his first run, I reflected on the first time Cameron had brought me here. I knew an ollie trick if nothing else, or so I'd thought. Cameron put me on the spot, wanting me to point out someone doing it right then. I searched around the bowl to find anyone doing an ollie but couldn't—not fast enough for him, anyway. So he showed me a few ollies, and explained why it was hard for me to recognize it. What he'd taught me was that an ollie's performed in many ways, often incorporated in many tricks.

And it's the most common and first trick skaters learn first. The skaters who'd skated already executed ollie tricks. Thanks to Cameron, I knew an ollie when I saw one now.

"Ooh." The skater fell hard missing his landing that my body quaked as he wrapped up an almost-perfect run. Cameron was next in line; his name lit up on the

scoreboard. Feeling her eyes on me, I turned to Stephanie.

"He's going to be fine, don't worry," Stephanie placed a hand over mine. My fingers were fidgeting over the ring, vaguely, yet she noticed and took for granted I was worried.

"What makes you think I'm worried?" I said just for the hell of it.

"Mmm-mmm...I know you," Stephanie said.

"Yeah. It's not that I don't have confidence in Cam, I do. It's just that it's all chopped up with this and that." I motioned my hand as if chopping "confidence" into three pieces. "I'll get it together here in a minute." I then brought the ring up to my chin, concentrating on it, thinking it my duty to do so. Because if Cameron believed in its magic, then so should I.

Watching Cameron, I was amazed all over again at how much he had improved in very little time. He rounded the edge of the bowl. Flipped his board and then dropped back into the bowl. Then skated up another side, rode the rim of it and again dipped back into the bowl. He skated with ferocity, his skateboard sticking with him like partners do. Partners destined to work together—he and that skateboard were just that good together. For a split-second, while he one-handedly held his body upside down at the bowl's edge, it seemed as if the skateboard glued to his feet. The illusion of that was amazing.

He now climbed the eight-foot wall and soared high above it. Grabbing the board, his body then formed into a twist and began flipping. I jumped to my feet along with others. *"Come on, Babe, land it."* I held balled hands close to my mouth, knees bending bouncing my body. *"You can do it..."*

He came out of the flipping at the upper curve of the bowl and landed, a little shaky but he kept his balance. And then the announcer blared, "*He just landed a 900!*" The stadium erupted in a window-shattering madness, especially when 60 illuminated next to his name, putting him in the lead of the first two skaters scores, 45 and 40.

I looked over my shoulder for a quick glance at Sebastian, but with so many people still standing and applauding, I could barely see him. But I saw enough to know that he was pleased with Cam's performance. I spotted Celine across the way; she looked my way and then...then nothing, nothing at all. I turned away, pretended I didn't see her.

Following Cameron were four other great skaters, Winston included, but neither of them topped his score. But that didn't matter, all skaters had four runs, or chances, to up their scores. The best part, only the top two would figure the players' final score. One down, three to go, and with one more skater to go in the first run, next up was Ferret.

He started his run in full force like everyone else, conquering the walls, executing many of the same tricks as the other skaters. As I watched intently, I wondered about his game plan. Would he play fair? Also, if he wanted to, could he turn off his immortality and become human, through and through? Just for a little while? Just until the judges announced the winner? If not, then I sure hoped he had the common decency of turning off his ego and just play fair. So that the hopefuls with real blood running through their veins would have a deserving chance.

Of course that made me think of Cameron and his superhuman strength. Could he regain that strength during the contest? Chewing over that, put other things at the threshold of my mind I wanted to slam the door on. Because it was Ferret, it had been him all along. I didn't want to have those thoughts about Cameron all over again. I trusted him, and I had long exonerated him of having anything to do with my visions, not to mention my disappearance.

Not Cam...it's been Ferret all along.

"Cameron...no," I mumbled to myself as I watched Ferret dash up and down the bowl. Watched as he crisscrossed it at all angles, completing tricks with flair and agility. *Fifteen seconds*, I noticed the time he had left on the scoreboard. *Not Cameron*, I said as speaking to him directly. I supposed I was. We'd had our moments of reading each other's mind. Earlier when he suggested Cameron knew what was going on, what had he hoped to accomplish? Cameron had no part in all of this—never. I was convinced and had been since that moment I saw the fear of death in his face when he thought we would crash in the Bermuda Triangle.

With a few seconds remaining, I grew anxious, squirming in my seat, expecting his most audacious move yet.

Ferret soared up the wall, grabbed the end of his board, and when his body curled, I realized his intention. By the second I grew tensed, but the stadium grew excited to see him pull this off. More people rose to their feet, holding back blinks to savor every moment as Ferret came out of the flip and made— "A perfect 900!" the

273

announcer blasted over the speaker.

Perfect, it was, but I had all kinds of boos in me, watching him throw his arms up and began pumping his skateboard in the air. Proudly, I may add.

I stared at the scoreboard, waiting for his score to pop up and when it did— "Sixty-one! Sixty-one!" I was so furious, I pounded the bench. "*That's not fair, look at the score,*" I hunched over to grab everyone's attention. "How can they do that? He did everything Cam did."

"Yeah, but it's only a one-point difference, and CJ *was* a little wobbly on his landing," Ariana said. Then Stephanie, "I don't know how they figure the score, but CJ's landing wasn't as smooth as Ebay's. Sorry," she frowned. I looked at Cristina wearing a twisted face, pretty much staying out of it.

"He didn't fall so that shouldn't matter," I scoffed and resumed an upright position, groaning to myself: *That wasn't fair....*

The second round began, and to perk things up, Cristina suggested, "Let's play a guessing game: who can guess the skaters' score. And the one who guesses it exactly, or off by just *'one digit',*" she stressed, poking fun at me, "will win a buck. And you must pay up immediately. Hope you got a buck," she laughed, digging hers out of her pocket.

I chuckled. "Your one dollar will do. We probably will be passing the same dollar back and forth, anyway."

"Hey! I got an idea," Stephanie looked like it was a brilliant one too. "Whoever is holding the dollar when it's over, is the winner. And the losers chip in and buy the winner something. Like a pint of ice cream," she giggled.

"Yeah, I like that," we all liked Stephanie's idea, giggling.

Starting with the current skater, we were at it playing judges. We played all through the second round, with Cristina's dollar commuting from hand to hand, at times staying still when neither of us guessed the score. It was so much fun trying to predict the scores whether we hit the mark or not.

We pressed on into the third round playing the game. Three exact guesses, but overall, much of the same with the dollar, and, the skaters. Some got good scores; some, not so good.

Staying calm under pressure, if only there was a trick for that.

But the bright side to all this: the skaters had one more round to go, then it'd be all over, a thing of the past, something nice to look back on.

One more round.

So far so good, things were going well.

So far so good, things were going well—*until!*

Chapter Twenty-Eight

Lights go Out

"This is what pros are made of. *Look out, whoa, he stomps a 1080!*" the commentator blasted with historic flavor. And then suddenly "Aaahh...," he moaned with pity when the skater collapsed. The hearts of onlookers moaned too, moaned in waves when he broke down, precisely one second before time ran out.

"*What the hell...*" Stunned, I sat straight up. My bulging eyes couldn't believe what they were seeing. Because they (my eyes) had already analyzed this guy, saw straight through him and found him not human and as cold as steel.

But as it appeared, Winston, *yes Winston*, wasn't what I thought. Had I been wrong about him all along? I wondered as I looked down on him radiating excruciating pain while his skateboard mourned slowly to a complete stop.

It's his ankle, it's strained, and it's probably broken. How he fell was freaky, like his legs just turned to jelly causing them to buckle. He grabbed the tail of his white t-shirt and mopped sweat from his face. Then he squirmed, tried to push himself up, only to collapse. So much pain in the ankle, it probably was broken for real, I thought.

Help rushed to his side and eased him up. He draped both arms over the men shoulders and hopped on his good foot, trying to help himself along, but his helpers lifted him and carried him off.

"He finished the trick before he fell." The word circulating reached my ears. Then as if the entire audience blew through a sound barrier, they cheered the instant 135 burned on the scoreboard, moving him from fifth to first place. The crowd continued showering him with praise, a heartfelt moment indeed, as he made his exit, leaving an indelible mark on this event. Of which could still land him the gold medal if no one topped it.

A heartfelt moment, yes, but I was still in a state of confusion. *His body can break into pieces, and even feel pain?*

Not once, *not once* had it crossed my mind that he might actually be human. So if he wasn't like Ferret, how did he know him and where did he come from? *And Celine?* I looked over to where she was sitting, but she had already left. She, he, how did they hook up with Ferret? No one knew Winston when he first came on the scene; didn't know where he lived and still didn't know as far as I knew.

Celine was a different story, however. How she fit in this mysterious equation, finding out would be remarkable, like a goose laying a golden egg. As I marveled over that it hit me: What if they were like Ferret but in a different way? Could be they knew him in another life. If so, that could only be possible if they remembered their past lives. Yeah, I nodded without nodding. It was logical, made perfect sense, but was I right?

The next skater careened into the bowl as the third round continued. I took another glance at the scoreboard. The scores of the remaining players were 121, 118, 97, 84, 75, 73, and 69. Cameron followed Ferret in second place, leading him by three points. I drew a breath of the sight and sound of the atmosphere, held it just a second or two then freed it.

"Hey, I need to take a restroom break," I said.

"Yeah, me too," Stephanie replied, looked over at Cristina and Ariana. "Y'all need to go to the restroom?"

"Yeah, but I don't want to lose our seats." Cristina had a point. This place was jam-packed, and to have a seat was a commodity. "We'll just go when you get back," she decided.

Stephanie and I got up and made our way up the aisle and through the double doors. On the other side, I reached into my purse strapped over my shoulder for my phone. Checking messages, I saw that Miss Lambert, my publishing agent, had called. There was a message, and as I stood in line, waiting to use the restroom, I listened to her message, smiling. She wanted to move forward publishing the diaries. I whispered the news to Stephanie. "Really, that's great!" she said smiling like jumping up and down, wanting to know more but I didn't have more to offer, not until I called Miss Lambert back. Now wasn't the time. I had the mind to get back inside as soon as possible, in time for Ferret's performance hopefully.

Stephanie went in, then I. Shortly thereafter, we were back relieving Cristina and Ariana, right as the fourth round was beginning. Unfortunately, I'd missed Ferret's third run. According to the board, he had a winning run. His best score was now 129, eight points he'd gained.

The fourth round started out tense with the first skater vying to knock down the legendary figure Winston left hanging. He upped his game, stretching himself limitless no matter the risk, executing incredible flips and spins that the commentators themselves were in the zone, watching him annihilate the bowl and commenting: *He skates with such ferocity that you could compare his talent to superman....* Yeah. They were in the zone.

"That's probably a 55," Stephanie said reflexively.

"Yep," I nodded absently. At this point all of us were emotionally involved in what was going on below that we weren't really playing the game anymore.

The skater completed his last run moving him into third place, placing Cameron now in fourth. Of course fans gave him a well-deserved applause. It occurred to me that it didn't matter much to them who won. Because the best was the best was the best. In the end that's all that mattered. To them anyway, because it mattered to me. And to Sebastian. I looked over my shoulder to get a glimpse. He was anxious, yes; I really didn't have to see it to know it. Skateboarding was his DNA, so how could he not be?

I peeked at the scoreboard before Cameron dove into the bowl. Soon it would reveal the winner.

I was more nervous than ever and was feeling feverish with chills about my arms. I began rubbing the length from shoulders to elbows, hoping it was just nerves and not me getting sick again. Remembering I had a bottled water at my feet, I reached for it, opened it and took a long swallow.

The coolness streaming through my lips spread across my chest, cooling it. I put the bottle on my forehead for a moment, doing it wonders, but very little did it help my nervousness.

This was the climax, the do-or-die moment. How could I be anything but nervous?

Watching Cam perform, my tensed body bent forward, elbows digging in quads. *Whatever techniques he pulls out of the bag had better be spectacular—better than spectacular,* I thought. Fate landed him here, so he had to win. He couldn't let Sebastian down, nor let himself down—and now me, he couldn't let me down. And the ring, it couldn't, it shouldn't let him down either. Not now.

I covered my clenched fist, and the ring. *I don't care how he pulls this off, but he has to,* I said to the ring, wielding my belief that anything was possible.

"He's in defiant mode, hacking the bowl," the sports commentator said as Cameron soared upward like tackling a wave. So high, never had I seen him sail so high before. He grabbed the tail of the board, and like being at the tongue of the wave, his body curled so achingly beautiful. Now he was flipping....

I eased up shaking my clasped hands, rubbing the ring. *Come on, Babe...you can do it.*

He's flipping and flipping—and then finally! "*He comes out of a 1440 flip and lands a 540! Unbelievable! I've never seen this in the history of skateboarding...,*" the commentator blared ecstatically. The elated audience applauded in their most joyous moment ever as they too achingly awaited to see the score. Then it popped up, *165,* Cam had taken the lead! Suddenly it was like a pandemonium with doors flying off the hinges when the audience exploded anew with cheer.

It took a moment for things to die down, but it did, and the next competitor started his last run.

All the skaters were good, skating with flair and agility. But the three leading, Cameron, Winston, Ferret, it was safe to say that it was how the universe planned it. My only concern was what would happen next.

As I watched the contender perform his best, I settled back into the same monotone I was in at the beginning. *They're good, but not good enough, because they "are" up against sharks. The kind of sharks they never knew existed, therefore, would never see coming.* That being the truth, it's not their fault for losing. They would lose being the best of the best ever to share the bowl with sharks.

The seventh challenger finished his run; his final score of 98 moved him up to fifth place. The scores now looked like this: *165, 135, 121, 117, 98, 94, 92 and 91.* And next up was the deciding moment. I sat in a slightly forward lean, my palms fists pressed to the bench, wondering what Ferret was going to do. Would he swipe the gold medal from up under Cam's feet?

He came out with a confidence that no one could put a damper on. All that he could possibly want, he shall have. Feel it, and he could have it in the palm of his hand. Imagine it, and it would form in a blink of an eye. He had the power to do just about anything. The question was, how badly he wanted this moment to be his?

The other question, would something else play a part in the outcome?

I watched intently as he climbed to the height of the walls. At times riding the board across the rim at an amazing distant, flipping the board as he angled his body upside down. Always dipping back into the bowl and coming back up with more tricks. He was "annihilating the bowl" as the commentator described it. Once again he soared up a wall, reaching an insurmountable height above the rim. Many times—in this day alone—I'd seen it done, yet it never ceased to amaze me. But as time ticked down, I knew he was saving his best for last, and again I asked myself, what was he going to do? As time ticked away, this was it; in a matter of seconds, I would know.

I wiped away anxious perspiration from my forehead as he again homed in on the deepest wall. This time like a daredevil, as though the wall was wicked, and he was about to teach it a lesson. *Or teach someone a lesson,* I thought as tension rose like there was a daredevil inside of me. So eager to see what's it going to be that my insides could explode.

But it wasn't all me. On-the-edge-of-your-seat tension and excitement intoxicated the air. We all drunk in it, watching as he conquered the bowl every which way (all the same for all skater, yet never a dull moment). For only a quick moment, he then thrust himself into a whopping downward spin, like a skater spinning on ice. So dizzily incredible, never had I seen it done in so many rotations before.

"He's a technical wizard...," the broadcaster said with such exuberance I could tell he expected Ferret to nail the landing. Because after all, what could go wrong, right? But...but the hype of the moment—incredibly—came to a crashing halt when Ferret somehow lost his footing and the skateboard popped up.

"Whoa," I hopped up. Looking like a panicky chipmunk biting my nails, I stared at the scoreboard. *Come on, come on...let it be....* And when *164* lit up, I was in a heart-stopping panic—I mean, my breathing began quivering that it might have stopped on the spot. Because I was choked up, paralyzed by a joy so enormous that when it broke through I went, "Aaaaaaahhhh. He did it! He did it!"

Jumping up and down, I grabbed Stephanie, hugged her. "He did it! He did it! And he did it by *one measly point,*" I said to the girls and gave each of them a high-five. He did it, and the best thing of all, it was finally over. Finally over!

As it was time to present the winners, the bravo calmed down. I was excited rubbing my arms as if warming away chills, only it wasn't chills I felt, but like something pricking at them. Lightheaded, I was starting to feel, too. *Not now,* I hoped I wasn't getting sick again. But as seconds flashed by, clearly something was wrong.

The sound of everything around me was going up and down as if in my head was a volume switch and somebody playing with it. Stephanie touched my arm, saying something to me but I couldn't understand with her voice going in and out. "Are you okay?" I heard her say but barely.

"No, no...something is seriously wrong," I said,

mopping away fresh sweat from my face with the back of my hand. "Something's...wrong..."

All sound faded away, the lights went out, and his voice chimed, "Time's up."

Chapter Twenty-Nine
Bypass Death

I breathed echoes of distinct voices in a dark place as the words *Time's* Up lay awake in my subconscious. I was sick, having another one of those weird dreams, I thought, and then I remembered.

"Ugh, where am I?" I fought the lethargy weighing on my eyes, but I managed to open them.

Covered in white linen, I lay flat on my back, my head propped slightly. Rails guarded me. My eyes shifted across the pale wall. To my right was a window hung with palish drapes. I obviously was in the hospital. I tried to lift myself up, and realized my arm taped to a tube running clear fluid in my vein, and even if I wanted to, I was too weak and feverish to do anything.

I turned, sensing someone about to enter the room, and saw squiggly lines, green and yellow, moving on a machine next to me. A heart monitor, I minded.

"Hey." Cameron entered. At once he picked up a

white cloth, dipped it in a pan of water on the stand next to me, and squeezed it out. "We gotta keep you cool, you're running a fever." He touched the cool cloth to my forehead, as he continued, dabbed it so lovingly over my cheeks, my neck.

"Why...what's wrong with me?"

"A virus or something. They're trying to figure it out."

"How long have I been here?" My voice weak and shallow.

"For about three hours now. You passed out. A good thing the man sitting behind you caught you. So your pretty little head didn't hit the floor. Stephanie already called your parents, so they'll be here soon," he smiled caring eyes down on me.

I nodded, "Where is Stephanie now?"

"They're all here. They just went down to get something to eat."

"Cam...I'm so sorry...sorry for spoiling your moment."

"Shhh. That's over. You are what's important."

I smiled hazily into his eyes. "You did it. You're a gold medalist. But where is it? Why aren't you wearing—?" I gasped.

"Just take it easy," he said, and patted my face some more with the towel. "I'm not wearing it because I gave it to Sebastian. I put it around his neck because he deserved it more. When I said I was doing it for him, I meant it."

"It was a miracle..." My throat tickled, and I coughed. "I'm just so glad things worked out the way it did."

"Yeah...but it won't take a miracle for you to get better. The doctors will figure out what's going on with you. And you'll be up and out of here in no time," he said. But I saw in his eyes, heard in his voice, how worried he was. He kissed the top of my head, brushed fingers across my cheek. "You're going to be fine."

I closed my tired eyes and tears welled up. I didn't know why, I didn't want to think about it, and yet I was afraid...afraid and ready for what it may be. Above all, I was thankful for Cam there next to me, safe and sound. Thankful for the miracle that'd come through for Sebastian. Nothing else could please me more.

Time's up. His voice again scrolled through my mind.

When? Now? Show me what it means.

My eyes opened as I released a sigh of desperation. I looked upon Cam's face, strained with pity and hope. "It's...it's not a coincidence I'm sick." I coughed, sniffled. "I think you know that."

"I know what you're thinking but don't... You will get better."

"We won't have any peace until it's over. Until that time comes. And according to him it's here. He said to me, time...is...up." I grew quiet, giving the words time to sink in.

"When did he say this?"

"Right before I blacked out, I heard his voice."

"Pia listen—" He became suddenly startled when Ferret appeared out of nowhere at the foot of my bed. "*What in the hell are you doing here?*" Cam said to him.

"Now really? Must you ask?" Ferret gave him a firm, conniving look.

"Oh, I see. You're still trying to brainwash Pia into thinking I'm in cahoots with you. But it'll never work...Old Nicky."

Ferret chortled. "You can't bring yourself to face what's right in front of you."

"And what might that be?" Cameron glowered at him, as Ferret glowered back. They were having a face-off glowering at each other, while I waited patiently to hear something I didn't know already. "Just what I thought, nothing," Cameron said finally. "You don't have legitimate business here. I mean, you have no business trying to reclaim unrequited love. So why don't you do all of us a favor and just get lost—and for good this time?" Cam ordered. And when Ferret didn't budge he said, "Fine, I'll get security."

"No, Cam, wait!" I raised my head and my heart raced out of my chest it seemed. At once my head collapsed back down on the pillow. I sputtered as I spoke, "I wish it was that simple, but we both know it won't do any good. It's time, Cam. It's time," I reminded him. I reached out my hand, and he took it with both his. His face drenched with a kind of pain I'd never seen on him before. "It's my fate. Our fate. It's time we face it...together," I panted, trying to catch my breath.

He bent closer, kissed my head, and then whispered in my ear, "Remember what I said about the ring. Because it's the only power we have against him. You have to trust...and believe." He looked me in the eyes, nodding, "Okay?"

I reciprocated a nod.

Cameron phone then went off. He quickly removed it from his pocket. "Sebastian, he's calling to check on you." Cameron answered and began updating him on my condition, smiled at me as he did. "Sebastian sends his love, said hang in there." He then removed the phone from his ear. "I gotta step out for a minute. I won't be long, and I'll be just outside the door." But when he turned to Ferret, I could see he was having second thoughts.

"It'll be fine, I'm not going anywhere. Isn't that right?" I looked for Ferret to respond.

"Yeah, sure," Ferret said dully. He then stepped over to the window and looked out. Cameron kissed my lips then left the room.

Now that we were alone, I had to know about the ring. Whether it had the kind of power Cameron believed it had. So I asked, "Was it your plan all alone, to let him win?"

"Mm, I see you lack confidence...even doubt all what he believes in," he said looking out the window still. And when I didn't respond, he looked over his shoulder. "Hm?"

"That's not the point."

"Then what is? What would I have to gain by letting him win?"

I thought about it, but of course, I didn't see the point. "How should I know? None of it makes sense to me, but to you...."

Our eyes locked for a measureless moment, and I grew amused, disappointingly so. Because looking into his eyes didn't give me the satisfaction of reading his mind, just this once, that I scoffed and gave up.

Despite my condition, a relaxing sensation came over me. I closed my eyes to it and it felt as though I was floating in the wind. Then the eyes in my head opened and there I saw a dove, a peculiar one, because it was half black, half white. The breath of its wings full and it was just sailing. Wings not flapping, just sailing...

Sailing, by its lonesome...sailing.

Sailing, sailing...the sky so beautifully dim...it's sailing into the sunset.

Sailing, ever so peacefully...no wings flapping...just sailing...far...and forever....

"Not now."

"Hah?" I opened my eyes and Ferret's standing over me.

"You dozed off," he said.

I grunted softly. "Didn't I hear you say something?"

"I wish it hadn't come to this." He avoided the question intentionally, I thought.

"What exactly...do you mean?" Did he mean it was time for me to die, I wondered. I'd been wondering about that ever since that day.

"I have a confession. About our mishap earlier."

"Okay." I felt around for the remote. "I want to lift my head up some. Do you—"

"I got it over here." He lifted it from the side of the bed, pressed the button. My head rose as Cameron reentered the room.

"Your confession, go on," I glanced up at Ferret on my right, then at Cameron on my left.

"I crossed the line with you, today. When I provoke you into fighting me—I shouldn't have done that. I was wrong," he said, talking to Cam. "I did it because I wanted to do all I could to help you remember. I thought if I put someone you cared about in a life-threatening situation, it would force you to remember. That's all it was, and I apologize. No harm done, and I assure you it won't happen again."

"I wondered if it was more to it than that. I mean, like something else was going on, like another force, present. But you would know if there was...," I implied, wanting him to elaborate. But he didn't, not how I intended, anyway.

"I wish it had been more: you, remembering something vital. Unfortunately, that didn't happen," he said.

"Yeah, if you say so," Cameron brooded openly.

"I'm sick. I've been sick off and on for days now. And I'm not better but worse—*look at me.* The doctors, they don't seem to know what's wrong with me." In a roundabout way I was asking him the question. Asking him the question that'd been in my head for days. No, not just that question, but the question of all questions I had long awaited the answer, and now, it was time....

Ferret nodded, "Yeah. It's time."

"*Time to fix her? Make her well?* You're indebted to making her better if nothing else and you—"

"Cam please! Well? I will get better, right?" I feebly asked for myself.

He put on a concerning expression. "I assure you that this will pass, and all will be forgotten. But can I change things, make you better? If only I could.... Right now, it's up to you; it's all in your hands what happens next."

"In my hands?" I repeated him. "I wonder...had I not come back to Florida, had I gone anywhere else,

291

would things be different?"

He dropped his head, looked away.

"Is that a no—I will never know—what?" I demanded.

"It's fate, Pia," he sounded. "No matter what you do or where you are, there's no avoiding fate."

"Then what is her fate, huh? Because the way I see it, we will always be together no matter what." The pain in his voice, the sorrow on his face, said it all, whether he believed in his heart that to be true or not. "She hasn't remembered anything. So why are you even here? Just, just do what you came here for and then leave!" Cameron said in a raised voice.

"*Cam, everyone on the floor can hear you.*" My tone, much weaker now.

"No need to worry. No one can disturb us; we can't disturb anybody," said Ferret.

"Yeah, right!" Cameron was even more pumped up, moving around as he was in disarray. "Will you just get on with it? Tell her what she needs to know so we can get on with our lives—without you in it!"

Ferret looked at me now, too long wearing a regretful expression.

"Tell me! Tell me what's wrong with me. I've been sick for days now. And it started the day I met you at the waterfront. I thought I might get better but no—and you said you can't heal me. So stop with the suspense."

"Just you take an easy," Ferret said as I caught my breath, and as Cameron wiped my face with a cool towel. Ferret's expression grew even more regretful, and I knew it was time to address the elephant in the room, Death.

Death.

Death!

"It's time you be totally honest with me. And don't think I can't take it because I can. So, tell me. Am...I dying?"

He dropped his head, nodded, "Yes, but—"

"You think I'm gonna stand here and let—"

"Cam!" I broke.

What was he thinking!

Chapter Thirty

Weeping Memories

He lashed out at Ferret!

In quick action Ferret raised his hand, shifted Cameron across the floor, outside the door and pinned him up on the wall. The way he did it, like moving an object across a computer screen with your fingertip. Like moving a piece of paper across a wall then tacking it in place. Like a monster sending him to a cornfield—at any moment just for the hell of it—if, he wanted to.

"Sorry, pal, but you have no say in this. I must do what I was sent here to do and there's nothing you or I can do to change it. You want to try to defeat me?" Ferret said to Cameron shimming against the wall trying to break loose, his facial muscles plumping like a mad Incredible Hulk.

"Please, stop. Cam, babe...it's no use making the situation worse."

"You're loving this—just look at that smug look on your face. If you can't have her then no one can—isn't that it? *You piece a shit.* You can't stand to see me win," Cameron griped miserably.

"I lost the gold medal to you. Oh, but that's different, huh?"

"You're so full of it. I guess that's what Pia—*oh wait—Perseaus*, loved about you *so much* that she—"

"*Enough!*" his voice shattered, and for a moment, no one, not even Cam, said a thing.

"Now, as I was about to say, there's a way to bypass that...a more favorable way out, if you will." Ferret turned to me, "But it's all up to you what course you choose to take."

I sat gaping. *Whether I died or not was up to me,* I dreaded what I may have to sacrifice.

"Now, like I said before, there's nothing you can do to change things here. It's in her hands, her choice to make. You think you can handle that? Or should I slam the door on you now?" Ferret's ultimatum perfectly clear.

Cameron's angered face softened. "Yeah, okay. Depends on the ultimatum," he said. Ferret took that as a yes and Cameron dropped to the floor. "Let's hear this other alternative you're talking about," Cameron said, re-entering the room.

"Yes, I'm curious," I consented as my heart raced impatiently. And as every breath in me and the soul in me heaved across very thin ice. And the thought of falling through and dying, dying at such a youthful age—my god I hadn't begun to live yet. I should have a full life to look forward to that how could I begin to understand and accept anything else?

"Why do I have to choose anything other than to be healthy and live a full life...happily ever after?" I said—

pleaded. I got lost in Cameron's eyes when he took my hand, and as we shared a special moment of what "happily ever after" meant to us. Thinking back to our prom day, this wasn't how we intended our life to be. The question still, why...why had it come to this?

"Because." Ferret began pacing the floor. "Because some things can't be changed. And because, had you remembered, maybe you wouldn't want to."

"What do you mean by that?" I asked.

"What I mean is that maybe, just maybe you would have decided to go back with me. But that's off the table; you don't have that choice."

"And that's a good thing because no way in hell would she agree to that, anyway." Cameron growled looking like he could bite his head off.

"Wait. You mean to tell me all this time you wanted me to remember was so...," I paused catching my breath, "was so you can take me back to Massouvia?"

"No. Not exactly. I wanted you to remember how you left things. If you'd remembered, if you remember now, you would understand everything."

"And yet, I don't understand. And you promised that I would, so..."

He nodded, then began. "You didn't leave Massouvia in good standing. I wasn't the only one who loved you, Perseaus, we all did; me, your friends, we didn't want to see you go. We wanted you to stay. So much so that you felt pressured by us trying to convince you to stay that you grew in rage and fired back. And the things you said...were so harsh, hurtful. So humiliating...you tore my soul apart."

"I-I...I can't imagine being this horrible person.

To you, to anyone, I can't imagine..."

"Neither could I; you took me by surprise. The things you said, and did...I don't know...," he dropped his slightly shaking head, exhaled. "I don't know what came over you. And now, for that reason, you can't go back. Not this way. Not unless you remember everything. And I mean everything. Not just remember how you left things but remember how our world functions, remember our way of life."

"You said 'I can't go back, not this way.' What did you mean by that?"

"What I mean is that I can't take you back. It means, that under the circumstances, I don't have the authority."

The room grew quiet, taking a moment to think and breathe and digest so to remain stable and not croak in the interim. An exaggeration, I knew, but dying was no joke. The room alone suddenly felt like a chamber, slowly smothering the life out of me.

"I need some water," I said to Cameron. Gazing into his eyes, as he poured water in a cup, I knew he wondered about the awful things I had said and done. And how could I blame him? I wondered the same thing myself. Had I been under so much pressure that it drove me to hurt someone I supposedly cared for? He'd revealed to me why I wanted to leave, and it seemed to me a good enough reason. Unless I was missing something, and that something, I wondered was it part of the reason I had to remember.

"I'm sorry. For whatever I did and said, I'm sorry. I don't know why I hurt you or anyone else, why I said the things that I said, but, I'm so, so sorry. I don't know

297

what came over me. Literally, I don't. But I wish...." I closed my eyes teary eyes, wiped away the tears. "I can't imagine the person I was then. Maybe it's why I can't remember."

Cameron snatched up a napkin and took over wiping away my tears. "Listen to me. It's okay. The why, the what—it doesn't matter because that was a lifetime ago. *A lifetime ago, you hear me.* And how can you fault yourself for doing what was in your heart? Don't you see?" He placed my hand on his beating chest. "The decision you made then brought you to me." His sincere, loving expression smiled down on me and mingled with my unspoken expression of *Yes, Yes.*

Ferret moved closer. "He's right. You were in your right to make that call. But Pia, in those last moments, you struggled with that decision, that it was killing you inside. You longed in such pain and regret. You were already missing the one thing you were leaving behind.

"The problem was that you wanted the best of both worlds. But that couldn't be. You crossed the threshold, into the birthing chamber then turned to me one last time. It should've been a happy moment. But I could see, every ounce of your soul quaking in sadness—and in pain, grief, regret. It's that moment I wish that you could remember. Because, even then you couldn't bring yourself to change what would be (was) irreversible. And when the door came down, slowly splitting us apart, it was then...too late. Too late for you...too late for us."

Choked up with emotions, pushing back tears, he turned and stepped away. His sentiments caught me by surprise as he went on. "And so, here we are, because something went wrong during the transition. We don't know for sure what caused the malfunction. But things do happen from time to time, affecting people in different ways. Some cases more severe than others. Usually affects the mind. Your case is different, rare," he said pacing. "No one seems to recall having a case like this before."

"But her life was normal until that night she went missing," Cameron reminded him. "You must have some idea what went wrong?"

I gazed at him, waiting to hear the answer.

"Yeah. I have an idea. Since birth, the defect laid dormant. But why it became active when it did, the night you went missing, I'm not sure. What caused the malfunction in the first place, I believe it had something to do with the emotional state you were in at the time, Perseaus. You were torn between two worlds, the one you were entering, and the one you were leaving; that somehow during the transition it affected your human DNA. In other words, you transitioned into this world bearing traces of Massouvia's DNA.

"Love is a powerful thing. And deep down, you couldn't stand the fact that you were leaving me," he added. But that didn't sit well with Cameron.

"But none of that matters now. Because that's the one thing you can't change and we both know it," Cameron denounced whatever Ferret's attentions were, as my sentiments for him grew. No matter the current situation, I'd once loved him; this I felt.

I felt it as I'd listened to him described our final moments together. It felt as though I was living it all over again, like my knowing it really did happen. Me weeping profusely on the inside, not so much on the outside, for I had made my decision and needed to stand strong—I could feel it, feel it as it was really happening. That moment in the birthing chamber, I could almost see it, feel myself inside it, as if I remembered it for real. Moment by moment, watching as the door came down, shutting of us apart. And when there was no more room for the door to shut, only then had I allowed my emotions to explode. By then it had been too late.

When the door came down, it was too late.

"How do we even know this is true?" Cameron's skepticism continued.

"And you think it's not?" Ferret hit back with a question.

Cameron scoffed him, turned to me then placed an open hand on my forehead. "Your forehead feels cool now. And you're looking much better. How do you feel?"

"B-better," I said, surprised myself that I was. But I was dying, and I had an alternative to dying. "I am feeling better now. Is there a chance...?" I hoped. For the love of god, I hoped.

But he shook his head. "I'm sorry. Nothing has changed. You're in the final stage, which means, time is near."

"Tell me about this alternative I have," I said.

"I can make it all go away. As if none of this ever happened." He gazed at me with raised eyebrows

I put on a sidelong expression, gazing back at him.

"That's right. But what that means is that you will remember absolutely nothing. What that means is that you will go on living life as Pia Wade, but only it'll be in a different timeline. Your life, how you know it now in the

300

here and now, will be as it never existed, happened. That's because you'll have no memory of it. All your memories will be in the new timeline.

"All the years of suffering, the visions, the nightmares, back to the day it all began, including the night you went missing, will never have happened. Your new life...will be the same, somewhat, but different. It would be how it would've been had none of this ever happened. You will still have your parents; you were born to them so that won't change. What you experience growing up, absent that night you went missing, will be different in ways. Naturally, because, the chain reactions stemming from that night would never have happened."

"So...so many times I wished it would all just—poof—disappear. That I would wake up from this nightmare, and, not remember it. For so long I wished for what you're offering me now. But, now, I-I... So, what about Cameron? Will he remember any of this? Will I remember him?" I asked, but I already knew.

"I'm sorry, but no. There will be no recollection of this timeline or that it ever existed. That's essential for this to work. It's how it should be. Just think about it."

"I'm thinking about it and I say no. No, no, no," Cam chimed in. "Either way I'd lose her and everything that we have together. Don't you see? I cannot lose her—I won't." He then got up, "Damn you! You think I don't know what this is? *If you can't have her, no one can.*"

"You're wrong! This isn't about me, nor is it about you!" said Ferret.

"Look, I think we should take our chances on this. We can't be sure about anything he's saying. What if it's a hoax? What if...it's all an illusion, not real, that time will only tell, only if we give it time?"

"I-I...I just don't know." I was more confused, at the same time, wanted to open my mind up to the possibility, but I couldn't see how to do that.

"If I leave this situation as it is now, I assure you, within 24 hours, she'd be dead. Do you really want to put her life in your hands?" said Ferret.

"What do you say, Pia, give it time? Let our faith in fate work this out? I don't want to lose you. I worship the day this insanity brought us together."

"Why now? Why did you wait until now to fix this? Obviously, that first night you realized something wrong, you could have fixed things then. So why?" I cried.

"Because. Because it was the only way for you to redeem yourself...to come back to...home. Because had you remembered you would have understood without question." His emotion was raw, understood, but it didn't matter.

"You were just being selfish! Thinking of no one but yourself!"

"Cam, whatever you want me to do I'll do it. I'll do it, you hear me." By now I was so angry and confused I wanted to put all my trust in him. I couldn't do it on my own, no more than I could bear the thought of losing him, and, the thought of dying.

Cameron turned away, deliriously scoured his hands over his face then clawed them over his head like pulling his hair out. He then let out a maddening howl, swagged over to the doorframe and collapsed his forehead in his arm against it. He didn't know what to do with himself or about this situation. But I waited patiently just the same, emotionally distraught myself faced with the fact that life would never be the same without him in it. Not the same because, we may never meet again—and if we did, we wouldn't have this, our special bond and what we shared together...once upon a timeline ago we would never know existed.

Cameron returned to my bedside pushing through choking emotions to speak, shedding tears. Pushing through emotions myself, "Please, will you give us a moment," I said to Ferret.

He nodded then walked out of the room.

I looked at Cam. Barely could I look him in the eyes with all the pain and sorrow. "I'm so sorry. You were right. I shouldn't have come back. I should've gone to Harvard—anywhere but here. Things wouldn't be as it is now. I believe this in all my heart, I don't care what he said. I put us in this mess, it's all my fault!" I said through dreadful eyes gushing with tears.

"No-no, stop. You're not to blame. And this isn't the end. This can't be the end. This can't be how it was meant to be. We found each other for a reason, and that reason was meant to last for a very long time, not to be cut short like this. You believe that don't you? Tell me you do and mean it."

"Yes, of course I do. I do, I do." What else could I say? And how could I not believe it? It's what I wanted to believe.

He placed a hand over my forehead. "You're burning up!" He got the towel out of the pale, wrung it out then began dabbing it all over my forehead.

"I can't do it, put your life in my hands. It would be wrong. It has to be your decision. Whatever you decide...I'll understand. Death is final. With death, we wouldn't have a chance at all." He nodded, "You hear me?"

He then moved the towel down to my neck, cooling and freshening me up there, and then continued. "But fate, I won't—I can't—give up on it. Because right now, my love, it's all we got. And if we don't give up on fate, it won't give up on us. You know what I mean?"

I looked at him believingly, and whispered, "Yes."

He took my hand, lifted it, and nudged the ring with his chin. "This is our fate. Our fate is in the ring." He then brought the ring to his lips and kissed it. His brows arched, *"But you have to believe, truly believe...nothing hinders the power of faith, especially now when we need it the most. I know this, Pia. And I want you to know it too. There's power in the ring. Don't worry, because from this moment on, I won't be. It will come through for us, I know...I know. In all the universe, I will, I shall hold the power vested in us...."*

The way he spoke, lyrical and hypnotic, as if he himself was becoming the ring, that I thought I felt it happening. The notion I should give his mother's ring back, wiped from my mind. No matter what, I had to wear it; he'd before made that clear. Whether I had any doubts then, surely, I didn't now.

Ferret re-entered moments later. "I hope I've given you enough time. Either way, it's time."

Gazing at me, Cameron nodded. He then lowered his lips to my ear, whispered, "There's always a pot of gold at the end of the rainbow. It's where we will find each other again. With the ring, Pia, we'll be again. You must believe. Say it, say that you believe," he wept softly, so close that his tears mingled with mine. A steady stream of our tears stained the pillow.

I held the back of his head, like holding a precious baby, always wanting to protect it, never wanting to let it go. "Yes, yes, I believe. I shall hold my memory of you, in my heart, to the end of time," I uttered tenderly, kissed him. "I believe."

"Will you allow me to do this now?" Ferret suggested softly.

Cameron sniffled as his head lifted from my embrace.

"I think so," I nodded, looking into Cam's eyes. He brushed my cheek and returned the nod.

Ferret approached my side. "May I?" he requested permission to take my hand. I handed him my right hand, and he wrapped it with both of his. Cameron scooted the chair back as he stood. He leaned over me, holding my other hand against his heart.

I lowered my head, staring at my body beneath the white sheet. "So...this is it. All that time...and this, this is what it has come to..." I trailed off, took a deep breath. Then I looked up at him. "But you haven't told me what really happened that night that brought us to this moment."

He tightened his lips, looked at me as if wondering if he should. "If I told you, you wouldn't believe me."

I scoffed, "You think? At this point I would believe anything."

"You came back to me, to Massouvia," he said, and I looked at him startled. "See? I told you you wouldn't believe me. You came all that way, and even then, you didn't remember a thing: where you were, and how you got there. The people who found you on the beach, Beth and Jason, they made sure you got back safely."

"B-but—"

"How?" He jumped in, knowing my mind. "Massouvia's DNA, all this time since birth, rooted inside of you. But not for much longer, my dear. No more questions; nothing else matters. It's over now...all over..."

I turned and locked eyes with Cameron, one last time. He had said he saw the visions only when I was around, and now, I understood why. "I love you," I sobbed.

"I love you more," he sobbed back.

For an enduring moment, we stared into each other's eyes, as if we were the only two people in the room, transfixed in an aura of *I love you.* Our eyes glutted with burning tears streaming down our cheeks, permeating them with everlasting stains. How unfair, the mere notion we'd never remember our lives together, remember us in this moment. Unfair indeed, but our souls had a mission now, and that mission was to search, find, and bring us together again. *And with love on the journey, how could we not? Nothing's stronger than love...,* I cried out thinking this.

Cameron held my face with both hands, "Believe in fate." He then lifted my hand, kissed the ring. "Fate."

Yes, yes, I nodded.

"Close your eyes now. Relax and think pleasant thoughts," Ferret voiced softly.

My eyes blinked intermittently, wanting to see Cam's face just one more time, again and again. Until finally, they relaxed and blinked no more. But my mind's eyes, they were wide-open, still looking into his dark brown eyes, conflicted with hope and despair.

I love you. I will always love you, Pia.

I love you, Perseaus. Always have, always will. Now you can have the life you always wanted, my love. Live it to the fullest. Until we meet again....

I love you...

I love you...

Their voices became soft echoes drifting in space...drifting...drifting.

I love you, too, forever...

Epilogue
Storm

Late September, 4 years later

The sky was dark like the end of the world. The rain was torrential, the thunder was fierce, and the wind was howling. And the black sky was ablaze with lightning.

The storm moved in about 9:30 and, according to the weatherman, was to last all day long and late into the night. But that wasn't the original forecast. Today was supposed to be perfect, full of sunshine. The storm formed without warning, catching the city off guard, including the meteorologists. I knew they had to have been scratching their heads wondering where it came from. And probably still was.

And scratching their heads wondering how it could be clearing up so fast. At the window looking up at the sky, I watched black clouds turn gray, then turn white, soon revealing patches of blue sky, all while the pouring rain came to a drizzle. In a matter of fifteen minutes, the rain stopped completely.

I grabbed my keys off the sofa and headed out the door. Didn't have a clue where I was going. But couldn't resist the urge to get out and be somewhere other than here. The power was out in my neighborhood. Had been for hours. I took a deep breath of the damp, earthy scented air, wondering about the extent of the outage. I looked up and down the street. Garbage cans, tree limbs were scattered everywhere. I would dodge a few leaving the subdivision.

The storm wreaked havoc everywhere with snapped trees and downed power lines. All kinds of things littered the city: sombreros, shoes, table awnings, more trash bins. Broken windows here and there, due to flying debris, lightning strikes, I assumed. Street flooding in some places. Some impassable. But no severe damage for what I could see; the down power lines were the worst of the storm's damage.

Not one measly cloud in sky when the storm hit. The storm formed fast and hit hard. No one, not even the meteorologists, saw it coming. I just couldn't get that out of my mind. I searched the east sky toward the ocean looking for the storm. No sign of it whatsoever, but, there was a rainbow. A rare, unusual one, I was drawn to it instantly.

In no time I was at the boardwalk. I parked behind it on a street, got out. *Four-thirty.* After checking the time, I stuffed the cellphone in my shirt pocket, and the keys in my pants. As I moved closer to the ocean, I couldn't shake this strange feeling. Maybe because how the storm appeared out of nowhere had me in a loop. That had to be it because nothing was different. Except for the rainbow it left behind. A multi-rainbow, so well formed, and it was huge. Never had I ever seen anything like it. Out of this world what it was. An unusual sight to see.

There were more people than I'd expected on the boardwalk. Like me, I supposed they all had come to see the rainbow. Everyone had their cellphones out snapping pictures. I removed mine, began taking pictures myself.

And when I thought I had gotten enough, I put the phone away and continued gazing at it. For a long while, I couldn't take my eyes off it. It was the most fascinating thing, the arcs, and the colossal bold colors, unfading as time went by. If only my mind could reach it; it drifted over the water, thinking about the good times and the bad times...my long-lost parents, and something magical happening. I missed them dearly. Life hadn't been the same without them. *If magic took them away, then magic could bring them back and....* I could get myself in trouble thinking like that, so I stopped.

I looked over my shoulder, noticed two girls nearby. Pretty girls, wearing flip-flops and shorts, they weren't there a moment ago. I recognized one of them but didn't know her name. The other one (she noticed me looking at her and smiled), had to be new to the area; I hadn't seen her around before. I smiled back as I looked the area over.

Moments later she said something to the other girl. The other girl looked in my direction and turned her nose up at me. I knew what that was all about; she was in that clique who despised me, thought I was a demon. It didn't matter what they thought, sometimes. Like today, like at this very moment, her turning up her nose at me wouldn't discourage me. Because what I was about to do wasn't what I would normally do, and for the life in me, I didn't know why. No more than I had a sudden desire to do so, and that my nerves were building up fast to get me moving because, it was now or never; she was getting away. I walked up behind her:

"Leaving so soon?" I said.

"Um...you talking to me?"

"Yeah. Just thought I would say hi. I don't think I've ever seen you around here before." I then put on a smile when her brown eyes sparkled.

Things were falling into place, the stars lining up. Something magical was truly happening, I could feel it. Something I would never dreamed of, not in a million years. Soon, I would understand why.

"Come on, we better get going," her friend said with urgency.

"Hey, what's your name?" I asked before she was whisked off.

"Pia," she said.

"Pia? What a coincidence. My mom's name was Pia." I was just thinking about her when I saw you, I thought. I looked off at the rainbow, "Some rainbow, huh?"

"Yeah, it is," she smiled.

"Will you come on," the other girl pressured her. Let's put some distance between us and him, she meant.

"Okay, in a minute. I didn't get your name," she said to me now.

"Cameron. But most people..." I broke as images of her flashed in my head. I shook my head, then said, "Sorry about that. But most people call me CJ."

"Well, it was nice meeting you, Cameron," she

311

hesitated saying, wearing a curious expression now.

"Yeah, same here."

She turned and walked away. They stopped in front of a shop for a little window-shopping. She glanced back at me, still that curious look on her face.

More images of her, of us this time, flashed in my head. I had never met this girl. So why was she in my head? Was I starting to hallucinate again? If so, it was different this time, not as freaky as before, though I was freaked out enough.

But the hallucination was too different. It was more like memories. Of us holding hands on the beach, of us at this skatepark I frequented, of us on some exotic island. Even images of us at a prom (she...so beautiful)— the images kept coming, exploding in my head. That it seemed I was becoming another person in a life I knew nothing about.

She was on the move again. I didn't know what to do but knew I had to do something.

"Wait, it's me, Cameron," I said. Foolish and gullible, and an insane thing to say to someone who didn't know you from thou.

She gave me a quick, angelic glance as she brushed hair out of her face and again, turned away.

Trancelike, I gazed after her. She didn't hear me—of course, she didn't. And how could she? I spoke the words but barely gave voice to them. Unless her hearing was laser-sharp, she couldn't have heard me.

It was a foolish attempt, because by now, I wasn't convinced of anything. Meaning, not yet could I claim the memories as my own. The images continued flooding my mind and it was starting to feel real, like it all really happened. So real, I felt I loved her, couldn't live without her, and couldn't let her go to save my soul. Then suddenly, it hit me, like the missing link I needed to put it all together that I hollered at the top of my lungs, "Pia! Pia! Wait, it's me, Cameron," making sure she heard me this time.

She quickly turned around, looking like "what the hell's going on?"

I ran to catch up to her, smiling of the huge breakthrough. As I approached, I repeated, "It's me, Cameron! Look, I know that doesn't mean a thing to you, and it sounds crazy. But I know, I know it'll all come back to you the way it did me."

"I can't believe it! You just met her and already you're going crazy on her. Come on, Pia, let's get out of here. I'm telling you he has a screw loose."

"Okay, but wait a minute," Pia waved her off while squaring me dead in the eyes. "Why do you think I know you?" she asked at the same time I said, "I know how this seems."

"Yeah, so what is this?" She glared, looking like "this better be damn good."

I knew Pia, knew how determined she could be. Was she determined now? And to what extent? How much of me would she put up with in this moment? With what little time I had, I had to be somehow convincing. All I had was the truth, and it was insane. But to not speak that truth...I had no other alternative but trust my gut. Trust the time I had in this moment to help me out because my god, we were halfway there.

"I don't know how to tell you this. I was standing over there all this time, thought I was losing my mind about this, but it's true."

"What?"

"That we were close once. Wait, before you say anything, let me ask you this. Do you believe you could have lived in another lifetime?"

"Well, yeah, but—"

"Okay hold that thought! Just listen to what I have to say and see if it comes back to you," I said kindly, and in a most sincere way. She opened her mouth to say something, but I charged on.

"*You're Pia Wade* from Texas. Your birthday is July 7. We met for the first time, right here, on the boardwalk..."

As I began sharing our history, Stephanie moved over to a nearby bench and sat. *What! Stephanie not putting her two cents in Pia's business?* I thought.

Miraculous how things were converging, like Moses parting the red sea, I knew right then Pia wouldn't be too quick to run off. The rainbow was a sign too: signifying timelines converging. It was fading now; at any moment it would disappear. I told her about us, about the island, though for now I left out the horrific details. I went on to telling her about how I, with the help of her parents, surprised her on the day of her senior prom.

"...You were so blown away when I stepped out of the limo. You were so happy—it was the happiest I had ever seen you, Pia. The dust settled perfectly for us that day, considering all we had been through. That time was precious. It was going to be our happily-ever-after from that moment on. Our happily-ever-after...." I trailed off, seeing the look in her face.

It was happening, the images bombarding her

mind—and like me, she thought she was losing it. She closed her eyes, rubbing her forehead as to rub away a sudden headache. But as it did with me, it would past. I wanted to tell her that but thought better not to.

For a moment she looked at me confused and in awe, about to say something but was overcome with even more fascination. Wondering what was being revealed to her at this moment, I looked at her in the same expression...in awe. Still disinclined to speak, I knew soon she would get "the kicker."

The kicker, that one thing that would collect all the pieces, and put them all in place.

That one thing that would have her understand where it's all coming from—and trust it and believe it.

That one thing that would ultimately...make her remember.

The kicker for me...seeing the moment I gave her my mother's ring. What might it be for her, I wondered, knowing that in that moment she would enter my heart all over again.

Then finally, her eyes ogling with a stunning glow, she said, "Cam."

A bonus for book clubs

Discussion Questions

1. What is the first thing that comes to mind after reading the last page of Perseaus? How does the story make you feel?

2. Preceding the opening of the story, Pia decides not to go to Harvard on a scholarship. Where does she decide to go instead? Discuss Pia's regrets for what she did to her parents to get her way.

3. Cameron's friend Sebastian has an accident that turns out to be a premonition. Explain why the incident terrifies Pia so. Why does she have a tough time explaining it to Cameron?

4. Because of their experience with the island last year, Cameron shouldn't doubt Pia on anything. So why when Pia expresses her concern about Ebay, Cameron discredits her? How do you feel about his behavior toward her? Discuss how he later comes around to seeing things her way.

5. Pia's friends—Stephanie, Cristina, Ariana—have much working against them while investigating Ebay. Discuss the details of this.

6. Do you think they go too far with Pia in the investigation?

7. Why does Pia hide the ring from Ebay?

8. You might say fate is why Pia returns to Florida and discovers something about herself she'd never thought possible. As for Cameron, give examples of what he learns about himself, if anything.

9. Why is Pia taken aback when Cameron presents his mother's ring?

10. Sebastian had a miraculous recovery. Pia believed Ferret was behind his accident which prompted Cameron to enter the competition. Do you share her belief? And why?

11. Why does Pia think Cameron and Ferret were rivals in a past life?

12. It's not clear how Cameron came about his strength in defending himself against Ferret. But is this an example of "the mean justifies the end"? Discuss.

13. "He's why you can't remember," Ferret says to Pia. Based on how things evolve, would you say he's right?

14. Ferret insists he only came because Pia summoned him. But does he play more of a selfish role than a business one? Explain your reason(s).

15. If you were Pia, would you prefer not to remember and have things play out as they do at the end?

16. Do you believe in the hereafter? If so, how do you see it? Do you think you would be satisfied living life anywhere else, or in another form other than human?

17. Magic is a fascination and a way of life in Massouvia (walking through water without getting wet, this fascinates Pia). Imagine our world without any form of magic. What would it be like? Be careful not to become delusional; imagination is a powerful entity.

18. Fate plays a powerful role in the story. But what if Pia had gone to Harvard instead, do you think things would have ended differently? If so, what does that say to you about fate?

19. The moldavite stone is known for its energy in communicating with the extraterrestrial. Discuss its suspicious timing as to Cameron and Pia, and ways it shapes their relationship.

20. How do you see Pia's and Cameron's future now?

21. When the author first heard the name Perseaus, she knew instantly her search for a title was over. What title would you have given the book, and why?

About the Author

For C.C., the joy of reading came later in life. When it did, it was as if she'd been placed under a spell with the desire to read. It wasn't until her imagination started going wild when she realized her desire to read had evolved into something else. At first, she didn't know what to do with the images; she just wanted them to go away so that she could get some sleep. But it didn't take long to realize that it was time to pick up a pen.

She resides in Arizona with family and friends.

Visit her at www.ccwyattbooks.com
Twitter: @1ccwyatt